CLONES

Edited by Jack Dann & Gardner Dozois

Edited by Jack Dann & Gardner Dozois

Edited by Terri Windling

CLONES

EDITED BY
JACK DANN & GARDNER DOZOIS

ACE BOOKS, NEW YORK

This book is an Ace original edition,
and has never been previously published.

CLONES

An Ace Book / published by arrangement with
the editors

PRINTING HISTORY
Ace edition / April 1998

All rights reserved.
Copyright © 1997 by Jack Dann & Gardner Dozois.
Cover art by Lee MacLeod.
Book design by Erin Lush.
This book may not be reproduced in whole or in part,
by mimeograph or any other means, without permission.
For information address: The Berkley Publishing Group,
a member of Penguin Putnam Inc.,
200 Madison Avenue, New York, NY 10016.

The Penguin Putnam Inc. World Wide Web site address is
http://www.penguinputnam.com

ISBN: 0-441-00522-5

ACE®
Ace Books are published by The Berkley Publishing Group,
a member of Penguin Putnam Inc.,
200 Madison Avenue, New York, NY 10016.
ACE and the "A" design are trademarks
belonging to Charter Communications, Inc.

PRINTED IN THE UNITED STATES OF AMERICA

10 9 8 7 6 5 4 3 2 1

Acknowledgment is made
for permission to reprint the following material:

"*Nine Lives*," by Ursula K. Le Guin. Copyright © 1975 by Ursula K. Le Guin. First published in *Playboy*, November 1969. Reprinted by permission of the author and the author's agent, Virginia Kidd.

"*Mary*," by Damon Knight. Copyright © 1964 by Galaxy Publishing Corporation. First published (under the title "An Ancient Madness") in *Galaxy*, June 1964. Reprinted by permission of the author.

"*The Extra*," by Greg Egan. Copyright © 1990 by Greg Egan. First published in *Eidolon #2*, August 1990. Reprinted by permission of the author.

"*Out of Copyright*," by Charles Sheffield. Copyright © 1989 by Mercury Press, Inc. First published in *The Magazine of Fantasy and Science Fiction*, May 1989. Reprinted by permission of the author.

"*The Phantom of Kansas*," by John Varley. Copyright © 1976 by UPD Publishing Corp. First published in *Galaxy*, February 1976. Reprinted by permission of the author and the author's agent.

"*Blood Sisters*," by Joe Haldeman. Copyright © 1979 by Playboy. First published in *Playboy*, July 1979. Reprinted by permission of the author.

"*Past Magic*," by Ian R. MacLeod. Copyright © 1990 by Interzone. First published in *Interzone 39*, September 1990. Reprinted by permission of the author and the author's agents, Owlswick Literary Agency.

CONTENTS

PREFACE

The birth of Dolly, arguably history's most famous sheep (although, admittedly, there's not a lot of intense *competition* for that title!) early in 1997, lead to a flood of speculation in the media that the cloning techniques used to produce Dolly would soon be adaptable to produce *human* clones as well. "Flood," in fact, is probably too understated a word to describe the torrent of sudden speculation about the feasibility—and the imminence—of human cloning: "tidal wave" or "tsunami" might describe that torrent of speculation better, as cover stories about cloning appeared in *Time* and *Newsweek* and on the front page of nearly every newspaper in the country—and, in fact, around the world. Footage of Dolly the cloned sheep—and a cute little thing she is, too—appeared on practically every TV news show that night, again worldwide, and would be shown over and over again for days to come. The tabloids, of course, went *totally* insane.

Suddenly, the general public was aware of the possibility that technology might someday be able to produce human clones; and that it was not only *possible* that this technology would one day be perfected but, in fact, that it was fairly *likely*. That human cloning was not an issue that would arise in some remote, misty future, but something that might well happen during the lifetimes of many of the people now alive—perhaps, according to the most optimistic estimates, a break-through no more than a decade or so away. (According to the tabloids, of course, it was a capability that we *already* possessed, with sinister secret government labs busily churning out clones of everyone from JFK to Elvis.) Something that would have to be dealt with *soon*. By *us*. Suddenly everyone was talking about clones, and the morality and legality of human cloning was being debated endlessly—and often vitrolically—on TV and radio talk shows, and even thundered about from pulpits and by the Vatican. Publishers were suddenly inundated with proposals for clone novels, with one book editor of our acquaintance saying that he'd received a half dozen or more pitches on the *same day* for novels about cloning Jesus (an idea dealt with in SF all the way back in 1979, in Gary Jenning's "The Relic"), and no doubt the first cloning movies and TV movies-of-the-week are being rushed into production even as these words are being typed. I wouldn't be at all surprised if a *sitcom* about clones was in development somewhere right now.

We can't be too self-righteous about this, of course, since the book that you hold in your hands is obviously also calculated to cash in on this very craze—but we *can* say that if you *really* want to know about the potentials and dangers of human cloning, if you really want to get a forecast of the profound and widespread (and sometimes extremely subtle) impact that human cloning could have on human society, then you are far better served by spending your money on this anthology than by buying supermarket tabloids with lurid headlines about JFK's clone, or by plonking down ten dollars for a ticket to the first big-budget clone movie to make it out of the gate.

For the idea of human cloning is old news to science fiction writers, who have been speculating about it for more than twenty-five years now, long before the average person in the street had even ever *heard* of the concept. And during that time, those science fiction writers have worked out the implications of cloning for society (some of which are much more widespread and profound than anything speculated about to date in the public press), examined the impact that cloning could have on the lives of every one of us, in far greater depth and detail, with far more imagination and ingenuity, and with enormously more technical sophistica-tion and clarity, than anything you're going to hear said on *Geraldo* or *Oprah* . . . or even on *60 Minutes*.

So if you want to *really* explore the miracles and terrors that cloning could bring to our lives, and get an advance look at the pitfalls and potentialities ahead long before your neighbor has any idea what's about to blindside him, and if you want to be thrilled and elated and moved while doing so (because, of course, the colorful, fast-paced, and imaginative stories that follow were written to *entertain*, not to inform . . . although, as it happens, they *also* do a pretty good job of informing as well) . . . or if you'd just like to have a good *read*, a few hours of imaginative entertainment, then put down those tabloids, shut off the television, put your feet up, open this book—and enjoy. Forget about Dolly! You ain't seen *nothing* yet! You're about to be transported to worlds wilder than anything you can imagine—so far!

NINE LIVES

Ursula K. Le Guin

Although science fiction has always been fascinated by the idea of the duplication of human beings, and has long used ingenious twists on the idea of matter-transmission, or sometimes time-travel paradox loops, to produce such dopplegangers (stories about android duplicates of human beings, one of Philip K. Dick's most obsessive themes, are clearly related as well—another few years, and most of the android stories of the fifties would have been clone stories instead, I'm willing to bet), the genre as a whole didn't begin talking about "clones" until the last few years of the sixties, after the appearance of Gordon Rattray Taylor's extremely influential nonfiction book, The Biological Time-Bomb. (Le Guin has explicitly acknowledged Taylor's influence on the story that follows; one of your editors was also writing an early clone story in 1969—"A Special Kind of Morning," published in 1971—before Le Guin's story hit print, and certainly Taylor was his inspiration as well; rarely, in fact, has a nonfiction book had as much impact on the evolution of the genre as Taylor's had.) Although there were earlier stories that dealt with some of the conceptual material of cloning—Theodore Sturgeon's "When You Care, When You Love," for instance, or Damon Knight's "Mary"—the eloquent and hard-hitting story that follows, "Nine Lives," is perhaps science fiction's first true clone story, and is probably the first to use the word "clone" in its true context.

It's a story that had a tremendous impact on the field, and one that is still as fresh and germane today as it was in 1969, telling the moving story of a young man who is suddenly left all alone in life in a way that no one has ever been alone before. . . .

Ursula K. Le Guin is probably one of the best known and most universally respected SF writers in the world today. Her famous novel The Left Hand of Darkness may have been the most influential SF novel of its decade and shows every sign

*of becoming one of the enduring classics of the genre. Even
ignoring the rest of Le Guin's work, the impact of this one
novel alone on future SF writers would be incalculably
strong. (Her 1968 fantasy novel,* A Wizard of Earthsea,
*would be almost as influential on future generations of High
Fantasy writers.)* The Left Hand of Darkness *won both the
Hugo and Nebula Awards, as did Le Guin's monumental
novel* The Dispossessed *a few years later. Her novel* Tehanu
*won her another Nebula in 1990, and she has also won three
other Hugo Awards and a Nebula Award for her short fiction,
as well as the National Book Award for Children's literature
for her novel* The Farthest Shore, *part of her acclaimed
Earthsea trilogy. Her other novels include* Planet of Exile,
The Lathe of Heaven, City of Illusions, Rocannon's World,
The Beginning Place, A Wizard of Earthsea, The Tombs of
Atuan, Tehanu, Searoad, *and the controversial multimedia
novel* Always Coming Home. *She has had six collections:*
The Wind's Twelve Quarters, Orsinian Tales, The Compass
Rose, Buffalo Gals and Other Animal Presences, A Fisher-
man of the Inland Sea, *and her most recent book,* Four Ways
to Forgiveness.

S*he was alive* inside but dead outside, her face a black and
dun net of wrinkles, tumors, cracks. She was bald and blind.
The tremors that crossed Libra's face were mere quiverings
of corruption. Underneath, in the black corridors, the halls
beneath the skin, there were crepitations in darkness,
ferments, chemical nightmares that went on for centuries.
"O the damned flatulent planet," Pugh murmured as the
dome shook and a boil burst a kilometer to the southwest,
spraying silver pus across the sunset. The sun had been
setting for the last two days. "I'll be glad to see a human
face."

"Thanks," said Martin.

"Yours is human to be sure," said Pugh, "but I've seen it
so long I can't see it."

Radvid signals cluttered the communicator which Martin

was operating, faded, returned as face and voice. The face filled the screen, the nose of an Assyrian king, the eyes of a samurai, skin bronze, eyes the color of iron: young, magnificent. "Is that what human beings look like?" said Pugh with awe. "I'd forgotten."

"Shut up, Owen, we're on."

"Libra Exploratory Mission Base, come in please, this is *Passerine* launch."

"Libra here. Beam fixed. Come on down, launch."

"Expulsion in seven E-seconds. Hold on." The screen blanked and sparkled.

"Do they all look like that? Martin, you and I are uglier men than I thought."

"Shut up, Owen. . . ."

For twenty-two minutes Martin followed the landing craft down by signal and then through the cleared dome they saw it, small star in the blood-colored east, sinking. It came down neat and quiet, Libra's thin atmosphere carrying little sound. Pugh and Martin closed the headpieces of their insuits, zipped out of the dome airlocks, and ran with soaring strides, Nijinsky and Nureyev, toward the boat. Three equipment modules came floating down at four-minute intervals from each other and hundred-meter intervals east of the boat. "Come on out," Martin said on his suit radio, "we're waiting at the door."

"Come on in, the methane's fine," said Pugh.

The hatch opened. The young man they had seen on the screen came out with one athletic twist and leaped down onto the shaky dust and clinkers of Libra. Martin shook his hand, but Pugh was staring at the hatch, from which another young man emerged with the same neat twist and jump, followed by a young woman who emerged with the same neat twist, ornamented by a wriggle, and the jump. They were all tall, with bronze skin, black hair, high-bridged noses, epicanthic fold, the same face. They all had the same face. The fourth was emerging from the hatch with a neat twist and jump. "Martin bach," said Pugh, "we've got a clone."

"Right," said one of them, "we're a tenclone. John Chow's the name. You're Lieutenant Martin?"

"I'm Owen Pugh."

"Alvaro Guillen Martin," said Martin, formal, bowing slightly. Another girl was out, the same beautiful face; Martin stared at her and his eye rolled like a nervous pony's. Evidently he had never given any thought to cloning and was suffering technological shock. "Steady," Pugh said in the Argentine dialect, "it's only excess twins." He stood close by Martin's elbow. He was glad himself of the contact.

It is hard to meet a stranger. Even the greatest extrovert meeting even the meekest stranger knows a certain dread, though he may not know he knows it. Will he make a fool of me wreck my image of myself invade me destroy me change me? Will he be different from me? Yes, that he will. There's the terrible thing: the strangeness of the stranger.

After two years on a dead planet, and the last half year isolated as a team of two, oneself and one other, after that it's even harder to meet a stranger, however welcome he may be. You're out of the habit of difference, you've lost the touch; and so the fear revives, the primitive anxiety, the old dread.

The clone, five males and five females, had got done in a couple of minutes what a man might have got done in twenty: greeted Pugh and Martin, had a glance at Libra, unloaded the boat, made ready to go. They went, and the dome filled with them, a hive of golden bees. They hummed and buzzed quietly, filled up all silences, all spaces with a honey-brown swarm of human presence. Martin looked bewildered at the long-limbed girls, and they smiled at him, three at once. Their smile was gentler than that of the boys, but no less radiantly self-possessed.

"Self-possessed," Owen Pugh murmured to his friend, "that's it. Think of it, to be oneself ten times over. Nine seconds for every motion, nine ayes on every vote. It would be glorious." But Martin was asleep. And the John Chows had all gone to sleep at once. The dome was filled with their quiet breathing. They were young, they didn't snore. Martin sighed and snored, his Hershey-bar-colored face relaxed in the dim afterglow of Libra's primary, set at last. Pugh had cleared the dome and stars looked in, Sol among them, a great company of lights, a clone of splendors. Pugh slept and dreamed of a one-eyed giant who chased him through the shaking halls of Hell.

From his sleeping bag Pugh watched the clone's awakening. They all got up within one minute except for one pair, a boy and a girl, who lay snugly tangled and still sleeping in one bag. As Pugh saw this there was a shock like one of Libra's earthquakes inside him, a very deep tremor. He was not aware of this and in fact thought he was pleased at the sight; there was no other such comfort on this dead hollow world. More power to them, who made love. One of the others stepped on the pair. They woke and the girl sat up flushed and sleepy, with bare golden breasts. One of her sisters murmured something to her; she shot a glance at Pugh and disappeared in the sleeping bag; from another direction came a fierce stare, from still another direction a voice: "Christ, we're used to having a room to ourselves. Hope you don't mind, Captain Pugh."

"It's a pleasure," Pugh said half truthfully. He had to stand up then wearing only the shorts he slept in, and he felt like a plucked rooster, all white scrawn and pimples. He had seldom envied Martin's compact brownness so much. The United Kingdom had come through the Great Famines well, losing less than half its population: a record achieved by rigorous food control. Black marketeers and hoarders had been executed. Crumbs had been shared. Where in richer lands most had died and a few had thriven, in Britain fewer died and none throve. They all got lean. Their sons were lean, their grandsons lean, small, brittle-boned, easily infected. When civilization became a matter of standing in lines, the British had kept queue, and so had replaced the survival of the fittest with the survival of the fair-minded. Owen Pugh was a scrawny little man. All the same, he was there.

At the moment he wished he wasn't.

At breakfast a John said, "Now if you'll brief us, Captain Pugh—"

"Owen, then."

"Owen, we can work out our schedule. Anything new on the mine since your last report to your Mission? We saw your reports when *Passerine* was orbiting Planet V, where they are now."

Martin did not answer, though the mine was his discovery and project, and Pugh had to do his best. It was hard to talk to them. The same faces, each with the same expression of intelligent interest, all leaned toward him across the table at almost the same angle. They all nodded together.

Over the Exploitation Corps insigne on their tunics each had a nameband, first name John and last name Chow of course, but the middle names different. The men were Aleph, Kaph, Yod, Gimel, and Samedh; the women Sadhe, Daleth, Zayin, Beth, and Resh. Pugh tried to use the names but gave it up at once; he could not even tell sometimes which one had spoken, for all the voices were alike.

Martin buttered and chewed his toast, and finally interrupted: "You're a team. Is that it?"

"Right," said two Johns.

"God, what a team! I hadn't seen the point. How much do you each know what the others are thinking?"

"Not at all, properly speaking," replied one of the girls, Zayin. The others watched her with the proprietary, approving look they had. "No ESP, nothing fancy. But we think alike. We have exactly the same equipment. Given the same stimulus, the same problem, we're likely to be coming up with the same reactions and solutions at the same time. Explanations are easy—don't even have to make them, usually. We seldom misunderstand each other. It does facilitate our working as a team."

"Christ yes," said Martin. "Pugh and I have spent seven hours out of ten for six months misunderstanding each other. Like most people. What about emergencies, are you as good at meeting the unexpected problem as a nor . . . an unrelated team?"

"Statistics so far indicate that we are," Zayin answered

readily. Clones must be trained, Pugh thought, to meet questions, to reassure and reason. All they said had the slightly bland and stilted quality of answers furnished to the Public. "We can't brainstorm as singletons can, we as a team don't profit from the interplay of varied minds; but we have a compensatory advantage. Clones are drawn from the best human material, individuals of IIQ ninety-ninth percentile, Genetic Constitution alpha double A, and so on. We have more to draw on than most individuals do."

"And it's multiplied by a factor of ten. Who is—who was John Chow?"

"A genius surely," Pugh said politely. His interest in cloning was not so new and avid as Martin's.

"Leonardo Complex type," said Yod. "Biomath, also a cellist and an undersea hunter, and interested in structural engineering problems and so on. Died before he'd worked out his major theories."

"Then you each represent a different facet of his mind, his talents?"

"No," said Zayin, shaking her head in time with several others. "We share the basic equipment and tendencies, of course, but we're all engineers in Planetary Exploitation. A later clone can be trained to develop other aspects of the basic equipment. It's all training; the genetic substance is identical. We *are* John Chow. But we are differently trained."

Martin looked shell-shocked. "How old are you?"

"Twenty-three."

"You say he died young—had they taken germ cells from him beforehand or something?"

Gimel took over: "He died at twenty-four in an air car crash. They couldn't save the brain, so they took some intestinal cells and cultured them for cloning. Reproductive cells aren't used for cloning, since they have only half the chromosomes. Intestinal cells happen to be easy to despecialize and reprogram for total growth."

"All chips off the old block," Martin said valiantly. "But how can . . . some of you be women . . . ?"

Beth took over: "It's easy to program half the clonal mass

back to the female. Just delete the male gene from half the cells and they revert to the basic, that is, the female. It's trickier to go the other way, have to hook in artificial Y chromosomes. So they mostly clone from males, since clones function best bisexually."

Gimel again: "They've worked these matters of technique and function out carefully. The taxpayer wants the best for his money, and of course clones are expensive. With the cell manipulations, and the incubation in Ngama Placentae, and the maintenance and training of the foster-parent groups, we end up costing about three million apiece."

"For your next generation," Martin said, still struggling, "I suppose you . . . you breed?"

"We females are sterile," said Beth with perfect equanimity. "You remember that the Y chromosome was deleted from our original cell. The males can interbreed with approved singletons, if they want to. But to get John Chow again as often as they want, they just reclone a cell from this clone."

Martin gave up the struggle. He nodded and chewed cold toast. "Well," said one of the Johns, and all changed mood, like a flock of starlings that change course in one wing-flick, following a leader so fast that no eye can see which leads. They were ready to go. "How about a look at the mine? Then we'll unload the equipment. Some nice new models in the roboats; you'll want to see them. Right?" Had Pugh or Martin not agreed they might have found it hard to say so. The Johns were polite but unanimous; their decisions carried. Pugh, Commander of Libra Base 2, felt a qualm. Could he boss around this superman/woman-entity-of-ten? and a genius at that? He stuck close to Martin as they suited for outside. Neither said anything.

Four apiece in the three large airjets, they slipped off north from the dome, over Libra's dun rugose skin, in starlight.

"Desolate," one said.

It was a boy and girl with Pugh and Martin. Pugh wondered if these were the two that had shared a sleeping bag last night. No doubt they wouldn't mind if he asked them. Sex must be as handy as breathing to them. Did you two breathe last night?

"Yes," he said, "it is desolate."

"This is our first time off, except training on Luna." The girl's voice was definitely a bit higher and softer.

"How did you take the big hop?"

"They doped us. I wanted to experience it." That was the boy; he sounded wistful. They seemed to have more personality, only two at a time. Did repetition of the individual negate individuality?

"Don't worry," said Martin, steering the sled, "you can't experience no-time because it isn't there."

"I'd just like to once," one of them said. "So we'd know."

The Mountains of Merioneth showed leprotic in starlight to the east, a plume of freezing gas trailed silvery from a vent-hole to the west, and the sled tilted groundward. The twins braced for the stop at one moment, each with a slight protective gesture to the other. Your skin is my skin, Pugh thought, but literally, no metaphor. What would it be like, then, to have someone as close to you as that? Always to be answered when you spoke; never to be in pain alone. Love your neighbor as you love yourself. . . . That hard old problem was solved. The neighbor was the self: the love was perfect.

And here was Hellmouth, the mine.

Pugh was the Exploratory Mission's E.T. geologist, and Martin his technician and cartographer; but when in the course of a local survey Martin had discovered the U-mine, Pugh had given him full credit, as well as the onus of prospecting the lode and planning the Exploitation Team's job. These kids had been sent out from Earth years before Martin's reports got there and had not known what their job would be until they got there. The Exploitation Corps simply sent out teams regularly and blindly as a dandelion sends out its seed, knowing there would be a job for them on Libra or the next planet out or one they hadn't even heard about yet. The government wanted uranium too urgently to wait while reports drifted home across the lightyears. The stuff was like gold, old-fashioned but essential, worth

mining extraterrestrially and shipping interstellar. Worth its
weight in people, Pugh thought sourly, watching the tall
young men and women go one by one, glimmering in
starlight, into the black hole Martin had named Hellmouth.

As they went in their homeostatic forehead-lamps brightened. Twelve nodding gleams ran along the moist, wrinkled
walls. Pugh heard Martin's radiation counter peeping twenty
to the dozen up ahead. "Here's the drop-off," said Martin's
voice in the suit intercom, drowning out the peeping and the
dead silence that was around them. "We're in a side-fissure,
this is the main vertical vent in front of us." The black void
gaped, its far side not visible in the headlamp beams. "Last
vulcanism seems to have been a couple of thousand years
ago. Nearest fault is twenty-eight kilos east, in the Trench.
This area seems to be as safe seismically as anything in the
area. The big basalt-flow overhead stabilizes all these
substructures, so long as it remains stable itself. Your central
lode is thirty-six meters down and runs in a series of five
bubble caverns northeast. It is a lode, a pipe of very high-
grade ore. You saw the percentage figures, right? Extrac-
tion's going to be no problem. All you've got to do is get the
bubbles topside."

"Take off the lid and let 'em float up." A chuckle. Voices
began to talk, but they were all the same voice and the suit
radio gave them no location in space. "Open the thing right
up. —Safer that way.—But it's a solid basalt roof, how
thick, ten meters here?—Three to twenty, the report said.—
Blow good ore all over the lot.—Use this access we're in,
straighten it a bit and run slider rails for the robos.—Import
burros.—Have we got enough propping material?—What's
your estimate of total payload mass, Martin?"

"Say over five million kilos and under eight."

"Transport will be here in ten E-months.—It'll have to go
pure. —No, they'll have the mass problem in NAFAL
shipping licked by now, remember it's been sixteen years
since we left Earth last Tuesday.—Right, they'll send the
whole lot back and purify it in Earth orbit.—Shall we go
down, Martin?"

"Go on. I've been down."

The first one—Aleph? (Heb., the ox, the leader)—
swung onto the ladder and down; the rest followed. Pugh
and Martin stood at the chasm's edge. Pugh set his intercom
to exchange only with Martin's suit, and noticed Martin
doing the same. It was a bit wearing, this listening to one
person think aloud in ten voices, or was it one voice
speaking the thoughts of ten minds?

"A great gut," Pugh said, looking down into the black pit,
its veined and warted walls catching stray gleams of
headlamps far below. "A cow's bowel. A bloody great
constipated intestine."

Martin's counter peeped like a lost chicken. They stood
inside the dead but epileptic planet, breathing oxygen from
tanks, wearing suits impermeable to corrosives and harmful
radiations, resistant to a 200-degree range of temperatures,
tear-proof, and as shock-resistant as possible given the soft
vulnerable stuff inside.

"Next hop," Martin said, "I'd like to find a planet that has
nothing whatever to exploit."

"You found this."

"Keep me home next time."

Pugh was pleased. He had hoped Martin would want to
go on working with him, but neither of them was used to
talking much about their feelings, and he had hesitated to
ask. "I'll try that," he said.

"I hate this place. I like caves, you know. It's why I came
in here. Just spelunking. But this one's a bitch. Mean. You
can't ever let down in here. I guess this lot can handle it,
though. They know their stuff."

"Wave of the future, whatever," said Pugh.

The wave of the future came swarming up the ladder,
swept Martin to the entrance, gabbled at and around him:
"Have we got enough material for supports?—If we convert
one of the extractor servos to anneal, yes.—Sufficient if we
miniblast?—Kaph can calculate stress." Pugh had switched
his intercom back to receive them; he looked at them, so
many thoughts jabbering in an eager mind, and at Martin
standing silent among them, and at Hellmouth and the

wrinkled plain. "Settled! How does that strike you as a preliminary schedule, Martin?"

"It's your baby," Martin said.

Within five E-days the Johns had all their material and equipment unloaded and operating and were starting to open up the mine. They worked with total efficiency. Pugh was fascinated and frightened by their effectiveness, their confidence, their independence. He was no use to them at all. A clone, he thought, might indeed be the first truly stable, self-reliant human being. Once adult it would need nobody's help. It would be sufficient to itself physically, sexually, emotionally, intellectually. Whatever he did, any member of it would always receive the support and approval of his peers, his other selves. Nobody else was needed.

Two of the clone stayed in the dome doing calculations and paperwork, with frequent sled trips to the mine for measurements and tests. They were the mathematicians of the clone, Zayin and Kaph. That is, as Zayin explained, all ten had had thorough mathematical training from age three to twenty-one, but from twenty-one to twenty-three she and Kaph had gone on with math while the others intensified study in other specialties, geology, mining, engineering, electronic engineering, equipment robotics, applied atomics, and so on. "Kaph and I feel," she said, "that we're the element of the clone closest to what John Chow was in his singleton lifetime. But of course he was principally in biomath, and they didn't take us far in that."

"They needed us most in this field," Kaph said, with the patriotic priggishness they sometimes evinced.

Pugh and Martin soon could distinguish this pair from the others, Zayin by gestalt, Kaph only by a discolored left fourth fingernail, got from an ill-aimed hammer at the age of six. No doubt there were many such differences, physical and psychological, among them; nature might be identical, nurture could not be. But the differences were hard to find. And part of the difficulty was that they never really talked to Pugh and Martin. They joked with them, were polite, got along fine. They gave nothing. It was nothing one could complain about; they were very pleasant, they had the standardized American friendliness. "Do you come from Ireland, Owen?"

"Nobody comes from Ireland, Zayin."

"There are lots of Irish-Americans."

"To be sure, but no more Irish. A couple of thousand in all the island, the last I knew. They didn't go in for birth control, you know, so the food ran out. By the Third Famine there were no Irish left at all but the priesthood, and they all celibate, or nearly all."

Zayin and Kaph smiled stiffly. The had no experience of either bigotry or irony. "What are you then, ethnically?" Kaph asked, and Pugh replied, "A Welshman."

"Is it Welsh that you and Martin speak together?"

None of your business, Pugh thought, but said, "No, it's his dialect, not mine: Argentinean. A descendant of Spanish."

"You learned it for private communication?"

"Whom had we here to be private from? It's just that sometimes a man likes to speak his native language."

"Ours is English," Kaph said unsympathetically. Why should they have sympathy? That's one of the things you give because you need it back.

"Is Wells quaint?" asked Zayin.

"Wells? Oh, Wales, it's called. Yes, Wales is quaint." Pugh switched on his rock-cutter, which prevented further conversation by a synapse-destroying whine, and while it whined he turned his back and said a profane word in Welsh.

That night he used the Argentine dialect for private communication. "Do they pair off in the same couples or change every night?"

Martin looked surprised. A prudish expression, unsuited to his features, appeared for a moment. It faded. He too was curious. "I think it's random."

"Don't whisper, man, it sounds dirty. I think they rotate."

"On a schedule?"

"So nobody gets omitted."

Martin gave a vulgar laugh and smothered it. "What about us? Aren't we omitted?"

"That doesn't occur to them."

"What if I proposition one of the girls?"

"She'd tell the others and they'd decide as a group."

"I am not a bull," Martin said, his dark, heavy face heating up. "I will not be judged—"

"Down, down, *machismo*," said Pugh. "Do you mean to proposition one?"

Martin shrugged, sullen. "Let 'em have their incest."

"Incest is it, or masturbation?"

"I don't care, if they'd do it out of earshot!"

The clone's early attempts at modesty had soon worn off, unmotivated by any deep defensiveness of self or awareness of others. Pugh and Martin were daily deeper swamped under the intimacies of its constant emotional-sexual-mental interchange: swamped yet excluded.

"Two months to go," Martin said one evening.

"To what?" snapped Pugh. He was edgy lately, and Martin's sullenness got on his nerves.

"To relief."

In sixty days the full crew of their Exploratory Mission were due back from their survey of the other planets of the system. Pugh was aware of this.

"Crossing off the days on your calendar?" he jeered.

"Pull yourself together, Owen."

"What do you mean?"

"What I say."

They parted in contempt and resentment.

Pugh came in after a day alone on the Pampas, a vast lava plain the nearest edge of which was two hours south by jet. He was tired but refreshed by solitude. They were not supposed to take long trips alone but lately had often done so. Martin stooped under bright lights, drawing one of his elegant masterly charts. This one was of the whole face of Libra, the cancerous face. The dome was otherwise empty, seeming dim and large as it had before the clone came. "Where's the golden horde?"

Martin grunted ignorance, cross-hatching. He straightened his back to glance round at the sun, which squatted feebly like a great red toad on the eastern plain, and at the clock, which said 18:45. "Some big quakes today," he said, returning to his map. "Feel them down there? Lots of crates were falling around. Take a look at the seismo."

The needle jigged and wavered on the roll. It never stopped dancing here. The roll had recorded five quakes of major intensity back in midafternoon; twice the needle had hopped off the roll. The attached computer had been activated to emit a slip reading. "Epicenter 61' N by 42'4" E."

"Not in the Trench this time."

"I thought it felt a bit different from usual. Sharper."

"In Base One I used to lie awake all night feeling the ground jump. Queer how you get used to things."

"Go spla if you didn't. What's for dinner?"

"I thought you'd have cooked it."

"Waiting for the clone."

Feeling put upon, Pugh got out a dozen dinnerboxes, stuck two in the Instobake, pulled them out. "All right, here's dinner."

"Been thinking," Martin said, coming to table. "What if some clone cloned itself? Illegally. Made a thousand duplicates—ten thousand. Whole army. They could make a tidy power grab, couldn't they?"

"But how many millions did this lot cost to rear? Artificial placentae and all that. It would be hard to keep secret, unless they had a planet to themselves. . . . Back before the Famines when Earth had national governments, they talked about that: clone your best soldiers, have whole regiments of them. But the food ran out before they could play that game."

They talked amicably, as they used to do.

"Funny," Martin said, chewing. "They left early this morning, didn't they?"

"All but Kaph and Zayin. They thought they'd get the first payload above ground today. What's up?"

"They weren't back for lunch."

"They won't starve, to be sure."

"They left at seven."

"So they did." Then Pugh saw it. The air tanks held eight hours' supply.

"Kaph and Zayin carried out spare cans when they left. Or they've got a heap out there."

"They did, but they brought the whole lot in to recharge." Martin stood up, pointing to one of the stacks of stuff that cut the dome into rooms and alleys.

"There's an alarm signal on every imsuit."

"It's not automatic."

Pugh was tired and still hungry. "Sit down and eat, man. That lot can look after themselves."

Martin sat down but did not eat. "There was a big quake, Owen. The first one. Big enough it scared me."

After a pause Pugh sighed and said, "All right."

Unenthusiastically, they got out the two-man sled that was always left for them and headed it north. The long sunrise covered everything in poisonous red jello. The horizontal light and shadow made it hard to see, raised walls of fake iron ahead of them which they slid through, turned the convex plain beyond Hellmouth into a great dimple full of bloody water. Around the tunnel entrance a wilderness of machinery stood, cranes and cables and servos and wheels and diggers and robocarts and sliders and control huts, all slanting and bulking incoherently in the red light. Martin jumped from the sled, ran into the mine. He came out again, to Pugh. "Oh God, Owen, it's down," he said. Pugh went in and saw, five meters from the entrance, the shiny moist, black wall that ended the tunnel. Newly exposed to air, it looked organic, like visceral tissue. The tunnel entrance, enlarged by blasting and double-tracked for robocarts, seemed unchanged until he noticed thousands of tiny spiderweb cracks in the walls. The floor was wet with some sluggish fluid.

"They were inside," Martin said.

"They may be still. They surely had extra air cans—"

"Look, Owen, look at the basalt flow, at the roof, don't you see what the quake did, look at it."

The low hump of land that roofed the caves still had the unreal look of an optical illusion. It had reversed itself, sunk down, leaving a vast dimple or pit. When Pugh walked on it he saw that it too was cracked with many tiny fissures. From some a whitish gas was seeping, so that the sunlight on the surface of the gas pool was shafted as if by the waters of a dim red lake.

"The mine's not on the fault. There's no fault here!"

Pugh came back to him quickly. "No, there's no fault, Martin—Look, they surely weren't all inside together."

Martin followed him and searched among the wrecked machines dully, then actively. He spotted the airsled. It had come down heading south, and stuck at an angle in a pothole of colloidal dust. It had carried two riders. One was half sunk in the dust, but his suit meters registered normal functioning; the other hung strapped onto the tilted sled. Her imsuit had burst open on the broken legs, and the body was frozen hard as any rock. That was all they found. As both regulation and custom demanded, they cremated the dead at once with the laser guns they carried by regulation and had never used before. Pugh, knowing he was going to be sick, wrestled the survivor onto the two-man sled and sent Martin off to the dome with him. Then he vomited and flushed the waste out of his suit, and finding one four-man sled undamaged, followed after Martin, shaking as if the cold of Libra had got through to him.

The survivor was Kaph. He was in deep shock. They found a swelling on the occiput that might mean concussion, but no fracture was visible.

Pugh brought two glasses of food concentrate and two chasers of aquavit. "Come on," he said. Martin obeyed, drinking off the tonic. They sat down on crates near the cot and sipped the aquavit.

Kaph lay immobile, face like beeswax, hair bright black to the shoulders, lips stiffly parted for faintly gasping breaths.

"It must have been the first shock, the big one," Martin said. "It must have slid the whole structure sideways. Till it fell in on itself. There must be gas layers in the lateral rocks,

like those formations in the Thirty-first Quadrant. But there
wasn't any sign—" As he spoke the world slid out from
under them. Things leaped and clattered, hopped and jigged,
shouted Ha! Ha! Ha! "It was like this at fourteen hours,"
said Reason shakily in Martin's voice, amidst the unfasten-
ing and ruin of the world. But Unreason sat up, as the tumult
lessened and things ceased dancing, and screamed aloud.

Pugh leaped across his spilt aquavit and held Kaph down.
The muscular body flailed him off. Martin pinned the
shoulders down. Kaph screamed, struggled, choked; his
face blackened. "Oxy," Pugh said, and his hand found the
right needle in the medical kit as if by homing instinct;
while Martin held the mask he stuck the needle home to the
vagus nerve, restoring Kaph to life.

"Didn't know you knew that stunt," Martin said, breathing hard.

"The Lazarus Jab, my father was a doctor. It doesn't often
work," Pugh said. "I want that drink I spilled. Is the quake
over? I can't tell."

"Aftershocks. It's not just you shivering."

"Why did he suffocate?"

"I don't know, Owen. Look in the book."

Kaph was breathing normally and his color was restored;
only the lips were still darkened. They poured a new shot of
courage and sat down by him again with their medical
guide. "Nothing about cyanosis or asphyxiation under
'Shock' or 'Concussion.' He can't have breathed in anything
with his suit on. I don't know. We'd get as much good out
of *Mother Mog's Home Herbalist*. . . . 'Anal Hemor-
rhoids,' fy!" Pugh pitched the book to a crate table. It fell
short, because either Pugh or the table was still unsteady.

"Why didn't he signal?"

"Sorry?"

"The eight inside the mine never had time. But he and the
girl must have been outside. Maybe she was in the entrance
and got hit by the first slide. He must have been outside, in
the control hut maybe. He ran in, pulled her out, strapped
her onto the sled, started for the dome. And all that time
never pushed the panic button in his imsuit. Why not?"

"Well, he'd had that whack on his head. I doubt he ever realized the girl was dead. He wasn't in his senses. But if he had been I don't know if he'd have thought to signal us. They looked to one another for help."

Martin's face was like an Indian mask, grooves at the mouth corners, eyes of dull coal. "That's so. What must he have felt, then, when the quake came and he was outside, alone—"

In answer Kaph screamed.

He came off the cot in the heaving convulsions of one suffocating, knocked Pugh right down with his flailing arm, staggered into a stack of crates and fell to the floor, lips blue, eyes white. Martin dragged him back onto the cot and gave him a whiff of oxygen, then knelt by Pugh, who was sitting up, and wiped at his cut cheekbone. "Owen, are you all right, are you going to be all right, Owen?"

"I think I am," Pugh said. "Why are you rubbing that on my face?"

It was a short length of computer tape, now spotted with Pugh's blood. Martin dropped it. "Thought it was a towel. You clipped your cheek on that box there."

"Is he out of it?"

"Seems to be."

They stared down at Kaph lying stiff, his teeth a white line inside dark parted lips.

"Like epilepsy. Brain damage maybe?"

"What about shooting him full of meprobamate?"

Pugh shook his head. "I don't know what's in that shot I already gave him for shock. Don't want to overdose him."

"Maybe he'll sleep it off now."

"I'd like to myself. Between him and the earthquake I can't seem to keep on my feet."

"You got a nasty crack there. Go on, I'll sit up a while."

Pugh cleaned his cut cheek and pulled off his shirt, then paused.

"Is there anything we ought to have done—have tried to do—"

"They're all dead," Martin said heavily, gently.

Pugh lay down on top of his sleeping bag and one instant

later was wakened by a hideous, sucking, struggling noise. He staggered up, found the needle, tried three times to jab it in correctly and failed, began to massage over Kaph's heart. "Mouth-to-mouth," he said, and Martin obeyed. Presently Kaph drew a harsh breath, his heartbeat steadied, his rigid muscles began to relax.

"How long did I sleep?"

"Half an hour."

They stood up sweating. The ground shuddered, the fabric of the dome sagged and swayed. Libra was dancing her awful polka again, her *Totentanz*. The sun, though rising, seemed to have grown larger and redder; gas and dust must have been stirred up in the feeble atmosphere.

"What's wrong with him, Owen?"

"I think he's dying with them."

"Them—But they're all dead, I tell you."

"Nine of them. They're all dead, they were crushed or suffocated. They were all him, he is all of them. They died, and now he's dying their deaths one by one."

"Oh, pity of God," said Martin.

The next time was much the same. The fifth time was worse, for Kaph fought and raved, trying to speak but getting no words out, as if his mouth were stopped with rocks or clay. After that the attacks grew weaker, but so did he. The eighth seizure came at about four-thirty; Pugh and Martin worked till five-thirty doing all they could to keep life in the body that slid without protest into death. They kept him, but Martin said, "The next will finish him." And it did; but Pugh breathed his own breath into the inert lungs, until he himself passed out.

He woke. The dome was opaqued and no light on. He listened and heard the breathing of two sleeping men. He slept, and nothing woke him till hunger did.

The sun was well up over the dark plains, and the planet had stopped dancing. Kaph lay asleep. Pugh and Martin drank tea and looked at him with proprietary triumph.

When he woke Martin went to him: "How do you feel, old man?" There was no answer. Pugh took Martin's place and looked into the brown, dull eyes that gazed toward but not into his own. Like Martin he quickly turned away. He heated food concentrate and brought it to Kaph. "Come on, drink."

He could see the muscles in Kaph's throat tighten. "Let me die," the young man said.

"You're not dying."

Kaph spoke with clarity and precision: "I am nine-tenths dead. There is not enough of me left alive."

That precision convinced Pugh, and he fought the conviction. "No," he said, peremptory. "They are dead. The others. Your brothers and sisters. You're not them, you're alive. You are John Chow. Your life is in your own hands."

The young man lay still, looking into a darkness that was not there.

Martin and Pugh took turns taking the Exploitation hauler and a spare set of robos over to Hellmouth to salvage equipment and protect it from Libra's sinister atmosphere, for the value of the stuff was, literally, astronomical. It was slow work for one man at a time, but they were unwilling to leave Kaph by himself. The one left in the dome did paperwork, while Kaph sat or lay and stared into his darkness and never spoke. The days went by, silent.

The radio spat and spoke: the Mission calling from the ship. "We'll be down on Libra in five weeks, Owen. Thirty-four E-days nine hours I make it as of now. How's tricks in the old dome?"

"Not good, chief. The Exploit team were killed, all but one of them, in the mine. Earthquake. Six days ago."

The radio crackled and sang starsong. Sixteen seconds' lag each way; the ship was out around Planet II now. "Killed, all but one? You and Martin were unhurt?"

"We're all right, chief."

Thirty-two seconds.

"*Passerine* left an Exploit team out here with us. I may put them on the Hellmouth project then, instead of the Quadrant Seven project. We'll settle that when we come down. In any case you and Martin will be relieved at Dome Two. Hold tight. Anything else?"

"Nothing else."

Thirty-two seconds.

"Right then. So long, Owen."

Kaph had heard all this, and later on Pugh said to him, "The chief may ask you to stay here with the other Exploit team. You know the ropes here." Knowing the exigencies of Far Out life, he wanted to warn the young man. Kaph made no answer. Since he had said, "There is not enough of me left alive," he had not spoken a word.

"Owen," Martin said on suit intercom, "he's spla. Insane. Psycho."

"He's doing very well for a man who's died nine times."

"Well? Like a turned-off android is well? The only emotion he has left is hate. Look at his eyes."

"That's not hate, Martin. Listen, it's true that he has, in a sense, been dead. I cannot imagine what he feels. But it's not hatred. He can't even see us. It's too dark."

"Throats have been cut in the dark. He hates us because we're not Aleph and Yod and Zayin."

"Maybe. But I think he's alone. He doesn't see us or hear us, that's the truth. He never had to see anyone else before. He never was alone before. He had himself to see, talk with, live with, nine other selves all his life. He doesn't know how you go it alone. He must learn. Give him time."

Martin shook his heavy head. "Spla," he said. "Just remember when you're alone with him that he could break your neck one-handed."

"He could do that," said Pugh, a short, soft-voiced man with a scarred cheekbone; he smiled. They were just outside the dome airlock, programming one of the servos to repair a damaged hauler. They could see Kaph sitting inside the great half-egg of the dome like a fly in amber.

"Hand me the insert pack there. What makes you think he'll get any better?"

"He has a strong personality, to be sure."

"Strong? Crippled. Nine-tenths dead, as he put it."

"But he's not dead. He's a live man: John Kaph Chow. He had a jolly queer upbringing, but after all every boy has got to break free of his family. He will do it."

"I can't see it."

"Think a bit, Martin bach. What's this cloning for? To repair the human race. We're in a bad way. Look at me. My IIQ and GC are half this John Chow's. Yet they wanted me so badly for the Far Out Service that when I volunteered they took me and fitted me with an artificial lung and corrected my myopia. Now if there were enough good sound lads about would they be taking one-lunged short-sighted Welshmen?"

"Didn't know you had an artificial lung."

"I do then. Not tin, you know. Human, grown in a tank from a bit of somebody; cloned, if you like. That's how they make replacement organs, the same general idea as cloning, but bits and pieces instead of whole people. It's my own lung now, whatever. But what I am saying is this, there are too many like me these days and not enough like John Chow. They're trying to raise the level of the human genetic pool, which is a mucky little puddle since the population crash. So then if a man is cloned, he's a strong and clever man. It's only logic, to be sure."

Martin grunted; the servo began to hum.

Kaph had been eating little; he had trouble swallowing his food, choking on it, so that he would give up trying after a few bites. He had lost eight or ten kilos. After three weeks or so, however, his appetite began to pick up, and one day he began to look through the clone's possessions, the sleeping bags, kits, papers which Pugh had stacked neatly in a far angle of a packing-crate alley. He sorted, destroyed a heap of papers and oddments, made a small packet of what remained, then relapsed into his walking coma.

Two days later he spoke. Pugh was trying to correct a flutter in the tape-player and failing; Martin had the jet out, checking their maps of the Pampas. "Hell and damnation!" Pugh said, and Kaph said in a toneless voice, "Do you want me to do that?"

Pugh jumped, controlled himself, and gave the machine to Kaph. The young man took it apart, put it back together, and left it on the table.

"Put on a tape," Pugh said with careful casualness, busy at another table.

Kaph put on the topmost tape, a chorale. He lay down on his cot. The sound of a hundred human voices singing together filled the dome. He lay still, his face blank.

In the next days he took over several routine jobs, unasked. He undertook nothing that wanted initiative, and if asked to do anything he made no response at all.

"He's doing well," Pugh said in the dialect of Argentina.

"He's not. He's turning himself into a machine. Does what he's programmed to do, no reaction to anything else. He's worse off than when he didn't function at all. He's not human any more."

Pugh sighed. "Well, good night," he said in English. "Good night, Kaph."

"Good night," Martin said; Kaph did not.

Next morning at breakfast Kaph reached across Martin's plate for the toast. "Why don't you ask for it?" Martin said with the geniality of repressed exasperation. "I can pass it."

"I can reach it," Kaph said in his flat voice.

"Yes, but look. Asking to pass things, saying good night or hello, they're not important, but all the same when somebody says something a person ought to answer. . . ."

The young man looked indifferently in Martin's direction; his eyes still did not seem to see clear through to the person he looked toward. "Why should I answer?"

"Because somebody has said something to you."

"Why?"

Martin shrugged and laughed. Pugh jumped up and turned on the rock-cutter.

Later on he said, "Lay off that, please, Martin."

"Manners are essential in small isolated crews, some kind of manners, whatever you work out together. He's been taught that, everybody in Far Out knows it. Why does he deliberately flout it?"

"Do you tell yourself good night?"

"So?"

"Don't you see Kaph's never known anyone but himself?"

Martin brooded and then broke out. "Then by God this cloning business is all wrong. It won't do. What are a lot of duplicate geniuses going to do for us when they don't even know we exist?"

Pugh nodded. "It might be wiser to separate the clones and bring them up with others. But they make such a grand team this way."

"Do they? I don't know. If this lot had been ten average inefficient E.T. engineers, would they all have got killed? What if, when the quake came and things started caving in, what if all those kids ran the same way, farther into the mine, maybe, to save the one who was farthest in? Even Kaph was outside and went in. . . . It's hypothetical. But I keep thinking, out of ten ordinary confused guys, more might have got out."

"I don't know. It's true that identical twins tend to die at about the same time, even when they have never seen each other. Identity and death, it is very strange. . . ."

The days went on, the red sun crawled across the dark sky, Kaph did not speak when spoken to, Pugh and Martin snapped at each other more frequently each day. Pugh complained of Martin's snoring. Offended, Martin moved his cot clear across the dome and also ceased speaking to Pugh for some while. Pugh whistled Welsh dirges until Martin complained, and then Pugh stopped speaking for a while.

The day before the Mission ship was due, Martin announced he was going over to Merioneth.

"I thought at least you'd be giving me a hand with the computer to finish the rock analyses," Pugh said, aggrieved.

"Kaph can do that. I want one more look at the Trench. Have fun," Martin added in dialect, and laughed, and left.

"What is that language?"

"Argentinean. I told you that once, didn't I?"

"I don't know." After a while the young man added, "I have forgotten a lot of things, I think."

"It wasn't important, to be sure," Pugh said gently, realizing all at once how important this conversation was. "Will you give me a hand running the computer, Kaph?"

He nodded.

Pugh had left a lot of loose ends, and the job took them

all day. Kaph was a good co-worker, quick and systematic, much more so than Pugh himself. His flat voice, now that he was talking again, got on the nerves; but it didn't matter, there was only this one day left to get through and then the ship would come, the old crew, comrades and friends.

During tea break Kaph said, "What will happen if the Explore ship crashes?"

"They'd be killed."

"To you, I mean."

"To us? We'd radio SOS signals and live on half rations till the rescue cruiser from Area Three Base came. Four and a half E-years away it is. We have life support here for three men for, let's see, maybe between four and five years. A bit tight, it would be."

"Would they send a cruiser for three men?"

"They would."

Kaph said no more.

"Enough cheerful speculations," Pugh said cheerfully, rising to get back to work. He slipped sideways and the chair avoided his hand; he did a sort of half-pirouette and fetched up hard against the dome hide. "My goodness," he said, reverting to his native idiom, "what is it?"

"Quake," said Kaph.

The teacups bounced on the table with a plastic cackle, a litter of papers slid off a box, the skin of the dome swelled and sagged. Underfoot there was a huge noise, half sound, half shaking, a subsonic boom.

Kaph sat unmoved. An earthquake does not frighten a man who died in an earthquake.

Pugh, white-faced, wiry black hair sticking out, a frightened man, said, "Martin is in the Trench."

"What trench?"

"The big fault line. The epicenter for the local quakes. Look at the seismograph." Pugh struggled with the stuck door of a still-jittering locker.

"Where are you going?"

"After him."

"Martin took the jet. Sleds aren't safe to use during quakes. They go out of control."

"For God's sake man, shut up."

Kaph stood up, speaking in a flat voice as usual. "It's unnecessary to go out after him now. It's taking an unnecessary risk."

"If his alarm goes off, radio me," Pugh said, shut the head-piece of his suit, and ran to the lock. As he went out Libra picked up her ragged skirts and danced a belly dance from under his feet clear to the red horizon.

Inside the dome, Kaph saw the sled go up, tremble like a meteor in the dull red daylight, and vanish to the northeast. The hide of the dome quivered, the earth coughed. A vent south of the dome belched up a slow-flowing bile of black gas.

A bell shrilled and a red light flashed on the central control board. The sign under the light read Suit 2 and scribbled under that, A. G. M. Kaph did not turn the signal off. He tried to radio Martin, then Pugh, but got no reply from either.

When the aftershocks decreased he went back to work and finished up Pugh's job. It took him about two hours. Every half hour he tried to contact Suit 1 and got no reply, then Suit 2 and got no reply. The red light had stopped flashing after an hour.

It was dinnertime. Kaph cooked dinner for one and ate it. He lay down on his cot.

The aftershocks had ceased except for faint rolling tremors at long intervals. The sun hung in the west, oblate, pale red, immense. It did not sink visibly. There was no sound at all.

Kaph got up and began to walk about the messy, half-packed-up, overcrowded, empty dome. The silence continued. He went to the player and put on the first tape that came to hand. It was pure music, electronic, without harmonies, without voices. It ended. The silence continued.

Pugh's uniform tunic, one button missing, hung over a stack of rock samples. Kaph stared at it a while.

The silence continued.

The child's dream: There is no one else alive in the world but me. In all the world.

Low, north of the dome, a meteor flickered.

Kaph's mouth opened as if he were trying to say something, but no sound came. He went hastily to the north wall and peered out into the gelatinous red light.

The little star came in and sank. Two figures blurred the airlock. Kaph stood close beside the lock as they came in. Martin's imsuit was covered with some kind of dust so that he looked raddled and warty like the surface of Libra. Pugh had him by the arm.

"Is he hurt?"

Pugh shucked his suit, helped Martin peel off his. "Shaken up," he said, curt.

"A piece of cliff fell onto the jet," Martin said, sitting down at the table and waving his arms. "Not while I was in it though. I was parked, see, and poking about that carbon-dust area when I felt things humping. So I went out onto a nice bit of early igneous I'd noticed from above, good footing and out from under the cliffs. Then I saw this bit of the planet fall off onto the flyer, quite a sight it was, and after a while it occurred to me the spare aircans were in the flyer, so I leaned on the panic button. But I didn't get any radio reception, that's always happening here during quakes, so I didn't know if the signal was getting through either. And things went on jumping around and pieces of the cliff coming off. Little rocks flying around, and so dusty you couldn't see a meter ahead. I was really beginning to wonder what I'd do for breathing in the small hours, you know, when I saw old Owen buzzing up the Trench in all that dust and junk like a big ugly bat—"

"Want to eat?" said Pugh.

"Of course I want to eat. How'd you come through the quake here, Kaph? No damage? It wasn't a big one actually, was it, what's the seismo say? My trouble was I was in the middle of it. Old Epicenter Alvaro. Felt like Richter fifteen there—total destruction of planet—"

"Sit down," Pugh said. "Eat."

After Martin had eaten a little his spate of talk ran dry. He very soon went off to his cot, still in the remote angle where he had removed it when Pugh complained of his snoring.

"Good night, you one-lunged Welshman," he said across the dome.

"Good night."

There was no more out of Martin. Pugh opaqued the dome, turned the lamp down to a yellow glow less than a candle's light, and sat doing nothing, saying nothing, withdrawn.

The silence continued.

"I finished the computations."

Pugh nodded thanks.

"The signal from Martin came through, but I couldn't contact you or him."

Pugh said with effort, "I should not have gone. He had two hours of air left even with only one can. He might have been heading home when I left. This way we were all out of touch with one another. I was scared."

The silence came back, punctuated now by Martin's long, soft snores.

"Do you love Martin?"

Pugh looked up with angry eyes: "Martin is my friend. We've worked together, he's a good man." He stopped. After a while he said, "Yes, I love him. Why did you ask that?"

Kaph said nothing, but he looked at the other man. His face was changed, as if he were glimpsing something he had not seen before; his voice too was changed. "How can you . . . How do you . . ."

But Pugh could not tell him. "I don't know," he said, "it's practice, partly. I don't know. We're each of us alone, to be sure. What can you do but hold your hand out in the dark?"

Kaph's strange gaze dropped, burned out by its own intensity.

"I'm tired," Pugh said. "That was ugly, looking for him in all that black dust and muck, and mouths opening and shutting in the ground. . . . I'm going to bed. The ship will be transmitting to us by six or so." He stood up and stretched.

"It's a clone," Kaph said. "The other Exploit Team they're bringing with them."

"Is it then?"

"A twelveclone. They came out with us on the *Passerine*."

Kaph sat in the small yellow aura of the lamp seeming to look past it at what he feared: the new clone, the multiple self of which he was not part. A lost piece of a broken set, a fragment, inexpert at solitude, not knowing even how you go about giving love to another individual, now he must face the absolute, closed self-sufficiency of the clone of twelve; that was a lot to ask of the poor fellow, to be sure. Pugh put a hand on his shoulder in passing. "The chief won't ask you to stay here with a clone. You can go home. Or since you're Far Out maybe you'll come on farther out with us. We could use you. No hurry deciding. You'll make out all right."

Pugh's quiet voice trailed off. He stood unbuttoning his coat, stooped a little with fatigue. Kaph looked at him and saw the thing he had never seen before, saw him: Owen Pugh, the other, the stranger who held his hand out in the dark.

"Good night," Pugh mumbled, crawling into his sleeping bag and half asleep already, so that he did not hear Kaph reply after a pause, repeating, across darkness, benediction.

MARY

Damon Knight

A multi-talented professional whose career as writer, editor, critic, and anthologist spans almost fifty years, Damon Knight has long been a major shaping force in the development of modern science fiction. He wrote the first important book of SF criticism, In Search of Wonder, *and won a Hugo Award for it. He was the founder of the Science Fiction Writers of America, co-founder of the prestigious Milford Writer's Conference, and, with his wife, writer Kate Wilhelm, was involved in the creation of the* Clarion *workshop for new young writers. He was the editor of* Orbit, *the longest running original anthology series in the history of American science fiction, and has also produced important works of genre history such as* The Futurians and Turning Points, *as well as dozens of influential reprint anthologies. Knight has also been highly influential as a writer, and may well be one of the finest short story writers ever to work in the genre. His books include the novels* A For Anything, The Other Foot, Hell's Pavement, The Man in the Tree, CV, *and* A Reasonable World, Why Do Birds, *and the collections* Rule Golden and Other Stories, Turning On, Far Out, The Best of Damon Knight, *and the recent* One Side Laughing. *His most recent book is the critically acclaimed novel* Humptey Dumptey: An Oval.*

Here, in one of the earliest clone stories in SF, from the days before the term "clone" itself was even coined, he brings us a future of quiet voices, cool shadows, shuttered stairwells, boats rocking at mooring, white ceramic islands on a placid blue sea, crystalline music, wine, new cloth. A drowsy civilized afternoon of life, full of pastels and pleasant silences, where all the pieces fit neatly together and everything works smoothly and calmly—except for one piece just a little out of kind . . .

Thirty sisters, alike as peas, were sitting at their looms in the court above the Gallery of Weavers. In the cool shadow, their white dresses rustled like the stirrings of doves, and their voices now murmured, now shrilled. Over the court-yard was a canopy of green glass, through which the sun appeared to swim like a golden-green fish: but over the roofs could be seen the strong blue of the sky, and even, at one or two places, the piercing white sparkle of the sea.

The sisters were ivory-skinned, strong-armed and straight of back, with eyebrows arched black over bright eyes. Some had grown fat, some were lean, but the same smiles dimpled their cheeks, the same gestures threw back their sleek heads when they laughed, and each saw herself mirrored in the others.

Only the youngest, Mary, was different. Hers was the clan face, but so slender and grave that it seemed a stranger's. She had been brought to birth to replace old Anna-one, who had fallen from the lookout and broken her neck sixteen springs ago; and some said it had been done too quick, that Mary was from a bad egg and should never have been let grow. Now the truth was that Mary had in her genes a long-recessive trait of melancholy and unwordliness, turned up by accident in the last cross; but the Elders, who after all knew best, had decided to give her the same chance as anyone. For in the floating island of Iliria, everyone knew that the purpose of life was happiness; and therefore to deprive anyone of life was a great shame.

At the far side of the court, Vivana called from her loom, "They say a new Fisher came from the mainland yester-day!" She was the eldest of the thirty, a coarse, good-natured woman with a booming laugh. "If he's handsome, I may take him, and give you others a chance at my Tino. Rose, how would you like that? Tino would be a good man for you." Her loom whirled, and rich, dark folds of liase rippled out. It was an artificial fiber, formed, spun, woven and dyed in the loom, hardening as it reached the air. A canister of the stuff, like tinted gelatin, stood at the top of every loom. It came from the Chemist clan, who concocted it by mysterious workings out of the sea water that tumbled through their vats.

"What, is he tiring of you already?" Rose called back. She was short and moon-faced, with strong, clever fingers that danced on the keyboard of her loom. "Probably you belched in his face once too often." She raised her shrill voice over the laughter. "Now let me tell you, Vivana, if the new Fisher is as handsome as that, I may take him myself, and let you have Mitri." Mounds of apple-green stuff tumbled into the basket at her feet.

Between them, Mary worked on, eyes cast down, without smiling.

"Gogo and Vivana!" someone shouted.

"Yes, that's right—never mind about the Fisher! Gogo and Vivana!" All the sisters were shouting and laughing. But Mary still sat quietly busy at her loom.

"All right, all right," shouted Vivana, wheezing with laughter. "I will try him, but then who's to have Gunner?"

"Me!"

"No, me!"

Gunner was the darling of the Weavers, a pink man with thick blond lashes and a roguish grin.

"No, let the youngsters have a chance," Vivana called reprovingly. "Joking aside, Gunner is too good for you old scows." Ignoring the shrieks of outrage, she went on, "I say let Viola have him. Better yet, wait, I have an idea—how about Mary?"

The chatter stilled; all eyes turned toward the silent girl where she sat, weaving slow cascades of creamy white liase. She flushed quickly, and bowed her head, unable to speak. She was sixteen, and had never taken a lover.

The women looked at her, and the pleasure faded out of their faces. Then they turned away, and the shouting began again:

"Rudi!"

"Ernestine!"

"Hugo!"

"Areta!"

Mary's slim hands faltered, and the intricate diapered pattern of her weaving was spoiled. Now the bolt would have to be cut off, unfinished. She stopped the loom, and drooped over it, pressing her forehead against the smooth metal. Tears burned her eyelids. But she held herself still, hoping Mia, at the next loom, would not see.

Below in the street, a sudden tumult went up. Heads turned to listen: there was the wailing of flutes, the thundering of drums, and the sound of men's rich voices, all singing and laughing.

A gate banged open, and a clatter of feet came tumbling up the stair. The white dresses rustled as the sisters turned expectantly toward the arch.

A knot of laughing, struggling men burst through, full into the midst of the women, toppling looms, while the sisters shrieked in protest and pleasure.

The men were Mechanics, dark-haired, gaunt, leavened by a few blond Chemists. They were wrestling, Mechanic against Chemist, arms locked about each other's necks, legs straining for leverage. One struggling pair toppled suddenly, overturning two more. The men scrambled up, laughing, red with exertion.

Behind them was a solitary figure whose stillness drew Mary's eyes. He was tall, slender and grave, with russet hair and a quiet mouth. While the others shouted and pranced, he stood looking around the courtyard. For an instant his calm gray eyes met hers, and Mary felt a sudden pain at the heart.

"Dear, what is it?" asked Mia, leaning closer.

"I think I am ill," said Mary faintly.

"Oh, not now!" Mia protested.

Two of the men were wrestling again. A heave, and the dark Mechanic went spinning over the other's hip.

A shout of applause went up. Through the uproar, Vivana's big voice came booming, "You fishheads, get out! Look at this, half a morning's work ruined! Are you all drunk? Get out!"

"We're all free for the day!" one of the Mechanics shouted. "You too—the whole district! It's in the Fisher's honor! So come on, what are you waiting for?"

The women were up, in a sudden flutter of voices and white skirts, the men beginning to spread out among them. The tall man still stood where he was. Now he was looking frankly at Mary, and she turned away in confusion, picking up the botched fabric with hands that did not feel it.

She was aware that two Mechanics had turned back, were leading the tall man across the courtyard, calling, "Violet— Clara!" She did not move: her breath stopped.

Then they were pausing before her loom. There was an awful moment when she thought she could not move or breathe. She looked up fearfully. He was standing there, hands in his pockets, slumped a little as he looked down at her.

He said, "What is your name?" His voice was low and gentle.

"Mary," she said.

"Will you go with me today, Mary?"

Around her, the women's heads were turning. A silence spread; she could sense the waiting, the delight held in check.

She could not! Her whole soul yearned for it, but she was too afraid, there were too many eyes watching. Miserably, she said, "No," and stopped, astonished, listening to the echo of her voice saying gladly, "Yes!"

Suddenly her heart grew light as air. She stood, letting the loom fall, and when he held out his hand, hers went into it as if it knew how.

"So you have a rendezvous with a Mainland Fisher?" the Doctor inquired jovially. He was pale-eyed and merry in his broad brown hat and yellow tunic; he popped open his little bag, took out a pill, handed it to Mary. "Swallow this, dear."

"What is it for, Doctor?" she asked, flushing.

"Only a precaution. You wouldn't want a baby to grow right in your belly, would you? Ha, ha, ha! That shocks you, does it? Well, you see, the Mainlanders don't sterilize the males, their clan customs forbid it, so they sterilize the females instead. We have to be watchful, ah, yes, we Doctors! Swallow it down, there's a good girl."

She took the pill, drank a sip of water from the flask he
handed her.

"Good, good—now you can go to your little meeting and
be perfectly safe. Enjoy yourself!" Beaming, he closed his
bag and went away.

On the high Plaza of Fountains, overlooking the quayside
and the sea, feasts of shrimp and wine, seaweed salad,
caviar, pasta, iced sweets had been laid out under canopies
of green glass. Orchestrinos were playing. Couples were
dancing on the old ceramic cobbles, white skirts swinging,
hair afloat in the brilliant air. Farther up, Mary and her
Fisher had found a place to be alone.

Under the bower in the cool shade, they lay clasped heart
to heart, their bodies still joined so that in her ecstasy she
could not tell where hers ended or his began.

"Oh, I love you, I love you!" she murmured.

His body moved, his head drew back a little to look at her.
There was something troubled in his gray eyes. "I didn't
know this was going to be your first time," he said. "How is
it that you waited so long?"

"I was waiting for you," she said faintly, and it seemed to
her that it was so, and that she had always known it. Her
arms tightened around him, wishing to draw him closer to
her body again.

But he held himself away, looking down at her with the
same vague uneasiness in his eyes. "I don't understand," he
said. "How could you have known I was coming?"

"I knew," she said. Timidly her hands began to stroke the
long, smooth muscles of his back, the man's flesh, so
different from her own. It seemed to her that her fingertips
knew him without being told; they found the tiny spots that
gave him pleasure, and lingered there, without her direction.

His body stiffened; his gray eyes half closed. "Oh, Mary,"
he said, and then he was close against her again, his mouth
busy on hers: and the pleasure began, more piercing and
sweet than she had ever dreamed it could be. Now she was
out of herself again, half aware that her body was moving,

writhing; that her voice was making sounds and speaking words that astonished her to hear . . .

Near the end she began to weep, and lay in his arms afterward with the luxurious tears wetting her cheeks, while his voice asked anxiously, "Are you all right? Darling, are you all right?" and she could not explain, but only held him tighter, and wept.

Later, hand in hand, they wandered down the bone-white stairs to the quayside strewn with drying nets, the glass floats sparkling sharp in the sun, spars, tackle and canvas piled everywhere. Only two boats were moored at the floating jetty below; the rest were out fishing, black specks on the glittering sea, almost at the horizon.

Over to eastward they saw the desolate smudge of the mainland and the huddle of stones that was Porto. "That's where you live," she said wonderingly.

"Yes."

"What do you do there?"

He paused, looked down at her with that startled unease in his glance. After a moment he shrugged. "Work. Drink a little in the evenings, make love. What else would I do?"

A dull pain descended suddenly on her heart and would not lift its wings. "You've made love to many women?" she asked with difficulty.

"Of course. Mary, what's the matter?"

"You're going back to Porto. You're going to leave me."

Now the unnamed thing in his eyes had turned to open incredulity. He held her arms, staring down at her. "What else?"

She put her head down obstinately, burying it against his chest. "I want to stay with you," she said in a muffled voice.

"But you *can't*. You're an Islander—I'm a Mainlander."

"I know."

"Then why this foolishness?"

"I don't know."

He turned her without speaking, and they stepped down from the promenade, went into the shadow of some storehouses that abutted on the quayside. The doors were open, breathing scents of spices and tar, new cordage, drying fish. Beyond them was a pleasant courtyard with boats piled upside down on one side, on the other a table, an umbrella, chairs, all cool in the afternoon shadow. From there they took a shallow staircase up into a maze of little streets full of the dim, mysterious blue light that fell from canopies of tinted glass between roofs. Passing a house with open shutters, they heard the drone of childish voices. They peered in: it was the nursery school—forty young Bakers, Chemists, Mechanics, fair skins and dark, each in a doll-like miniature of his clan costume, all earnestly reciting together while the shovel-hatted Teacher stood listening at the greenboard. Cool, neutral light came from the louvered skylights; the small faces were clear and innocent, here a tiny Cook in his apron, there two Carters sitting together, identical in their blue smocks, there a pale Doctor, and beside him Mary saw with a pang, a little Weaver in white. The familiar features were childishly blunted and small, the ivory skin impossibly pure, the bright eyes wide. "Look— that one," she whispered, pointing.

He peered in. "She looks like you. More like you than the others. You're different from all the rest, Mary—that's why I like you." He looked down at her with a puzzled expression; his arms tightened around her. "I've never felt quite this way about a girl before; what are you doing to me?" he said.

She turned to him, embracing him, letting her body go soft and compliant against his. "Loving you, darling," she said, smiling up, her eyes half-closed.

He kissed her fiercely, then pushed her away, looking almost frightened. "See here, Mary," he said abruptly, "we've got to understand something."

"Yes?" she said faintly, clinging to him.

"I'm going to be back in Porto tomorrow morning," he said.

"Tomorrow!" she said. "I thought—"

"My work was done this morning. It was a simple adjustment of the sonics. You'll catch plenty of fish from now on . . . There's nothing more for me to do here."

She was stunned; she could not believe it. Surely there
would be at least another night . . . that was little enough
to ask.

"Can't you stay?" she said.

"You know I can't." His voice was rough and strained. "I
go where they tell me, come when they say come."

She tried to hold back the time, but it slipped away, ran
through her fingers. The sky darkened slowly from cerulean
to Prussian blue, the stars came out and the cool night wind
stirred over the jetty.

Below her, in a cluster of lights, they were making the
boat ready. Orchestrinos were playing up the hillside, and
there was a little crowd of men and women gathering to say
good-bye. There was laughter, joking, voices raised good-
naturedly in the evening stillness.

Klef, pale in the lights, came up the stairs to where she
stood, his head tilted as he came, his grave eyes holding
hers.

"I'm not going to cry," she said.

His hands took her arms, gripping her half in tenderness,
half impatiently. "Mary, you know this is wrong. Get over
it. Find yourself other men—be happy."

"Yes, I'll be happy," she said.

He stared down at her in uncertainty, then bent his head
and kissed her. She held herself passive in his arms, not
responding or resisting. After a moment he let her go and
stepped back. "Good-bye, Mary."

"Good-bye, Klef."

He turned, went quickly down the steps. The laughing
voices surrounded him as he went toward the boat; after a
moment she heard his voice, too, lifted in cheerful farewells.

In the morning she awoke knowing that he was gone. A
frightening knowledge of loss seized her, and she sat up
with her heart leaping.

Down the high dormitory, smelling faintly of cinnamon
oil and fresh linens, the sisters were beginning to rustle
sleepily out of their cubicles, murmuring and yawning. The

familiar hiss of the showers began at the far end of the room. The white-curtained windows were open, and from her bed Mary could see the cream and terra-cotta roofs spread out in a lazy descent. The air was cool and still and mysteriously pure: it was the best moment of the day.

She rose, washed herself and dressed mechanically. "What is it, dear?" asked Mia, bending toward her anxiously.

"Nothing. Klef is gone."

"Well, there'll be others." Mia smiled and patted her hand, and went away. There was a closeness between them, they were almost of an age, and yet even Mia could not be comfortable long in Mary's company.

Mary sat with the others at table, silent in the steaming fragrances of coffee and new bread, the waves of cheerful talk that flowed around her. Carrying her loom, she went down with the rest into the court and sat in her usual place. The work began.

Time stretched away wearily into the future. How many mornings in her life would she sit here, where she sat now, beginning to weave as she did now? How could she endure it? How had she ever endured it? She put her fingers on the controls of the loom, but the effort to move them appalled her. A tear dropped bright on the keyboard.

Mia leaned over toward her. "Is there anything the matter? Don't you feel well?"

Her fists clenched uselessly. "I can't—I can't—" was all she could utter. Hot tears were running down her face; her jaw was shaking. She bowed her head over the loom.

Iliria was neither wearisomely flat, nor cone-shaped nor pyramidal in its construction, like some of the northern islands, but was charmingly hollowed, like a cradle. The old cobblestoned streets rose and fell; there were stairways, balconies, arcades; never a vista, always a new prospect. The buildings were pleasingly various, some domed and spired, others sprawling. Cream was the dominant color, with accents of cool light blue, yellow, and rose. For more than three hundred years the island had been afloat, just as

it now was: the same plazas with their fountains, the same
shuttered windows, the same rooftops.

During the last century, some colonies had been creeping
back onto the land as the contamination diminished; but
every Ilirian knew that only island life was perfect. Above,
the unchanging streets and buildings served each generation
as the last; down below, the storage chambers, engine
rooms, seines, preserving rooms, conveniently out of sight
and hearing, went on functioning as they always had.
Unsinkable, sheathed in ceramic above and below, the
island would go on floating just as it now was, forever.

It was strange to Mary to see the familiar streets so
empty. The morning light lay softly along the walls; in
corners, blue shadow gathered. Behind every door and
window there was a subdued hum of activity; the clans were
at their work. All the way to the church circle, she passed no
one but a Messenger and two Carters with their loads: all
three looked at her curiously until she was out of sight.

Climbing the Hill of Carpenters, she saw the gray dome
of the church rising against the sky—a smooth, unrelieved
ovoid, with a crescent of morning light upon it. Overhead,
a flock of gulls hung in the air, wings spread, rising and
dipping. They were gray against the light.

She paused on the porch step to look down. From this
height she could see the quays and the breakwater, and the
sun on the brightwork of the moored launches; and then the
long rolling back of the sea, full of whitecaps in the freshening
breeze; and beyond that, the dark smudge of the land, and
the clutter of brown windowed stone that was Porto. She
stood looking at it for a moment, dry-eyed, then went into
the shadowed doorway.

Clabert the Priest rose up from his little desk and came
toward her with ink-stained fingers, his skirt flapping
around his ankles. "Good morning, cousin, have you a
trouble?"

"I'm in love with a man who has gone away."

He stared at her in perplexity for a moment, then darted
down the corridor to the left. "This way, cousin." She
followed him past the great doors of the central harmonion.

He opened a smaller door, curved like the end of an egg, and motioned her in.

She stepped inside; the room was gray, egg-shaped, and the light came uniformly from the smooth ceramic walls. "Twenty minutes," said Clabert, and withdrew his head. The door shut, joining indistinguishably with the wall around it.

Mary found herself standing on the faintly sloping floor, with the smooth single curve of the wall surrounding her. After a moment she could no longer tell how far away the big end of the ovicle was; the room seemed first quite small, only a few yards from one end to the other; then it was gigantic, bigger than the sky. The floor shifted uncertainly under her feet, and after another moment she sat down on the cool hollow slope.

The silence grew and deepened. She had no feeling of confinement; the air was fresh and in constant slight movement. She felt faintly and agreeably dizzy, and put her arms behind her to steady herself. Her vision began to blur; the featureless gray curve gave her no focus for her eyes. Another moment passed, and she became aware that the muffled silence was really a continual slow hush of sound, coming from all points at once, like the distant murmuring of the sea. She held her breath to listen, and at once, like dozens of wings flicking away in turn, the sound stopped. Now, listening intently, she could hear a still fainter sound, a soft, rapid patterning that stopped and came again, stopped and came again . . . and listening, she realized that it was the multiple echo of her own heartbeat. She breathed again, and the slow hush flooded back.

The wall approached, receded . . . gradually it became neither close nor far away; it hung gigantically and mistily just out of reach. The movement of air imperceptibly slowed. Lying dazed and unthinking, she grew intensely aware of her own existence, the meaty solidness of her flesh, the incessant pumping of blood, the sigh of breath, the heaviness and pressure, the pleasant beading of perspiration on her skin. She was whole and complete, all the way from fingers to toes. She was uniquely herself; somehow she had forgotten how important that was . . .

"Feeling better?" asked Clabert, as he helped her out of the chamber.

"Yes . . ." She was dazed and languid; walking was an extraordinary effort.

"Come back if you have these confusions again," Clabert called after her, standing in the porch doorway.

Without replying, she went down the slope in the brilliant sunshine. Her head was light, her feet were amusingly slow to obey her. In a moment she was running to catch up with herself, down the steep cobbled street in a stumbling rush, with faces popping out of shutters behind her, and fetched up laughing and gasping with her arms around a light column at the bottom.

A stout Carter in blue was grinning at her out of his tanned face. "What's the joke, woman?"

"Nothing," she stammered. "I've just been to church . . ."

"Ah," he said, with a finger beside his nose, and went on.

She found herself taking the way downward to the quays. The sunlit streets were empty; no one was in the pools. She stripped and plunged in, gasping at the pleasure of the cool fresh water on her body. And even when two Baker boys, an older one and a younger, came by and leaned over the wall shouting, "Pretty! Pretty!" she felt no confusion, but smiled up at them and went on swimming.

Afterward, she dressed and strolled, wet as she was, along the sea-wall promenade. Giddily she began to sing as she walked, "Open your arms to me, sweetheart, for when the sun shines it's pleasant to be in love . . ." The orchestrinos had been playing that, that night when—

She felt suddenly ill, and stopped with her hand at her forehead.

What was wrong with her? Her mind seemed to topple, shake itself from one pattern into another. She swung her head up, looking with sharp anxiety for the brown tangle of buildings on the mainland.

At first it was not there, and then she saw it, tiny, almost lost on the horizon. The island was drifting, moving away, leaving the mainland behind.

She sat down abruptly; her legs lost their strength. She put her face in her arms and wept: "Klef! Oh, Klef!"

This love that had come to her was not the easy, pleasant thing the orchestrinos sang of; it was a kind of madness. She accepted that, and knew herself to be mad, yet could not change. Waking and sleeping, she could think only of Klef.

Her grief had exhausted itself; her eyes were dry. She could see herself now as the others saw her—as something strange, unpleasant, ill-fitting. What right had she to spoil their pleasure?

She could go back to church, and spend another dazed time in the ovicle. "If you have these confusions again," the Priest had said. She could go every morning, if need be, and again every afternoon. She had seen one who needed to do as much, silly Marget Tailor who always nodded and smiled, drooling a little, no matter what was said to her, and who seemed to have a blankness behind the glow of happiness in her eyes. That was years ago; she remembered the sisters always complained of the wet spots Marget left on her work. Something must have happened to her; others cut and stitched for the Weavers now.

Or she could hug her pain to herself, scourge them with it, make them do something . . . She had a vision of herself running barefoot and ragged through the streets, with people in their doorways shouting, "Crazy Mary! Crazy Mary!" If she made them notice her, made them bring Klef back . . .

She stopped eating except when the other sisters urged her, and grew thinner day by day. Her cheeks and eyes were hollow. All day she sat in the courtyard, not weaving, until at length the other women's voices grew melancholy and seldom. The weaving suffered; there was no joy in the clan house. Many times Vivana and the others reasoned with her, but she could only give the same answers over again, and at last she stopped replying at all.

"But what do you want?" the women asked her, with a note of exasperation in their voices.

What did she want? She wanted Klef to be beside her

every night when she went to sleep, and when she wakened in the morning. She wanted his arms about her, his flesh joined to hers, his voice murmuring in her ear. Other men? It was not the same thing. But they could not understand.

"But why do you want me to make myself pretty?" Mary asked with dull curiosity.

Mia bent over her with a tube of cosmetic, touching the pale lips with crimson. "Never mind, something nice. Here, let me smooth your eyebrows. Tut, how thin you've got! Never mind, you'll look very well. Put on your fresh robe, there's a dear."

"I don't know what difference it makes." But Mary stood up wearily, took off her dress, stood thin and pale in the light. She put the new robe over her head, shrugged her arms into it.

"Is that all right?" she asked.

"Dear Mary," said Mia, with tears of sympathy in her eyes. "Sweet, no, let me smooth your hair. Stand straighter, can't you, how will any man—"

"Man?" said Mary. A little color came and went in her cheeks. "Klef!"

"*No*, dear, forget Klef, will you?" Mia's voice turned sharp with exasperation.

"Oh." Mary turned her head away.

"Can't you think of anything else? Do try, dear, just try."

"All right."

"Now come along, they're waiting for us."

Mary stood up submissively and followed her sister out of the dormitory.

In bright sunlight the women stood talking quietly and worriedly around the bower. With them was a husky Chemist with golden brows and hair; his pink face was good-natured and peaceful. He pinched the nearest sister's buttocks, whispered something in her ear; she slapped his hand irritably.

"Quick, here they come," said one suddenly. "Go in now, Gunner."

With an obedient grimace, the blond man ducked his head
and disappeared into the bower. In a moment Mia and Mary
came into view, the thin girl hanging back when she saw the
crowd, and the bower.

"What is it?" she complained. "I don't want—Mia, let
me go."

"No, dear, come along, it's for the best, you'll see," said
the other girl soothingly. "Do give me a hand here, one of
you, won't you?"

The two women urged the girl toward the bower. Her face
was pale and frightened. "But what do you want me
to—You said Klef wasn't—Were you only teasing me? Is
Klef—?"

The women gave each other looks of despair. "Go in,
dear, and see, why don't you?"

A wild expression came into Mary's eyes. She hesitated,
then stepped nearer the bower; the two women let her go.
"Klef?" she called plaintively. There was no answer.

"Go in, dear."

She looked at them appealingly, then stooped and put her
head in. The women held their breaths. They heard her gasp,
then saw her backing out again.

"Crabs and mullets!" swore Vivana. "Get her in, you
fools!"

The girl was crying out, weakly and helplessly, as four
women swarmed around her, pushed her into the bower.
One of them lingered, peered in.

"Has he got her?"

"Yes, now he's got her." Stifled mewing sounds were
coming from the bower. "Hang onto her, you fool!"

"She bit!" came Gunner's indignant voice. Then silence.

"Sst, leave them alone," whispered Vivana. The woman
at the bower entrance turned, tiptoed away. Together the
women withdrew a few yards, found themselves seats on the
old steps under the portico, and sat down comfortably close
to one another.

There was a scream.

The women leaped up, startled and white. Not one of
them could remember hearing such a sound before.

Gunner's hoarse voice bawled something, then there was a stir. Mary appeared in the entrance to the bower. Her skirt was ripped, and she was clutching it to her lap with one hand. Her eyes were filmed, pink-rimmed. "Oh!" she said, moving past them blindly.

"Mary—" said one, reaching out a hand.

"Oh!" she said hopelessly, and moved on, clutching her garment to her body.

"What's the matter?" they asked each other. "What did Gunner do?"

"I did what I was supposed to do," said Gunner, sulkily appearing. There was a red bruise on his cheek. "Gut me and clean me if I ever do it with that one again, though."

"You fool, you must have been too rough. Go after her, someone."

"Well, then serve her yourself the next time, if you know so much." Prodding his cheek gently with a finger, the Chemist went away.

Up the slope, an orchestrino began playing. *"If you would not be cruel, torment me no more. Do not deny me ever; let it be now or never. Give me your love, then, as you promised me before . . ."*

"Shut that thing off!" cried Vivana angrily.

Her ageship, Laura-one, the eldest Weaver, was pacing up and down the sea-wall promenade, knotting her fingers together in silent agitation. Once she paused to look over the parapet; below her the wall dropped sheer to blue water. She glanced over at the blur of Porto, half concealed in the morning haze, and at the stark hills above with their green fur of returning vegetation. Her eyes were still keen; halfway across the distance, she could make out a tiny dark dot, moving toward the island.

Footsteps sounded in the street below; in a moment Vivana appeared, holding Mary by the arm. The younger woman's eyes were downcast; the older looked worried and anxious.

"Here she is, your ageship," said Vivana. "They found her at the little jetty, throwing bottles into the sea."

"Again?" asked the old woman. "What was in the bottles?"

"Here's one of them," said Vivana, handing over a crumpled paper.

"'Tell Klef the Fisher of the town of Porto that Mary Weaver still loves him,'" the old woman read. She folded the paper slowly and put it into her pocket. "Always the same," she said. "Mary, my child, don't you know that these bottles never can reach your Klef?"

The young woman did not raise her head or speak.

"And twice this month the Fishers have had to catch you and bring you back when you stole a launch," the old woman continued. "Child, don't you see that this must end?"

Mary did not answer.

"And these things that you weave, when you weave at all," said Laura-one, taking a wadded length of cloth from her apron pocket. She spread it taut and held it to the light. In the pattern, visible only when the light fell glancingly upon it, was woven the figure of a seated woman with a child in her arms. Around them were birds with spread wings among the intertwined stems of flowers.

"Who taught you to weave like this, child?" she asked.

"No one," said Mary, not looking up.

The old woman looked down at the cloth again. "It's beautiful work, but—" She sighed and put the cloth away. "We have no place for it. Child, you weave so well, why can't you weave the usual patterns?"

"They are dead. This one is alive."

The old woman sighed again. "And how long is it that you have been demanding your Klef back, dear?"

"Seven months."

"But now think." The old woman paused, glanced over her shoulder. The black dot on the sea was much nearer, curving in toward the jetty below. "Suppose this Klef did receive one of your messages; what then?"

"He would know how much I love him," said Mary, raising her head. Color came into her cheeks; her eyes brightened.

"And that would change his whole life, his loyalties, everything?"

"Yes!"

"And if it did not?"

Mary was silent.

"Child, if that failed, would you confess that you have been wrong—would you let us help you?"

"It wouldn't fail," Mary said stubbornly.

"But if it did?" the older woman insisted gently. "Just suppose—just let yourself imagine."

Mary was silent a moment. "I would want to die," she said.

The two elder Weavers looked at each other, and for a moment neither spoke.

"May I go now?" Mary asked.

Vivana cast a glance down at the jetty, and said quickly, "Maybe it's best, your ageship. Tell them—"

Laura-one stopped her with a raised hand. Her lips were compressed. "And if you go, child, what will you do now?"

"Go and make more messages, to put into bottles."

The old woman sighed. "You see?" she said to Vivana.

Footsteps sounded faintly on the jetty stair. A man's head appeared; he was an island Fisher, stocky, dark-haired, with a heavy black mustache. "Your ageship, the man is here," he said, saluting Laura-one. "Shall I—?"

"No," said Vivana involuntarily. "Don't— Send him back—"

"What would be the good of that?" the old woman asked reasonably. "No, bring him up, Alec."

The Fisher nodded, turned and was gone down the stair. Mary's head had come up. She said, "The man—?"

"There, it's all right," said Vivana, going to her.

"Is it Klef?" she asked fearfully.

The older woman did not reply. In a moment the black-mustached Fisher appeared again; he stared at them, climbed to the head of the stair, stood aside.

Behind him, after a moment, another head rose out of the stairwell. Under the russet hair, the face was grave and thin. The gray eyes went to Laura-one, then to Mary; they stared at her, as the man continued to climb the steps. He reached the top, and stood waiting, hands at his sides. The black-mustached Fisher turned and descended behind him.

Mary had begun to tremble all over.

"There, dear, it's all right," said Vivana, pressing her arms. As if the words had released her, Mary walked to the Fisher. Tears were shining on her face. She clutched his tunic with both hands, staring up at him. "Klef?" she said.

His hands came up to hold her. She threw herself against him then, so violently that he staggered, and clutched him as if she wished to bury herself in his body. Strangled, hurt sounds came out of her.

The man looked over her head at the two older women. "Can't you leave us alone for a moment?" he asked.

"Of course," said Laura-one, a little surprised. "Why not? Of course." She gestured to Vivana, and the two turned, walked away a little distance down the promenade to a bench, where they sat looking out over the sea-wall.

Gulls mewed overhead. The two women sat side by side without speaking or looking at one another. They were not quite out of earshot.

"Is it really you?" Mary asked, holding his face between her hands. She tried to laugh. "Darling, I can't see . . . you're all blurred."

"I know," said Klef quietly. "Mary, I've thought about you many times."

"Have you?" she cried. "Oh, that makes me so happy. Oh, Klef, I could die now! Hold me, hold me."

His face hardened. His hands absently stroked her back, up and down. "I kept asking to be sent back," he said. "Finally I persuaded them—they thought you might listen to me. I'm supposed to cure you."

"Of loving you?" Mary laughed. At the sound, his hands tightened involuntarily on her back. "How foolish they were! How foolish, Klef!"

"Mary, we have only these few minutes," he said.

She drew back a little to look at him. "I don't understand."

"I'm to talk to you, and then go back. That's all I'm here for."

She shook her head in disbelief. "But you told me—"

"Mary, listen to me. There is nothing else to do. Nothing."

"Take me back with you, Klef." Her hands gripped him hard. "That's what I want—just to be with you. Take me back."

"And where will you live—in the Fishers' dormitory with forty men?"

"I'll live anywhere, in the streets, I don't care—"

"They would never allow it. You know that, Mary."

She was crying, holding him, shuddering all over. "Don't tell me that, don't say it. Even if it's true, can't you pretend a little? Hold me, Klef, tell me that you love me."

"I love you," he said.

"Tell me that you'll keep me, never let me go, no matter what they say."

He was silent a moment. "It's impossible."

She raised her head.

"Try to realize," he said, "this is a sickness, Mary. You must cure yourself."

"Then you're sick too!" she said.

"Maybe I am, but I'll get well, because I know I have to. And you must get well too. Forget me. Go back to your sisters and your weaving."

She put her cheek against his chest, gazing out across the bright ocean. "Let me just be quiet with you a moment," she added. "I won't cry anymore. Klef—"

"Yes?"

"Is that all you have to say to me?"

"It has to be all." His eyes closed, opened again. "Mary, I didn't want to feel this way. It's wrong, it's unhealthy, it hurts. Promise me, before I go. Say you'll let them cure you."

She pushed herself away, wiped her eyes and her cheeks with the heel of one hand. Then she looked up. "I'll let them cure me," she said.

His face contorted. "Thank you. I'll go now, Mary."

"One more kiss!" she cried, moving toward him involuntarily. "Only one more!"

He kissed her on the lips, then wrenched himself away, and looking down to where the two women sat, he made an angry motion with his head.

As they rose and came nearer, he held Mary at arm's length. "Now I'm really going," he said harshly. "Good-bye, Mary."

"Good-bye, Klef." Her fingers were clasped tight at her waist.

The man waited, looking over her head, until Vivana came up and took her arms gently. Then he moved away. At the head of the stairs he looked up at her once more; then he turned and began to descend.

"Dear, it will be better now, you'll see," said Vivana uncertainly.

Mary said nothing. She stood still, listening to the faint sounds that echoed up from the stairwell: footsteps, voices, hollow sounds.

There was a sudden clatter, then footsteps mounting the stair. Klef appeared again, chest heaving, eyes bright. He seized both of Mary's hands in his. "Listen!" he said. "I'm mad. You're mad. We're both going to die."

"I don't care!" she said. Her face was glowing as she looked up at him.

"They say some of the streams are running pure, in the hills. Grass is growing there—there are fish in the streams, even the wild fowl are coming back. We'll go there, Mary, together—just you and I. Alone. Do you understand?"

"Yes, Klef, yes, darling."

"Then come on!"

"Wait!" cried Laura-one shrilly after them as they ran down the stair. "How will you live? What will you eat? Think what you are doing!"

Faint hollow sounds answered her, then the purr of a motor.

Vivana moved to Laura-one's side, and the two women stood watching, silent, as the dark tiny shape of the launch moved out into the brightness. In the cockpit they could make out the two figures close together, dark head and light. The launch moved steadily toward the land; and the two women stood staring, unable to speak, long after it was out of sight.

THE EXTRA

Greg Egan

Here's a razor-sharp little cautionary tale that proves once again that you should be careful what you wish for—you just might get it.

Only a few years into the decade, it's already a fairly safe bet to predict that Australian writer Greg Egan is going to come to be recognized (if indeed he hasn't already) as being one of the big new names to emerge in SF in the nineties. In the last few years, he has become a frequent contributor to Interzone *and* Asimov's Science Fiction, *and has made sales as well to* Pulphouse, Analog, Aurealis, Eidolon, *and elsewhere; many of his stories have also appeared in various "Best of the Year" series, and he was on the Hugo Final Ballot in 1995 for his story "Cocoon," which won the Ditmar Award and the* Asimov's Readers Award. *His first novel,* Quarantine, *appeared in 1992, to wide critical acclaim, and was followed by a second novel in 1994,* Permutation City, *which won the John W. Campbell Memorial Award. His most recent books are a collection of his short fiction,* Axiomatic, *and a new novel,* Distress. *Upcoming is another new novel,* Diaspora.

Daniel Gray didn't merely arrange for his Extras to live in a building within the grounds of his main residence—although that in itself would have been shocking enough. At the height of his midsummer garden party, he had their trainer march them along a winding path which took them within meters of virtually every one of his wealthy and powerful guests.

There were five batches, each batch a decade younger than the preceding one, each comprising twenty-five Extras (less one or two here and there; naturally, some depletion had occurred, and Gray made no effort to hide the fact). Batch A were forty-four years old, the same age as Gray himself. Batch E, the four-year-olds, could not have kept up with the others on foot, so they followed behind, riding an electric float.

The Extras were as clean as they'd ever been in their lives, and their hair—and beards in the case of the older ones—had been laboriously trimmed, in styles that amusingly parodied the latest fashions. Gray had almost gone so far as to have them clothed—but after much experimentation he'd decided against it; even the slightest scrap of clothing made them look *too* human, and he was acutely aware of the boundary between impressing his guests with his daring, and causing them real discomfort. Of course, naked, the Extras looked *exactly* like naked humans, but in Gray's cultural milieu, stark naked humans *en masse* were not a common sight, and so the paradoxical effect of revealing the creatures' totally human appearance was to make it easier to think of them as less than human.

The parade was a great success. Everyone applauded demurely as it passed by—in the context, an extravagant gesture of approval. They weren't applauding the Extras themselves, however impressive they were to behold; they were applauding Daniel Gray for his audacity in breaking the taboo.

Gray could only guess how many people in the world had Extras; perhaps the wealthiest ten thousand, perhaps the wealthiest hundred thousand. Most owners chose to be discreet. Keeping a stock of congenitally brain-damaged clones of oneself—in the short term, as organ donors; in the long term (once the techniques were perfected), as the recipients of brain transplants—was not illegal, but it wasn't widely accepted. Any owner who went public could expect a barrage of anonymous hate mail, intense media scrutiny, property damage, threats of violence—all the usual behavior associated with the public debate of a subtle point of ethics. There had been legal challenges, of course, but time and again the highest courts had ruled that Extras

were not human beings. Too much cortex was missing; if
Extras deserved human rights, so did half the mammalian
species on the planet. With a patient, skilled trainer, Extras
could learn to run in circles, and to perform the simple,
repetitive exercises that kept their muscles in good tone, but
that was about the limit. A dog or a cat would have needed
brain tissue *removed* to persuade it to live such a boring life.

Even those few owners who braved the wrath of the
fanatics, and bragged about their Extras, generally had them
kept in commercial stables—in the same city, of course, so
as not to undermine their usefulness in a medical emergency, but certainly not within the electrified boundaries of
their own *homes*. What ageing, dissipated man or woman
would wish to be surrounded by reminders of how healthy
and vigorous they might have been, if only they'd lived their
lives differently?

Daniel Gray, however, found the contrasting appearance
of his Extras entirely pleasing to behold, given that he, and not
they, would be the ultimate beneficiary of their good health. In
fact, his athletic clean-living brothers had already supplied him
with two livers, one kidney, one lung, and quantities of coro-
nary artery and mucous membrane. In each case, he'd had
the donor put down, whether or not it had remained strictly
viable; the idea of having imperfect Extras in his collection
offended his aesthetic sensibilities.

After the appearance of the Extras, nobody at the party
could talk about anything else. Perhaps, one stereovision
luminary suggested, now that their host had shown such
courage, it would at last become fashionable to flaunt one's
Extras, allowing full value to be extracted from them; after
all, considering the cost, it was a crime to make use of them
only in emergencies, when their pretty bodies went beneath
the surgeon's knife.

Gray wandered from group to group, listening contentedly, pausing now and then to pluck and eat a delicate
spice-rose or a juicy claret-apple (the entire garden had been
designed specifically to provide the refreshments for this
annual occasion, so everything was edible, and everything
was in season). The early afternoon sky was a dazzling

uplifting blue and he stood for a moment with his face raised to the warmth of the sun. The party was a complete success. Everyone was talking about him. He hadn't felt so happy in years.

"I wonder if you're smiling for the same reason I am."

He turned. Sarah Brash, the owner of Continental Bio-Logic, and a recent former lover, stood beside him, beaming in a faintly unnatural way. She wore one of the patterned scarves which Gray had made available to his guests; a variety of gene-tailored insects roamed the garden, and her particular choice of scarf attracted a bee whose painless sting contained a combination of a mild stimulant and an aphrodisiac.

He shrugged. "I doubt it."

She laughed and took his arm, then came still closer and whispered, "I've been thinking a very wicked thought."

He made no reply. He'd lost interest in Sarah a month ago, and the sight of her in this state did nothing to rekindle his desire. He had just broken off with her successor, but he had no wish to repeat himself. He was trying to think of something to say that would be offensive enough to drive her away, when she reached out and tenderly cupped his face in her small, warm hands.

Then she playfully seized hold of his sagging jowls, and said, in tones of mock aggrievement, "Don't you think it was terribly selfish of you, Daniel? You gave me your body . . . but you didn't give me your *best* one."

Gray lay awake until after dawn. Vivid images of the evening's entertainment kept returning to him, and he found them difficult to banish. The Extra that Sarah had chosen— C7, one of the twenty-four-year-olds—had been muzzled and tightly bound throughout, but it had made copious noises in its throat, and its eyes had been remarkably expressive. Gray had learnt, years ago, to keep a mask of mild amusement and boredom on his face, whatever he was feeling; to see fear, confusion, distress, and ecstasy, nakedly displayed on features that, in spite of everything, were unmistakably his own, had been rather like a nightmare of losing control.

Of course, it had also been as inconsequential as a nightmare; *he* had not lost control for a moment, however much his animal look-alike had rolled its eyes, and moaned, and trembled. His appetite for sexual novelty aside, perhaps he had agreed to Sarah's request for that very reason: to see this primitive aspect of himself unleashed, without the least risk to his own equilibrium.

He decided to have the creature put down in the morning; he didn't want it corrupting its clone-brothers, and he couldn't be bothered arranging to have it kept in isolation. Extras had their sex drives substantially lowered by drugs, but not completely eliminated—that would have had too many physiological side-effects—and Gray had heard that it took just one clone who had discovered the possibilities to trigger widespread masturbation and homosexual behavior throughout the batch. Most owners would not have cared, but Gray wanted his Extras to be more than merely healthy; he wanted them to be *innocent*, he wanted them to be *without sin*. He was not a religious man, but he could still appreciate the emotional power of such concepts. When the time came for his brain to be moved into a younger body, he wanted to begin his new life with a sense of purification, a sense of rebirth.

However sophisticated his amorality, Gray freely admitted that at a certain level, inaccessible to reason, his indulgent life sickened him, as surely as it sickened his body. His family and his peers had always, unequivocally, encouraged him to seek pleasure, but perhaps he had been influenced—subconsciously and unwillingly—by ideas which still prevailed in other social strata. Since the late twentieth century, when—in affluent countries—cardiovascular disease and other "diseases of lifestyle" had become the major causes of death, the notion that health was a reward for virtue had acquired a level of acceptance unknown since the medieval plagues. A healthy lifestyle was not just pragmatic, it was *righteous*. A heart attack or a stroke, lung cancer or liver disease—not to mention

AIDS—was clearly a *punishment* for some vice that the sufferer had chosen to pursue. Twenty-first century medicine had gradually weakened many of the casual links between lifestyle and life expectancy—and the advent of Extras would, for the very rich, soon sever them completely—but the outdated moral overtones persisted nonetheless.

In any case, however fervently Gray approved of his gluttonous, sedentary, drug-hazed, promiscuous life, a part of him felt guilty and unclean. He could not wipe out his past, nor did he wish to, but to discard his ravaged body and begin again in blameless flesh would be the perfect way to neutralize this irrational self-disgust. He would attend his own cremation, and watch his "sinful" corpse consigned to "hellfire"! Atheists, he decided, are not immune to religious metaphors; he had no doubt that the experience would be powerfully moving, liberating beyond belief.

Three months later, Sarah Brash's lawyers informed him that she had conceived a child (which, naturally she'd had transferred to an Extra surrogate), and that she cordially requested that Gray provide her with fifteen billion dollars to assist with the child's upbringing.

His first reaction was a mixture of irritation and amusement at his own naïveté. He should have suspected that there'd been more to Sarah's request than sheer perversity. Her wealth was comparable to his own, but the prospect of living for centuries seemed to have made the rich greedier than ever; a fortune that sufficed for seven or eight decades was no longer enough.

On principle, Gray instructed his lawyers to take the matter to court—and then he began trying to ascertain what his chances were of winning. He'd had a vasectomy years ago, and could produce records proving his infertility, at least on every occasion he'd had a sperm count measured. He couldn't *prove* that he hadn't had the operation temporarily reversed, since that could now be done with hardly a trace, but he knew perfectly well that the Extra was the father of the child, and he could prove *that*. Although the Extras' brain damage resulted solely from fetal microsur-

gery, rather than genetic alteration, all Extras were geneti-
cally tagged with a coded serial number, written into
portions of DNA which had no active function, at over a
thousand different sites. What's more, these tags were
always on *both* chromosomes of each pair, so any child
fathered by an Extra would necessarily inherit all of them.
Gray's biotechnology advisers assured him that stripping
these tags from the zygote was, in practice, virtually
impossible.

Perhaps Sarah planned to freely admit that the Extra was
the father, and hoped to set a precedent making its owner
responsible for the upkeep of its human offspring. Gray's
legal experts were substantially less reassuring than his
geneticists. Gray could prove that the Extra hadn't raped
her—as she no doubt knew, he'd taped everything that had
happened that night—but that wasn't the point; after all,
consenting to intercourse would not have deprived her of
the right to an ordinary paternity suit. As the tapes also
showed, Gray had known full well what was happening, and
had clearly approved. That the late Extra had been unwilling
was, unfortunately, irrelevant.

After wasting an entire week brooding over the matter,
Gray finally gave up worrying. The case would not reach
court for five or six years, and was unlikely to be resolved
in less than a decade. He promptly had his remaining Extras
vasectomized—to prove to the courts, when the time came,
that he was not irresponsible—and then he pushed the
whole business out of his mind.

Almost.

A few weeks later, he had a dream. Conscious all the
while that he was dreaming, he saw the night's events
re-enacted, except that this time it was *he* who was bound
and muzzled, slave to Sarah's hands and tongue, while the
Extra stood back and watched.

But . . . had they merely swapped places, he wondered,
or had they swapped *bodies*? His dreamer's point of view
told him nothing—he saw all three bodies from the
outside—but the lean young man who watched bore Gray's
own characteristic jaded expression, and the middle-aged

man in Sarah's embrace moaned and twitched and shuddered, exactly as the Extra had done.

Gray was elated. He still knew that he was only dreaming, but he couldn't suppress his delight at the inspired idea of keeping *his old body* alive with the Extra's brain, rather than consigning it to flames. What could be more controversial, more outrageous, than having not just his Extras, but *his own discarded corpse*, walking the grounds of his estate? He resolved at once to do this, to abandon his long-held desire for a symbolic cremation. His friends would be shocked into the purest admiration—as would the fanatics, in their own way. True infamy had proved elusive; people had talked about his last stunt for a week or two, and then forgotten it—but the midsummer party at which the guest of honor was Daniel Gray's old body would be remembered for the rest of his vastly prolonged life.

Over the next few years, the medical research division of Gray's vast corporate empire began to make significant progress on the brain transplant problem.

Transplants between newborn Extras had been successful for decades. With identical genes, and having just emerged from the very same womb (or from anatomically and biochemically indistinguishable wombs of two clone-sister Extras), any differences between donor and recipient were small enough to be overcome by a young, flexible brain.

However, older Extras—even those raised identically—had shown remarkable divergencies in many neural structures, and whole-brain transplants between them had been found to result in paralysis, sensory dysfunction, and sometimes even death. Gray was no neuroscientist, but he could understand roughly what the problem was: Brain and body grow and change together throughout life, becoming increasingly reliant on each other's idiosyncrasies, in a feed-back process riddled with chaotic attractors—hence the unavoidable differences, even between clones. In the body of a human (or an Extra), there are thousands of sophisticated control systems which may *include* the brain, but are certainly not contained within it, involving everything from the spinal cord and the peripheral nervous system to hormonal feedback loops, the immune system, and, ultimately, almost every organ in the body. Over time, all of these elements adapt in some degree to the particular demands placed upon them—and the brain grows to rely upon the specific characteristics that these external systems acquire. A brain transplant throws this complex interdependence into disarray—at least as badly as a massive stroke, or an extreme somatic trauma.

Sometimes, two or three years of extensive physiotherapy could enable the transplanted brain and body to adjust to each other—but only between clones of equal age and indistinguishable lifestyles. When the brain donor was a model of a likely human candidate—an intentionally over-fed, under-exercised, drug-wrecked Extra, twenty or thirty years older than the body donor—the result was always death or coma.

The theoretical solution, if not the detailed means of achieving it, was obvious. Those portions of the brain responsible for motor control, the endocrine system, the low-level processing of sensory data, and so on, had to be retained in the body in which they had matured. Why struggle to make the donor brain adjust to the specifics of a new body, when that body's original brain already contained neural systems fine-tuned to perfection for the task? If the aim was to transplant memory and personality, why transplant anything else?

After many years of careful brain-function mapping, and the identification and synthesis of growth factors which could trigger mature neurons into sending forth axons across the boundaries of a graft, Gray's own team had been the first to try partial transplants. Gray watched tapes of the operations, and was both repelled and amused to see oddly shaped lumps of one Extra's brain being exchanged with the corresponding regions of another's; repelled by visceral instinct, but amused to see the seat of reason—even in a mere Extra—being treated like so much vegetable matter.

The forty-seventh partial transplant, between a sedentary, ailing fifty-year-old, and a fit, healthy twenty-year-old, was an unqualified success. After a mere two months of recuperation, both Extras were fully mobile, with all five senses completely unimpaired.

Had they swapped memories and "personalities"? Apparently, yes. Both had been observed by a team of psychologists for a year before the operation, and their behavior extensively characterized, and both had been trained to perform different sets of tasks for rewards. After the selective brain swap, the learned tasks, and the observed behavioral idiosyncrasies, were found to have followed the transplanted tissue. Of course, eventually the younger, fitter Extra began to be affected by its newfound health, becoming substantially more active than it had been in its original body—and the Extra now in the older body soon showed signs of acquiescing to its ill-health. But regardless of any post-transplant adaption to their new bodies, the fact remained that the Extras' identities—such as they were—had been exchanged.

After a few dozen more Extra-Extra transplants, with virtually identical outcomes, the time came for the first human-Extra trials.

Gray's parents had both died years before (on the operating table—an almost inevitable outcome of their hundreds of non-essential transplants), but they had left him a valuable legacy; thirty years ago, their own scientists had (illegally) signed up fifty men and women in their early twenties, and Extras had been made for them. These volunteers had been well paid, but not so well paid that a far larger sum, withheld until after the actual transplant, would lose its appeal. Nobody had been coerced, and the seventeen who'd dropped out quietly had not been punished. An eighteenth had tried blackmail—even though she'd had no idea who was doing the experiment, let alone who was financing it—and had died in a tragic ferry disaster, along with three hundred and nine other people. Gray's people believed in assassinations with a low signal-to-noise ratio.

Of the thirty-two human-Extra transplants, twenty-nine were pronounced completely successful. As with the Extra-Extra trials, both bodies were soon fully functional, but now the humans in the younger bodies could—after a month or two of speech therapy—respond to detailed interrogation by experts, who declared that their memories and personalities were intact.

Gray wanted to speak to the volunteers in person, but knew that was too risky, so he contented himself with watching tapes of the interviews. The psychologists had their barrages of supposedly rigorous tests, but Gray preferred to listen to the less formal segments, when the volunteers spoke of their life histories, their political and religious beliefs, and so on—displaying at least as much consistency across the transplant as any person who is asked to discuss such matters on two separate occasions.

The three failures were difficult to characterize. They too learnt to use their new bodies, to walk and talk as proficiently as the others, but they were depressed, withdrawn, and uncooperative. No physical difference could be found—scans showed that their grafted tissue, and the residual portions of their Extra's brain, had forged just as many interconnecting pathways as the brains of the other volunteers. They seemed to be unhappy with a perfectly successful result—they seemed to have simply decided that they didn't *want* younger bodies, after all.

Gray was unconcerned; if these people were disposed to be ungrateful for their good fortune, that was a character defect that he knew he did not share. *He* would be utterly delighted to have a fresh young body to enjoy for a while—before setting out to wreck it, in the knowledge that, in a decade's time, he could take his pick from the next batch of Extras and start the whole process again.

There were "failures" amongst the Extras as well, but that was hardly surprising—the creatures had no way of even beginning to comprehend what had happened to them. Symptoms ranged from loss of appetite to extreme, uncontrollable violence; one Extra had even managed to batter itself to death on a concrete floor, before it could be tranquilized. Gray hoped his own Extra would turn out to be well-behaved—he wanted his old body to be clearly subhuman, but not utterly berserk—but it was not a critical factor, and he decided against diverting resources toward the problem. After all, it was the fate of *his* brain in the Extra's body that was absolutely crucial; success with the other half of the swap would be an entertaining bonus, but if it wasn't achieved, well, he could always revert to cremation.

Gray scheduled and canceled his transplant a dozen times. He was not in urgent need by any means—there was nothing currently wrong with him that required a single new organ, let alone an entire new body—but he desperately wanted to be *first*. The penniless volunteers didn't count—and that was why he hesitated: trials on humans from those lower social classes struck him as not much more reassuring than trials on Extras. Who was to say that a process that left a rough-hewn, culturally deficient personality intact, would preserve his own refined, complex sensibilities? Therein lay the dilemma: he would only feel safe if he knew that an equal—a rival—had undergone a transplant before him, in which case he would be deprived of all the glory of being a path-breaker. Vanity fought cowardice; it was a battle of titans.

It was the approach of Sarah Brash's court case that finally pushed him into making a decision. He didn't much care how the case itself went; the real battle would be for the best publicity; the media would determine who won and who lost, whatever the jury decided. As things stood, he looked like a naïve fool, an easily manipulated voyeur, while Sarah came across as a smart operator. She'd shown initiative; he'd just let himself (or rather, his Extra) get screwed. He needed an edge, he needed a gimmick—something that would overshadow her petty scheming. If he swapped bodies with an Extra in time for the trial—becoming, officially, the first human to do so—nobody would waste time covering the obscure details of Sarah's side of the case. His mere presence in court would be a matter of planet-wide controversy; the legal definition of identity was still based on DNA fingerprinting and retinal patterns, with some clumsy exceptions thrown in to allow for gene therapy and retina transplants. The laws would soon be changed—he was arranging it—but as things stood, the subpoena would apply to his old body. He could just imagine sitting in the public gallery, unrecognized, while Sarah's lawyer tried to cross-examine the quivering, confused, wild-eyed Extra that his discarded "corpse" had become! Quite possibly he, or his lawyers, would end up being charged with contempt of court, but it would be worth it for the spectacle.

So, Gray inspected Batch D, which were now just over nineteen years old. They regarded him with their usual idiotic, friendly expression. He wondered, not for the first time, if any of the Extras ever realized that *he* was their clone-brother, too. They never seemed to respond to him any differently than they did to other humans—and yet a fraction of a gram of fetal brain tissue was all that had kept him from being one of them. Even Batch A, his "contemporaries," showed no sign of recognition. If he had stripped naked and mimicked their grunting sounds, would they have accepted him as an equal? He'd never felt inclined to find out; Extra "anthropology" was hardly something he wished to encourage, let alone participate in. But he decided he would return to visit Batch D in his new body; it would certainly be amusing to see just what they made of a clone-brother who vanished, then came back three months later with speech and clothes.

The clones were all in perfect health, and virtually indistinguishable. He finally chose one at random. The trainer examined the tattoo on the sole of its foot, and said, "D12, sir."

Gray nodded, and walked away.

He spent the week before the transplant in a state of constant agitation. He knew exactly what drugs would have prevented this, but the medical team had advised him to stay clean, and he was too afraid to disobey them.

He watched D12 for hours, trying to distract himself with the supposedly thrilling knowledge that those clear eyes, that smooth skin, those taut muscles, would soon be his. The only trouble was, this began to seem a rather paltry reward for the risk he would be taking. Knowing all his life that this

day would come, he'd learnt not to care at all what he
looked like; by now, he was so used to his own appearance
that he wasn't sure he especially *wanted* to be lean and
muscular and rosy-cheeked. After all, if that really had been
his fondest wish, he could have achieved it in other ways;
some quite effective pharmaceuticals and tailored viruses
had existed for decades, but he had chosen not to use them.
He had *enjoyed* looking the part of the dissolute billionaire,
and his wealth had brought him more sexual partners than
his new body would ever attract through its own merits. In
short, he neither wanted nor needed to change his appearance at all.

So, in the end it came down to longevity, and the hope
of immortality. As his parents had proved, any transplant
involved a small but finite risk. A whole new body every ten
or twenty years was surely a far safer bet than replacing
individual organs at an increasing rate, for diminishing
returns. And a whole new body *now*, long before he needed
it, made far more sense than waiting until he was so frail
that a small overdose of anaesthetic could finish him off.

When the day arrived, Gray thought he was, finally,
prepared. The chief surgeon asked him if he wished to
proceed; he could have said no, and she would not have
blinked—not one of his employees would have dared to
betray the least irritation, had he canceled their laborious
preparations a thousand times.

But he didn't say no.

As the cool spray of the anaesthetic touched his skin, he
suffered a moment of absolute panic. *They were going to cut
up his brain*. Not the brain of a grunting, drooling Extra, not
the brain of some ignorant slum-dweller, but *his* brain, full
of memories of great music and literature and art, full
of moments of joy and insight from the finest psychotropic
drugs, full of ambitions that, given time, might change the
course of civilization.

He tried to visualize one of his favorite paintings, to
provide an image he could dwell upon, a memory that
would prove that the essential Daniel Gray had survived the
transplant. *That Van Gogh he'd bought last year*. But he

couldn't recall the name of it, let alone what it looked like. He closed his eyes and drifted helplessly into darkness.

When he awoke, he was numb all over, and unable to move or make a sound, but he *could* see. Poorly, at first, but over a period that might have been hours, or might have been days—punctuated as it was with stretches of enervating, dreamless sleep—he was able to identify his surroundings. A white ceiling, a white wall, a glimpse of some kind of electronic device in the corner of one eye; the upper section of the bed must have been tilted, mercifully keeping his gaze from being strictly vertical. But he couldn't move his head, or his eyes, he couldn't even close his eyelids, so he quickly lost interest in the view. The light never seemed to change, so sleep was his only relief from the monotony. After a while, he began to wonder if in fact he had woken many times, before he had been able to see, but had experienced nothing to mark the occasions in his memory.

Later he could hear, too, although there wasn't much to be heard; people came and went, and spoke softly, but not, so far as he could tell, to him; in any case, their words made no sense. He was too lethargic to care about the people, or to fret about his situation. In time he would be taught to use his new body fully, but if the experts wanted him to rest right now, he was happy to oblige.

When the physiotherapists first set to work, he felt utterly helpless and humiliated. They made his limbs twitch with electrodes, while *he* had no control, no say at all in what his body did. Eventually, he began to receive sensations from his limbs, and he could at least *feel* what was going on, but since his head just lolled there, he couldn't watch what they were doing to him, and they made no effort to explain anything. Perhaps they thought he was still deaf and blind, perhaps his sight and hearing at this early stage were freak effects that had not been envisaged. Before the operation, the schedule for his recovery had been explained to him in great detail, but his memory of it was hazy now. He told himself to be patient.

When, at last, one arm came under his control, he raised it, with great effort, into his field of view.

It was his arm, his *old* arm—not the Extra's.

He tried to emit a wail of despair, but nothing came out.

Something must have gone wrong, late in the operation, forcing them to cancel the transplant *after* they had cut up his brain. Perhaps the Extra's life-support machine had failed; it seemed unbelievable, but it wasn't impossible—as his parents' deaths had proved, there was always a risk. He suddenly felt unbearably tired. He now faced the prospect of spending months merely to regain the use of his very own body; for all he knew, the newly forged pathways across the wounds in his brain might require as much time to become completely functional as they would have if the transplant had gone ahead.

For several days, he was angry and depressed. He tried to express his rage to the nurses and physiotherapists, but all he could do was twitch and grimace—he couldn't speak, he couldn't even gesture—and they paid no attention. How could his people have been so incompetent? How could they put him through months of trauma and humiliation, with nothing to look forward to but ending up exactly where he'd started?

But when he'd calmed down, he told himself that his doctors weren't incompetent at all; in fact, he knew they were the best in the world. Whatever had gone wrong must have been completely beyond their control. He decided to adopt a positive attitude to the situation; after all, he was lucky: the malfunction might have killed *him*, instead of the Extra. He was alive, he was in the care of experts, and what was three months in bed to the immortal he would still, eventually, become? This failure would make his ultimate success all the more of a triumph—personally, he could have done without the setback, but the media would lap it up.

The physiotherapy continued. His sense of touch, and then his motor control, were restored to more and more of his body, until, although weak and uncoordinated, he felt without a doubt that this body was *his*. To experience familiar aches and twinges was a relief, more than a disappointment, and several times he found himself close to tears, overcome with mawkish sentiment at the joy of regaining what he had lost, imperfect as it was. On these occasions, he swore he would never try the transplant again; he would be faithful to his own body, in sickness and in health. Only by methodically reminding himself of all his reasons for proceeding in the first place could he put this foolishness aside.

Once he had control of the muscles of his vocal cords, he began to grow impatient for the speech therapists to start work. His hearing, as such, seemed to be fine, but he could still make no sense of the words of the people around him, and he could only assume that the connections between the parts of his brain responsible for understanding speech, and the parts which carried out the lower-level processing of sound, were yet to be refined by whatever ingenious regime the neurologists had devised. He only wished they'd start soon; he was sick of this isolation.

One day, he had a visitor—the first person he'd seen since the operation who was not a health professional clad in white. The visitor was a young man, dressed in brightly colored pajamas, and traveling in a wheelchair.

By now, Gray could turn his head. He watched the young man approaching, surrounded by a retinue of obsequious doctors. Gray recognized the doctors; every member of the transplant team was there, and they were all smiling proudly, and nodding ceaselessly. Gray wondered why they had taken so long to appear; until now, he'd presumed that they were waiting until he was able to fully comprehend the explanation of their failure, but he suddenly realized how absurd that was—how could they have left him to make his own guesses? It was outrageous! It was true that speech, and no doubt writing too, meant nothing to him, but surely they could have devised some method of communication! And why did they look so pleased, when they ought to have been abject?

Then Gray realized that the man in the wheelchair was

the Extra, D12. *And yet he spoke.* And when he spoke, the doctors shook with sycophantic laughter.

The Extra brought the wheelchair right up to the bed, and spent several seconds staring into Gray's face. Gray stared back; obviously he was dreaming, or hallucinating. The Extra's expression hovered between boredom and mild amusement, just as it had in the dream he'd had all those years ago.

The Extra turned to go. Gray felt a convulsion pass through his body. Of course he was dreaming. What other explanation could there be?

Unless the transplant *had* gone ahead, after all.

Unless the remnants of his brain in this body retained enough of his memory and personality to make him believe that he, too, was Daniel Gray. Unless the brain function studies that had localized identity had been correct, but incomplete—unless the processes that constituted human self-awareness were redundantly duplicated in the most primitive parts of the brain.

In which case, there were now two Daniel Grays.

One had everything: The power of speech. Money. Influence. Ten thousand servants. And now, at last, immaculate health.

And the other? He had one thing only.

The knowledge of his helplessness.

It was, he had to admit, a glorious afternoon. The sky was cloudless, the air was warm, and the clipped grass beneath his feet was soft but dry.

He had given up trying to communicate his plight to the people around him. He knew he would never master speech, and he couldn't even manage to convey meaning in his gestures—the necessary modes of thought were simply no longer available to him, and he could no more plan and execute a simple piece of mime than he could solve the latest problems in grand unified field theory. For a while he had simply thrown tantrums—refusing to eat, refusing to cooperate. Then he had recalled his own plans for his old body, in the event of such recalcitrance. *Cremation*. And realized that, in spite of everything, he didn't want to die.

He acknowledged, vaguely, that in a sense he really wasn't Daniel Gray, but a new person entirely, a composite of Gray and the Extra D12—but this was no comfort to him, whoever, whatever, he was. All his memories told him he was Daniel Gray; he had none from the life of D12, in an ironic confirmation of his long-held belief in human superiority over Extras. Should he be happy that he'd also proved—if there'd ever been any doubt—that human consciousness was the most physical of things, a spongy gray mess that could be cut up like a starfish, and survive in two separate parts? Should he be happy that the other Daniel Gray—without a doubt, the more complete Daniel Gray—had achieved his lifelong ambition?

The trainer yanked on his collar.

Meekly, he stepped onto the path.

The lush garden was crowded as never before—this was indeed the party of the decade—and as he came into sight, the guests began to applaud, and even to cheer.

He might have raised his arms in acknowledgment, but the thought did not occur to him.

OUT OF COPYRIGHT

Charles Sheffield

One of the best contemporary "hard science" writers, British-born Charles Sheffield is a theoretical physicist who has worked on the American space program, and is currently chief scientist of the Earth Satellite Corporation. Sheffield is also the only person who has ever served as president of both the American Astronautical Society and the Science Fiction Writers of America. He won the Hugo Award in 1994 for his story, "Georgia on My Mind." His books include the bestselling nonfiction title Earthwatch, *the novels* Sight of Proteus, The Web Between the Worlds, Hidden Variables, My Brother's Keeper, Between the Strokes of Night, The Nimrod Hunt, Trader's World, Proteus Unbound, Summertide, Divergence, Transcendence, Cold As Ice, Brother To Dragons, *and* The Mind Pool, *and the collections* Erasmus Magister, The McAndrew Chronicles, *and* Dancing With Myself. *His most recent books are the novels* Godspeed *and* The Ganymede Club, *and a new collection,* Georgia on My Mind and Other Places. *He lives in Silver Spring, Maryland.*

Here he slyly suggests that finding the right tool for the right job is more than half the battle—particularly if you're smart enough to know which jobs are really *the important ones . . . and just what kind of tools you need to do them right.*

Troubleshooting. A *splendid* idea, and one that I agree with totally in principle. Bang! One bullet, and trouble bites the dust. But unfortunately, trouble doesn't know the rules. Trouble won't stay dead.

I looked around the table. My top troubleshooting team was here. I was here. Unfortunately, they were supposed to be headed for Jupiter, and I ought to be down on Earth. In less than twenty-four hours, the draft pick would begin. That wouldn't wait, and if I didn't leave in the next thirty minutes, I would never make it in time. I needed to be in two places at once. I cursed the copyright laws and the single-copy restriction, and went to work.

"You've read the new requirement," I said. "You know the parameters. Ideas, anyone?"

A dead silence. They were facing the problem in their own unique ways. Wolfgang Pauli looked half-asleep, Thomas Edison was drawing little doll-figures on the table's surface, Enrico Fermi seemed to be counting on his fingers, and John von Neumann was staring impatiently at the other three. I was doing none of those things. I knew very well that wherever the solution would come from, it would not be from inside my head. My job was much more straightforward: I had to see that when we had a possible answer, it *happened*. And I had to see that we got *one* answer, not four.

The silence in the room went on and on. My brain trust was saying nothing, while I watched the digits on my watch flicker by. I had to stay and find a solution; and I had to get to the draft picks. But most of all and hardest of all, I had to remain quiet, to let my team do some thinking.

It was small consolation to know that similar meetings were being held within the offices of the other three combines. Everyone must be finding it equally hard going. I knew the players, and I could imagine the scenes, even though all the troubleshooting teams were different. NETSCO had a group that was intellectually the equal of ours at Romberg AG: Niels Bohr, Theodore von Karman, Norbert Weiner, and Marie Curie. MMG, the great Euro-Mexican combine of Magrit-Marcus Gesellschaft, had focused on engineering power rather than pure scientific understanding and creativity, and, in addition to the Soviet rocket designer Sergey Korolev and the American Nikola Tesla, they had reached farther back (and with more risk) to the great nineteenth-century English engineer Isambard Kingdom Brunel. He had been one of the outstanding successes of the program; I wished he were working with me, but MMG had always refused to look at a trade. MMG's one bow to theory was a strange one, the Indian mathematician Srinivasa Ramanujan, but the unlikely quartet made one hell of a team.

And finally there was BP Megation, whom I thought of as confused. At any rate, I didn't understand their selection logic. They had used billions of dollars to acquire a strangely mixed team: Erwin Schrödinger, David Hilbert, Leo Szilard, and Henry Ford. They were all great talents, and all famous names in their fields, but I wondered how well they could work as a unit.

All the troubleshooting teams were now pondering the same emergency. Our problem was created when the Pan-National Union suddenly announced a change to the Phase B demonstration program. They wanted to modify impact conditions, as their contracts with us permitted them to do. They didn't have to tell us how to do it, either, which was just as well for them, since I was sure they didn't know. How do you take a billion tons of mass, already launched to reach a specific target at a certain point of time, and redirect it to a different end point with a different arrival time?

There was no point in asking them *why* they wanted to change rendezvous conditions. It was their option. Some of our management saw the action on PNU's part as simple bloody-mindedness, but I couldn't agree. The four multinational combines had each been given contracts to perform the biggest space engineering exercise in human history: small asteroids (only a kilometer or so across—but massing a billion tons each) had to be picked up from their natural orbits and redirected to the Jovian system, where they were to make precise rendezvous with assigned locations of the moon Io. Each combine had to select the asteroid and the method of moving it, but deliver within a tight transfer-energy budget and a tight time schedule.

For that task the PNU would pay each group a total of $8 billion. That sounds like a fair amount of money, but I knew our accounting figures. To date, with the project still not finished (rendezvous would be in eight more days), Romberg AG had spent $14.5 billion. We are looking at a probable cost overrun by a factor of two. I was willing to bet that the other three groups were eating very similar losses. Why?

Because this was only Phase B of a four-phase project. Phase A had been a system design study, which led to four Phase B awards for a demonstration project. The Phase B effort that the four combines were working on now was a proof-of-capability run for the full European Metamorphosis. The real money came in the future, in Phases C and D. Those would be awarded by the PNU to a single combine, and the award would be based largely on Phase B performance. The next phases called for the delivery of fifty asteroids to impact points on Europa (Phase C), followed by thermal mixing operations on the moon's surface (Phase D). The contract value of C and D would be somewhere up around $800 billion. That was the fish that all the combines were after, and it was the reason we all overspend lavishly on this phase.

By the end of the whole program, Europa would have a forty-kilometer-deep water ocean over all its surface. And then the real fun would begin. Some contractor would begin the installation of the fusion plants, and the seeding of the sea-farms with the first prokaryotic bacterial forms.

The stakes were high; and to keep everybody on their toes, PNU did the right thing. They kept throwing in these little zingers, to mimic the thousand and one things that would go wrong in the final project phases.

While I was sitting and fidgeting, my team had gradually come to life. Fermi was pacing up and down the room—always a good sign; and Wolfgang Pauli was jabbing impatiently at the keys of a computer console. John von Neumann hadn't moved, but since he did everything in his head anyway, that didn't mean much.

I looked again at my watch. I had to go. "Ideas?" I said again.

Von Neumann made a swift chopping gesture of his hand. "We have to make a choice, Al. It can be done in four or five ways."

The others were nodding. "The problem is only one of efficiency and speed," added Fermi. "I can give you an order-of-magnitude estimate of the effects on the overall program within half an hour."

"Within fifteen minutes." Pauli raised the bidding.

"No need to compete this one." They were going to settle down to a real four-way fight on methods—they always did—but I didn't have the time to sit here and referee. The important point was that they said it could be done. "You don't have to rush it. Whatever you decide, it will have to wait until I get back." I stood up. "Tom?"

Edison shrugged. "How long will you be gone, Al?"

"Two days, maximum. I'll head back right after the draft picks." (That wasn't quite true; when the draft picks were over, I had some other business to attend to that did not include the troubleshooters, but two days should cover everything.)

"Have fun." Edison waved his hand casually. "By the time you get back, I'll have the engineering drawings for you."

One thing about working with a team like mine—they may not always be right, but they sure are always cocky.

"Make room there. Move over!" The guards were pushing ahead to create a narrow corridor through the wedged mass of people. The one in front of me was butting with his helmeted head, not even looking to see whom he was shoving aside. "Move!" he shouted. "Come on now, out of the way."

We were in a hurry. Things had been frantically busy Topside before I left, so I had cut it fine on connections to begin with, then been held up half an hour at reentry. We had broken the speed limits on the atmospheric segment, and there would be PNU fines for that, but still we hadn't managed to make up all the time. Now the first draft pick was only seconds away, and I was supposed to be taking part in it.

A thin woman in a green coat clutched at my arm as we bogged down for a moment in the crush of people. Her face was gray and grim, and she had a placard hanging round her neck. "You could wait longer for the copyright!" She had to shout to make herself heard. "It would cost you nothing—and look at the misery you would prevent. What you're doing is immoral! TEN MORE YEARS."

Her last words were a scream as she called out this year's slogan. TEN MORE YEARS! I shook my arm free as the guard in front of me made sudden headway, and dashed along in his wake. I had nothing to say to the woman; nothing that she would listen to. If it were immoral, what did ten more years have to do with it? Ten more years; if by some miracle they were granted ten more years on the copyrights, what then? I knew the answer. They would try to talk the Pan-National Union into fifteen more years, or perhaps twenty. When you pay somebody off, it only increases their demands. I know, only too well. They are never satisfied with what they get.

Joe Delacorte and I scurried into the main chamber and shuffled sideways to our seats at the last possible moment. All the preliminary nonsense was finished, and the real business was beginning. The tension in the room was terrific. To be honest, a lot of it was being generated by the media. They were all poised to make maximum noise as they shot the selection information all over the System. If it were not for the media, I don't think the PNU would hold live draft picks at all. We'd all hook in with video links and do our business the civilized way.

The excitement now was bogus for other reasons, too. The professionals—I and a few others—would not become interested until the ten rounds were complete. Before that, the choices were just too limited. Only when they were all made, and the video teams were gone, would the four groups get together off-camera and begin the horse trading. "*My ninth round plus my fifth for your second.*" "*Maybe, if you'll throw in $10 million and a tenth-round draft pick for next year. . . .*"

Meanwhile, BP Megation had taken the microphone. "First selection," said their representative. "Robert Oppenheimer."

I looked at Joe, and he shrugged. No surprise. Oppenheimer was the perfect choice—a brilliant scientist, but also practical, and willing to work with other people. He had died in 1967, so his original copyright had expired within the past twelve months. I knew his family had appealed for a copyright extension and been refused. Now BP Megation had sole single-copy rights for another lifetime.

"Trade?" whispered Joe.

I shook my head. We would have to beggar ourselves for next year's draft picks to make BP give up Oppenheimer. Other combine reps had apparently made the same decision. There was the clicking of data entry as the people around me updated portable databases. I did the same thing with a stub of pencil and a folded sheet of yellow paper, putting a check mark alongside his name. Oppenheimer was taken care of, I could forget that one. If by some miracle one of the four teams had overlooked some other top choice, I had to be ready to make an instant revision to my own selections.

"First selection, by NETSCO," said another voice. "Peter Joseph William Debye."

It was another natural choice. Debye had been a Nobel prizewinner in physics, a theoretician with an excellent grasp of applied technology. He had died in 1966. Nobel laureates in science, particularly ones with that practical streak, went fast. As soon as their copyrights expired, they would be picked up in the draft the same year.

That doesn't mean it always works out well. The most famous case, of course, was Albert Einstein. When his copyright had expired in 2030, BP Megation had had first choice in the draft pick. They had their doubts, and they must have sweated blood over their decision. The rumor mill said they spent over $70 million in simulations alone, before they decided to take him as their top choice. The same rumor mill said that the cloned form was now showing amazing ability in chess and music, but no interest at all in physics or mathematics. If that was true, BP Megation had dropped $2 billion down a black hole: $1 billion straight to the PNU for acquisition of copyright, and another $1 billion for the clone process. Theorists were always tricky; you could never tell how they would turn out.

Magrit-Marcus Gesellschaft had now made their first draft pick, and chosen another Nobel laureate, John Cockroft. He also had died in 1967. So far, every selection was completely predictable. The three combines were picking the famous scientists and engineers who had died in 1966 and 1967, and who were now, with the expiration of family retention of copyrights, available for cloning for the first time.

The combines were being logical, but it made for a very dull draft pick. Maybe it was time to change that. I stood up to announce our first take.

"First selection, by Romberg AG," I said. "Charles Proteus Steinmetz."

My announcement caused a stir in the media. They had presumably never heard of Steinmetz, which was a disgraceful statement of their own ignorance. Even if they hadn't spent most of the past year combing old files and records, as we had, they should have heard of him. He was one of the past century's most colorful and creative scientists, a man who had been physically handicapped (he was a hunchback), but mentally able to do the equivalent of a hundred one-hand push-ups without even breathing hard. Even I had heard of him, and you'd not find many of my colleagues who'd suggest I was interested in science.

The buzzing in the media told me they were consulting their own historical data files, digging farther back in time. Even when they had done all that, they would still not understand the first thing about the true process of clone selection. It's not just a question of knowing who died over seventy-five years ago, and will therefore be out of copyright. That's a trivial exercise, one that any yearbook will solve for you. You also have to evaluate other factors. Do you know where the body is—are you absolutely *sure*? Remember, you can't clone anyone with a cell or two from the original body. You also have to be certain that it's who you think it is. All bodies seventy-five years old tend to look the same. And then, if the body happens to be really old—say, more than a couple of centuries—there are other peculiar problems that are still not understood at all. When

NETSCO pulled its coup a few years ago by cloning Gottfried Wilhelm Leibniz, the other three combines were envious at first. Leibniz was a real universal genius, a seventeenth-century superbrain who was good at everything. NETSCO had developed a better cell-growth technique, and they had also succeeded in locating the body of Leibniz in its undistinguished Hanover grave.

They walked tall for almost a year at NETSCO, until the clone came out of the forcing chambers for indoctrination. He looked nothing like the old portraits of Leibniz, and he could not grasp even the simplest abstract concepts. Oops! said the media. Wrong body.

But it wasn't as simple as that. The next year, MMG duplicated the NETSCO cell-growth technology and tried for Isaac Newton. In this case there was no doubt that they had the correct body, because it had lain undisturbed since 1727 beneath a prominent plaque in London's Westminster Abbey. The results were just as disappointing as they had been for Leibniz.

Now NETSCO and MMG have become very conservative, in my opinion, far too conservative. But since then, nobody has tried for a clone of anyone who died before 1850. The draft picking went on its thoughtful and generally cautious way, and was over in a couple of hours except for the delayed deals.

The same group of protesters were picketing the building when I left. I tried to walk quietly through them, but they must have seen my picture on one of the exterior screens showing the draft-pick process. I was buttonholed by a man in a red jumpsuit and the same thin woman in green, still carrying her placard.

"Could we speak with you for just one moment?" The man in red was very well-spoken and polite.

I hesitated, aware that news cameras were on us. "Very briefly. I'm trying to run a proof-of-concept project, you know."

"I know. Is it going well?" He was a different type from most of the demonstrators, cool and apparently intelligent. And therefore potentially more dangerous.

"I wish I could say yes," I said. "Actually, it's going rather badly. That's why I'm keen to get back out."

"I understand. All I wanted to ask you was why you— and I don't mean *you*, personally; I mean the combines— why do you find it *necessary* to use clones? You could do your work without them, couldn't you?"

I hesitated. "Let me put it this way. We could do the work without them, in just the same way as we could stumble along somehow if we were denied the use of computer power, or nuclear power. The projects would be possible, but they would be enormously more difficult. The clones augment our available brainpower, at the highest levels. So let me ask you: Why *should* we do without the clones, when they are available and useful?"

"Because of the families. You have no right to subject the families to the misery and upset of seeing their loved ones cloned, without their having any rights in the matter. It's cruel, and unnecessary. Can't you see that?"

"No, I can't. Now, you listen to me for a minute." The cameras were still on me. It was a chance to say something that could never be said often enough. "The family holds copyright for seventy-five years after a person's death. So if you, personally, *remember* your grandparent, you have to be pushing eighty years old—and it's obvious from looking at you that you're under forty. So ask yourself, Why are all you petitioners people who are in their thirties? It's not *you* who's feeling any misery."

"But there are relatives—," he said.

"Oh yes, the relatives. Are you a relative of somebody who has been cloned?"

"Not yet. But if this sort of thing goes on—"

"Listen to me for one more minute. A long time ago, there were a lot of people around who thought that it was wrong to let books with sex in them be sold to the general public. They petitioned to have the books banned. It wasn't that they claimed to be buying the books themselves, and finding them disgusting; because if they said that was the case, then people would have asked them *why* they were buying what they didn't like. Nobody was forcing anybody to buy those books. No, what the petitioners wanted was for *other* people to be stopped from buying what the *petitioners* didn't like. And you copyright-extension people are just the same. You are making a case on behalf of the relatives of the ones who are being cloned. But you never seem to ask yourself this: If cloning is so bad, why aren't the *descendants* of the clones the ones doing the complaining? They're not, you know. You never see them around here."

He shook his head. "Cloning is immoral!"

I sighed. Why bother? Not one word of what I'd said had got through to him. It didn't much matter—I'd really been speaking for the media anyway—but it was a shame to see bigotry masquerading as public-spirited behavior. I'd seen enough of that already in my life.

I started to move off toward my waiting aircar. The lady in green clutched my arm again. "I'm going to leave instructions in my will that I want to be cremated. You'll never get me!"

You have my word on that, lady. But I didn't say it. I headed for the car, feeling an increasing urge to get back to the clean and rational regions of space. There was one good argument against cloning, and only one. It increased the total number of people, and to me that number already felt far too large.

I had been gone only thirty hours, total; but when I arrived back at Headquarters, I learned that in my absence five new problems had occurred. I scanned the written summary that Pauli had left behind.

First, one of the thirty-two booster engines set deep in the surface of the asteroid did not respond to telemetry requests for a status report. We had to assume it was defective, and eliminate it from the final firing pattern. Second, a big solar flare was on the way. There was nothing we could do about that, but it did mean we would have to recompute the strength of the magnetic and electric fields close to Io. They would change with the strength of the Jovian magnetosphere, and that was important because the troubleshooting team in my absence had agreed on their preferred solution to

the problem of adjusting impact point and arrival time. It
called for strong coupling between the asteroid and the
5-million-amp flux tube of current between Io and its parent
planet, Jupiter, to modify the final collision trajectory.

Third, we had lost the image data stream from one of our
observing satellites, in synchronous orbit with Io. Fourth,
our billion-ton asteroid had been struck by a larger-than-
usual micrometeorite. This one must have massed a couple
of kilograms, and it had been moving fast. It had struck
off-axis from the center of mass, and the whole asteroid was
now showing a tendency to rotate slowly away from our
preferred orientation. Fifth, and finally, a new volcano had
become very active down on the surface of Io. It was
spouting sulfur up for a couple of hundred kilometers, and
obscuring the view of the final-impact landmark.

After I had read Pauli's terse analysis of all the problems—
nobody I ever met or heard of could summarize as clearly
and briefly as he did—I switched on my communications
set and asked him the only question that mattered: "Can you
handle them all?"

There was a delay of almost two minutes. The troubleshooters were heading out to join the rest of our project
team for their on-the-spot analyses in the Jovian system;
already the light-travel time was significant. If I didn't
follow in the next day or two, radio-signal delay would
make conversation impossible. At the moment, Jupiter was
forty-five light-minutes from Earth.

"We can, Al," said Pauli's image at last. "Unless others
come up in the next few hours, we can. From here until
impact, we'll be working in an environment with increasing
uncertainties."

"The PNU people planned it that way. Go ahead—but
send me full transcripts." I left the system switched on, and
went off to the next room to study the notes I had taken of
the five problem areas. As I had done with every glitch that
had come up since the Phase B demonstration project began,
I placed the problem into one of two basic categories: act of
nature, or failure of man-made element. For the most recent
five difficulties, the volcano on Io and the solar flare belonged

to the left-hand column: Category One, clearly natural and unpredictable events. The absence of booster-engine telemetry and the loss of satellite-image data were Category Two, failures of our system. They went in the right-hand column. I hesitated for a long time over the fifth event, the impact of the meteorite; finally, and with some misgivings, I assigned it also as a Category One event.

As soon as possible, I would like to follow the engineering teams out toward Jupiter for the final hours of the demonstration. However, I had two more duties to perform before I could leave. Using a coded link to Romberg AG HQ in synchronous Earth orbit, I queried the status of all the clone tanks. No anomalies were reported. By the time we returned from the final stages of Phase B, another three finished clones would be ready to move to the indoctrination facility. I needed to be there when it happened.

Next, I had to review and approve acquisition of single-use copyright for all the draft picks we had negotiated down on Earth. To give an idea of the importance of these choices, we were looking at an expenditure of $20 billion for those selections over the next twelve months. It raised the unavoidable question, Had we made the best choices?

At this stage of the game, *every* combine began to have second thoughts about the wisdom of their picks. All the old failures came crowding into your mind. I already mentioned NETSCO and their problem with Einstein, but we had had our full share at Romberg AG: Gregor Mendel, the originator of the genetic ideas that stood behind all the cloning efforts, had proved useless; so had Ernest Lawrence, inventor of the cyclotron, our second pick for 1958. We had (by blind luck!) traded him along with $40 million for Wolfgang Pauli. Even so, we had made a bad error of judgment, and the fact that others made the same mistake was no consolation. As for Marconi, even though he looked like the old pictures of him, and was obviously highly intelligent, the clone who emerged turned out to be so indolent and casual about everything that he ruined any project he worked on. I had placed him in a cushy and undemanding position and allowed him to fiddle about with his own interests, which were mainly sports and good-looking women. (As Pauli acidly remarked, "And you say that *we're* the smart ones, doing all the work?")

It's not the evaluation of a person's past record that's difficult, because we are talking about famous people who have done a great deal; written masses of books, articles, and papers; and been thoroughly evaluated by their own contemporaries. Even with all that, a big question still remains: Will the things that made the original man or woman great still be there in the cloned form? In other words, *Just what is it that is inherited?*

That's a very hard question to answer. The theory of evolution was proposed 170 years ago, but we're still fighting the old Nature-versus-Nurture battle. Is a human genius decided mainly by heredity, or by the way the person was raised? One old argument against cloning for genius was based on the importance of Nurture. It goes as follows: an individual is the product of both heredity (which is all you get in the clone) and environment. Since it is impossible to reproduce someone's environment, complete with parents, grandparents, friends, and teachers, you can't raise a clone that will be exactly like the original individual.

I'll buy that logic. We can't make ourselves an intellectually exact copy of anyone.

However, the argument was also used to prove that cloning for superior intellectual performance would be impossible. But of course, it actually proves nothing of the sort. If you take two peas from the same pod, and put one of them in deep soil next to a high wall, and the other in shallow soil out in the open, they *must* do different things if both are to thrive. The one next to the wall has to make sure it gets enough sunshine, which it can do by maximizing leaf area; the one in shallow soil has to get enough moisture, which it does through putting out more roots. The *superior* strain of peas is the one whose genetic composition allows it to adapt to whatever environment it is presented with.

People are not peas, but in one respect they are not very different from them: some have superior genetic composition to others. That's all you can ask for. If you clone someone from a century ago, the last thing you want is someone who is *identical* to the original. They would be stuck in a twentieth-century mind-set. What is needed is someone who can adapt to and thrive in *today's* environment—whether that is now the human equivalent of shade, or of shallow soil. The success of the original clone-template tells us a very important thing, that we are dealing with a superior physical brain. What that brain thinks is the year 2040 *should* be different from what it would have thought in the year 1940—otherwise the clone would be quite useless. And the criteria for "useless" change with time, too.

All these facts and a hundred others were running around inside my head as I reviewed the list for this year. Finally I made a note to suggest that J.B.S. Haldane, whom we had looked at and rejected three years ago on the grounds of unmanageability, ought to be looked at again and acquired if possible. History shows that he had wild views on politics and society, but there was no question at all about the quality of his mind. I thought I had learned a lot about interfacing with difficult scientific personalities in the past few years.

When I was satisfied with my final list, I transmitted everything to Joe Delacorte, who was still down on Earth, and headed for the transition room. A personal shipment pod ought to be waiting for me there. I hoped I would get a good one. At the very least, I'd be in it for the next eight days. Last time I went out to the Jovian system, the pod's internal lighting and external antenna failed after three days. Have you ever sat in the dark for seventy-two hours, a hundred million miles from the nearest human, unable to send or receive messages? I didn't know if anyone realized I was in trouble. All I could do was sit tight—and I mean tight; pods are *small*—and stare out at the stars.

This time the pod was in good working order. I was able to participate in every problem that hit the project over the next four days. There were plenty of them, all small, and all significant. One of the fuel-supply ships lost a main ion drive. The supply ship was not much more than a vast bag of volatiles and a small engine, and it had almost no brain at all in its computer, not even enough to figure out an optimal use of its drives. We had to chase after and corral it as though we were pursuing a great lumbering elephant. Then three members of the impact-monitoring team came down with food poisoning—salmonella, which was almost certainly their own fault. You can say anything you like about throwing away spoiled food, but you can't get a sloppy crew to take much notice.

Then, for variety, we lost a sensor through sheer bad program design. In turning one of our imaging systems from star sensing to Io-Jupiter sensing, we tracked it right across the solar disk and burned out all the photocells. According to the engineers, that's the sort of blunder you don't make after kindergarten—but somebody did it.

Engineering errors are easy to correct. It was much trickier when one of the final-approach-coordination groups, a team of two men and one woman, chose the day before the Io rendezvous to have a violent sexual argument. They were millions of kilometers away from anyone, so there was not much we could do except talk to them. We did that, hoped they wouldn't kill each other, and made plans to do without their inputs if we had to.

Finally, one day before impact, an unplanned and anomalous firing of a rocket on the asteroid's forward surface caused a significant change of velocity of the whole body.

I ought to explain that I did little or nothing to solve any of these problems. I was too slow, too ignorant, and not creative enough. While I was still struggling to comprehend what the problem parameters were, my troubleshooters were swarming all over it. They threw proposals and counterproposals at each other so fast that I could hardly note them, still less contribute to them. For example, in the case of the anomalous rocket firing that I mentioned, compensation for the unwanted thrust called for an elaborate balancing act of lateral and radial engines, rolling and nudging the asteroid back into its correct approach path. The team had mapped out the methods in minutes, written the necessary optimization programs in less than half an hour, and implemented their solution before I understood the geometry of what was going on.

So what did I do while all this was happening? I continued to make my two columns: act of nature, or failure of man-made element. The list was growing steadily, and I was spending a lot of time looking at it.

We were coming down to the final few hours now, and all the combines were working flat out to solve their own problems. In an engineering project of this size, many thousands of things could go wrong. We were working in extreme physical conditions, hundreds of millions of kilometers away from Earth and our standard test environments. In the intense charged-particle field near Io, cables broke at loads well below their rated capacities, hard-vacuum welds showed air-bleed effects, and lateral jets were fired and failed to produce the predicted attitude adjustments. And on top of all this, the pressure, isolation, and bizarre surroundings were too much for some of the workers. We had human failure to add to engineering failure. The test was tougher than anyone had realized—even PNU, who was supposed to make the demonstration project just this side of impossible.

I was watching the performance of the other three combines only a little less intently than I was watching our own. At five hours from contact time, NETSCO apparently suffered a communications loss with their asteroid-control system. Instead of heading for Io impact, the asteroid veered away, spiraling in toward the bulk of Jupiter itself.

BP Megation lost it at impact minus three hours, when a vast explosion on one of their asteroid forward boosters threw the kilometer-long body into a rapid tumble. Within an hour, by some miracle of improvisation, their engineering team had found a method of stabilizing the wobbling mass. But by then it was too late to return to nominal impact time and place. Their asteroid skimmed into the surface of Io an hour early, sending up a long, tear-shaped mass of ejecta from the moon's turbulent surface.

That left just two of us, MMG and Romberg AG. We both had our hands full. The Jovian system is filled with electrical, magnetic, and gravitational energies bigger than anything in the Star System except the Sun itself. The two remaining combines were trying to steer their asteroid into a pinpoint landing through a great storm of interference that made every control command and every piece of incoming telemetry suspect. In the final hour I didn't even follow the exchanges between my troubleshooters. Oh, I could *hear* them easily enough. What I couldn't do was comprehend them, enough to know what was happening.

Pauli would toss a scrap of comment at von Neumann, and, while I was trying to understand that, von Neumann would have done an assessment, keyed in for a databank status report, gabbled a couple of questions to Fermi and an instruction to Edison, and at the same time be absorbing scribbled notes and diagrams from those two. I don't know if what they were doing was *potentially* intelligible to me or not; all I know is they were going about fifty times too fast for me to follow. And it didn't much matter what I understood—they were getting the job done. I was still trying to divide all problems into my Category One-Category Two columns, but it got harder and harder.

In the final hour I didn't look or listen to what my own team was doing. We had one band of telemetry trained on the MMG project, and more and more that's where my attention was focused. I assumed they were having the same kind of communications trouble as we were—that crackling discharge field around Io made everything difficult. But their team was handling it. They were swinging smoothly into impact.

And then, with only ten minutes to go, the final small adjustment was made. It should have been a tiny nudge from the radial jets; enough to fine-tune the impact position for a few hundred meters, and no more. Instead, there was a joyous roar of a radial jet at full, uncontrolled thrust. The MMG asteroid did nothing unusual for a few seconds (a billion tons is a lot of inertia), then began to drift lazily sideways, away from its nominal trajectory.

The jet was still firing. And that should have been

impossible, because the first thing that the MMG team would do was send a POWER-OFF signal to the engine.

The time for impact came when the MMG asteroid was still a clear fifty kilometers out of position, and accelerating away. I saw the final collision, and the payload scraped along the surface of Io in a long, jagged scar that looked nothing at all like the neat, punched hole that we were supposed to achieve.

And we did achieve it, a few seconds later. Our asteroid came in exactly where and when it was supposed to, driving in exactly vertical to the surface. The plume of ejecta had hardly begun to rise from Io's red-and-yellow surface before von Neumann was pulling a bottle of bourbon from underneath the communications console.

I didn't object—I only wished I were there physically to share it, instead of being stuck in my own pod, short of rendezvous with our main ship. I looked at my final list, still somewhat incomplete. Was there a pattern to it? Ten minutes of analysis didn't show one. No one had tried anything—this time. Someday, and it might be tomorrow, somebody on another combine would have a bright idea; and then it would be a whole new ball game.

While I was still pondering my list, my control console began to buzz insistently. I switched it on expecting contact with my own troubleshooting team. Instead, I saw the despondent face of Brunel, MMG's own team leader—the man above all others that I would have liked to work on my side.

He nodded at me when my picture appeared on the screen. He was smoking one of his powerful black cigars, stuck in the side of his mouth. The expression on his face was as impenetrable as ever. He never let his feelings show there. "I assume you saw it, didn't you?" he said around the cigar. "We're out of it. I just called to congratulate you—again."

"Yeah, I saw it. Tough luck. At least you came second."

"Which, as you know very well, is no better than coming last." He sighed and shook his head. "We still have no idea what happened. Looks like either a programming error, or a valve sticking open. We probably won't know for weeks. And I'm not sure I care."

I maintained a sympathetic silence.

"I sometimes think we should just give up, Al," he said. "I can beat those other turkeys, but I can't compete with you. That's six in a row that you've won. It's wearing me out. You've no idea how much frustration there is in that."

I had never known Brunel to reveal so much of his feelings before.

"I think I do understand your problems," I said.

And I did. I knew exactly how he felt—more than he would believe. To suffer through a whole, endless sequence of minor, niggling mishaps was heartbreaking. No single trouble was ever big enough for a trouble-shooting team to stop, isolate it, and be able to say, there's dirty work going on here. But their cumulative effect was another matter. One day it was a morass of shipments missing their correct flights, another time a couple of minus signs dropped into computer programs, or a key worker struck down from a few days by a random virus, permits misfiled, manifests mislaid, or licenses wrongly dated.

I knew all those mishaps personally. I should, because I invented most of them. I think of it as the death of a thousand cuts. No one can endure all that and still hope to win a Phase B study.

"How would you like to work on the Europan Metamorph?" I asked. "I think you'd love it."

He looked very thoughtful, and for the first time, I believe I could actually read his expression. "Leave MMG, you mean?" he said. "Maybe. I don't know what I want anymore. Let me think about it. I'd like to work with you, Al—you're a genius."

Brunel was wrong about that, of course. I'm certainly no genius. All I can do is what I've always done—handle people, take care of unpleasant details (quietly!), and make sure things get done that need doing. And of course, do what I do best: make sure that some things that need doing *don't* get done.

There *are* geniuses in the world, real geniuses. Not me,

though. The man who decided to clone me, secretly—*there* I'd suggest you have a genius.

"*Say, don't you remember, they called me AL.* . . ."

Of course, I don't remember. That song was written in the 1930s, and I didn't die until 1947, but no clone remembers anything of the forefather life. The fact that we tend to be knowledgeable about our originals' period is an expression of interest in those individuals, not memories from them. I know the Chicago of the Depression years intimately, as well as I know today; but it is all learned knowledge. I have no actual recollection of events. I don't *remember*.

So even if you don't remember, call me Al anyway. Everyone did.

THE PHANTOM
OF KANSAS

John Varley

*John Varley appeared on the SF scene in 1975, and by the
end of 1976—in what was a meteoric rise to prominence
even for a field known for meteoric rises—he was already
being recognized as one of the hottest new writers of the
seventies. His books include the novels* Ophiuchi Hotline,
Titan, Wizard, *and* Demon, *and the collections* The Persis-
tence of Vision, The Barbie Murders, Picnic on Nearside, *and*
Blue Champagne. *His most recent book is a major new novel,*
Steel Beach. *He has won two Nebulas and two Hugos for his
short fiction.*

*In the vivid and wildly inventive high-tech thriller that
follows, one of SF's best murder mysteries, he demonstrates
that identity, like beauty, is in the eye of the beholder . . .*

I *do* my banking at the Archimedes Trust Association. Their
security is first-rate, their service is courteous, and they
have their own medico facility that does nothing but take
recordings for their vaults.

And they had been robbed two weeks ago.

It was a break for me. I had been approaching my regular
recording date and dreading the chunk it would take from
my savings. Then these thieves break into my bank, steal a
huge amount of negotiable paper, and in an excess of
enthusiasm they destroy all the recording cubes. Every last
one of them, crunched into tiny shards of plastic. Of course
the bank had to replace them all, and very fast, too. They
weren't stupid; it wasn't the first time someone had used
such a bank robbery to facilitate a murder. So the bank had

to record everyone who had an account, and do it in a few days. It must have cost them more than the robbery.

How that scheme works, incidentally, is like this. The robber couldn't care less about the money stolen. Mostly it's very risky to pass such loot, anyway. The programs written into the money computers these days are enough to foil all but the most exceptional robber. You have to let that kind of money lie for on the order of a century to have any hope of realizing gains on it. Not impossible, of course, but the police types have found out that few criminals are temperamentally able to wait that long. The robber's real motive in a case where memory cubes have been destroyed is murder, not robbery.

Every so often someone comes along who must commit a crime of passion. There are very few left open, and murder is the most awkward of all. It just doesn't satisfy this type to kill someone and see them walking around six months later. When the victim sues the killer for alienation of personality— and collects up to 99% of the killer's worldly goods—it's just twisting the knife. So if you really hate someone, the temptation is great to *really* kill them, forever and ever, just like in the old days, by destroying their memory cube first then killing the body.

That's what the ATA feared, and I had rated a private bodyguard over the last week as part of my contract. It was sort of a status symbol to show your friends, but otherwise I hadn't been much impressed until I realized that ATA was going to pay for my next recording as part of their crash program to cover all their policy holders. They had contracted to keep me alive forever, so even though I had been scheduled for a recording in only three weeks they had to pay for this one. The courts had rules that a lost or damaged cube must be replaced with all possible speed.

So I should have been very happy. I wasn't, but tried to be brave.

I was shown into the recording room with no delay and told to strip and lie on the table. The medico, a man who looked like someone I might have met several decades ago, busied himself with his equipment as I tried to control my breathing. I was grateful when he plugged the computer lead into my occipital socket and turned off my motor control. Now I didn't have to worry about whether to ask if I knew him or not. As I grow older, I find that's more of a problem. I must have met twenty thousand people by now and talked to them long enough to make an impression. It gets confusing.

He removed the top of my head and prepared to take a multiholo picture of me, a chemical analog of everything I ever saw or thought or remembered or just vaguely dreamed. It was a blessed relief when I slid over into unconsciousness.

The coolness and sheen of stainless steel beneath my fingertips. There is the smell of isopropyl alcohol, and the hint of acetone.

The medico's shop. Childhood memories tumble over me, triggered by the smells. Excitement, change, my mother standing by while the medico carves away my broken finger to replace it with a pink new one. I lie in the darkness and remember.

And there is light, a hurting light from nowhere and I feel my pupil contract as the only movement in my entire body.

"She's in," I hear. But I'm not, not really. I'm just lying here in the blessed dark, unable to move.

It comes in a rush, the repossession of my body. I travel down the endless nerves to bang up hard against the insides of my hands and feet, to whirl through the pools of my nipples and tingle in my lips and nose, *Now* I'm in.

I sat up quickly into the restraining arms of the medico. I struggled for a second before I was able to relax. My fingers were buzzing and cramped with the clamminess of hyperventilation.

"Whew," I said, putting my head in my hands. "Bad dream. I thought . . ."

I looked around me and saw that I was naked on the steel-topped table with several worried faces looking at me from all sides. I wanted to retreat into the darkness again and let my insides settle down. I saw my mother's face, blinked, and failed to make it disappear.

"Carnival?" I asked her ghost.

"Right here, Fox," she said, and took me in her arms. It was awkward and unsatisfying with her standing on the floor and me on the table. There were wires trailing from my body. But the comfort was needed. I didn't know where I was. With a chemical rush as precipitous as the one just before I awoke, the people solidified around me.

"She's all right now," the medico said, turning from his instruments. He smiled impersonally at me as he began removing the wires from my head. I did not smile back. I knew where I was now, just as surely as I had ever known anything. I remembered coming in here only hours before.

But I knew it had been more than a few hours. I've read about it: the disorientation when a new body is awakened with transplanted memories. And my mother wouldn't be here unless something had gone badly wrong.

I had died.

I was given a mild sedative, help in dressing, and my mother's arm to lead me down plush-carpeted hallways to the office of the bank president. I was still not fully awake. The halls were achingly quiet but for the brush of our feet across the wine-colored rug. I felt like the pressure was fluctuating wildly, leaving my ears popped and muffled. I couldn't see too far away. I was grateful to leave the vanishing points in the hall for the panelled browns of wood veneer and the coolness and echoes of a white marble floor.

The bank president, Mr. Leander, showed us to our seats. I sank into the purple velvet and let it wrap around me. Leander pulled up a chair facing us and offered us drinks. I declined. My head was swimming already and I knew I'd have to pay attention.

Leander fiddled with a dossier on his desk. Mine, I imagine. It had been freshly printed out from the terminal at his right hand. I'd met him briefly before; he was a pleasant sort of person, chosen for this public-relations job for his willingness to wear the sort of old-man body that inspires confidence and trust. He seemed to be about sixty-five. He was probably more like twenty.

It seemed that he was never going to get around to the briefing so I asked a question. One that was very important to me at the moment.

"What's the date?"

"It's the month of November," he said, ponderously. "And the year is 342."

I had been dead for two and a half years.

"Listen," I said, "I don't want to take up any more of your time. You must have a brochure you can give me to bring me up to date. If you'll just hand it over, I'll be on my way. Oh, and thank you for your concern."

He waved his hand at me as I started to rise.

"I would appreciate it if you stayed a bit longer. Yours is an unusual case, Ms. Fox. I . . . well, it's never happened in the history of the Archimedes Trust Association."

"Yes?"

"You see, you've died, as you figured out soon after we woke you. What you couldn't have known is that you've died more than once since your last recording."

"More than once?" So it wasn't such a smart question; so what was I supposed to ask?

"Three times."

"Three?"

"Yes, three separate times. We suspect murder."

The room was perfectly silent for a while. At last I decided I should have that drink. He poured it for me, and I drained it.

"Perhaps your mother should tell you more about it," Leander suggested. "She's been closer to the situation. I was only made aware of it recently. Carnival?"

I found my way back to my apartment in a sort of daze. By the time I had settled in again the drug was wearing off and I could face my situation with a clear head. But my skin was crawling.

Listening in the third person to things you've done is not the most pleasant thing. I decided it was time to face some facts that all of us, including myself, do not like to think about. The first order of business was to recognize that the things that were done by those three previous people were not done by *me*. I was a new person, fourth in the line of succession. I had many things in common with the previous incarnations, including all my memories up to that day. I surrendered myself to the memory recording machine. But the *me* of that time and place had been killed.

She lasted longer than the others. Almost a year, Carnival had said. Then her body was found at the bottom of Hadley Rille. It was an appropriate place for her to die; both she and myself liked to go hiking out on the surface for purposes of inspiration.

Murder was not suspected that time. The bank, upon hearing of my—no, *her*—death, started a clone from the tissue sample I had left with my recording. Six lunations later, a copy of me was infused with my memories and told that she had just died. She had been shaken, but seemed to be adjusting well when she, too, was killed.

This time there was much suspicion. Not only had she survived for less than a lunation after her reincarnation, but the circumstances were unusual. She had been blown to pieces in a tube-train explosion. She had been the only passenger in a two-seat capsule. The explosion had been caused by a home-made bomb.

There was still the possibility that it was a random act, possibly by political terrorists. The third copy of me had not thought so. I don't know why. That is the most maddening thing about memory recording: being unable to profit by the experiences of your former selves. Each time I was killed, it moved me back to square one, the day I was recorded.

But Fox 3 had reason to be paranoid. She took extraordinary precautions to stay alive. More specifically, she tried to prevent circumstances that could lead to her murder. It worked for five lunations. She died as the result of a fight, that much was certain. It was a very violent fight, with blood all over the apartment. The police at first thought she must have fatally injured her attacker, but analysis showed all the blood to have come from her body.

So where did that leave me, Fox 4? An hour's careful thought left the picture gloomy indeed. Consider: each time my killer succeeded in murdering me, he or she learned more about me. My killer must be an expert on Foxes by now, knowing things about me that I myself did not know. Such as how I handle myself in a fight. I gritted my teeth when I thought of that. Carnival told me that Fox 3, the canniest of the lot, had taken lessons in self-defense. Karate, I think she said. Did I have the benefit of it? Of course not. If I wanted to defend myself I had to start all over, because those skills died with Fox 3.

No, all the advantages were with my killer. The killer starts off with the advantage of surprise—since I had no notion of who it was—and in this case learned more about me every time he or she succeeded in killing me.

What to do? I didn't even know where to start. I ran through everyone I knew, looking for an enemy, someone who hated me enough to kill me again and again. I could find no one. Most likely it was someone Fox 1 had met during that year she lived after the recording.

The only answer I could come up with was emigration. Just pull up stakes and go to Mercury, or Mars, or even Pluto. But would that guarantee my safety? My killer seemed to be an uncommonly persistent person. No, I'd have to face it here, where at least I knew the turf.

It was the next day before I realized the extent of my loss. I had been robbed of an entire symphony.

For the last thirty years I had been an Environmentalist. I had just drifted into it while it was still an infant art-form. I had been in charge of the weather machines at the Transvaal disneyland, which was new at the time and the biggest and most modern of all the environmental parks in Luna. A few of us had started tinkering with the weather programs, first for our own amusement. Later we invited friends to watch the storms and sunsets we concocted. Before we knew it, friends were inviting friends and the Transvaal people began selling tickets.

I gradually made a name for myself, and found I could

make more money being an artist than being an engineer. At the time of my last recording I had been one of the top three Environmentalists on Luna.

Then Fox 1 went on to compose *Liquid Ice*. From what I read in the reviews, two years after the fact, it was seen as the high point of the art to date. It had been staged in the Pennsylvania disneyland, before a crowd of three hundred thousand. It made me rich.

The money was still in my bank account, but the memory of creating it was forever lost. And it mattered.

Fox 1 had written it, from beginning to end. Oh, I recalled having had some vague ideas of a winter composition, things I'd think about later and put together. But the whole creative process had gone on in the head of that other person who had been killed.

How is a person supposed to cope with that? For one bitter moment I considered calling the bank and having them destroy my memory cube. If I died this time, I'd rather die completely. The thought of a Fox 5 rising from that table . . . it was almost too much to bear. She would lack everything that Fox 1, 2, 3, and me, Fox 4, had experienced. So far I'd had little time to add to the personality we all shared, but even the bad times are worth saving.

It was either that, or have a new recording made every day. I called the bank, did some figuring, and found that I wasn't wealthy enough to afford that. But it was worth exploring. If I had a new recording taken once a week I could keep at it for about a year before I ran out of money.

I decided I'd do it, for as long as I could. And to make sure that no future Fox would ever have to go through this again, I'd have one made today. Fox 5, if she was ever born, would be born knowing at least as much as I knew now.

I felt better after the recording was made. I found that I no longer feared the medico's office. That fear comes from the common misapprehension that one will wake up from the recording to discover that one has died. It's a silly thing to believe, but it comes from the distaste we all have for really looking at the facts.

If you'll consider human consciousness, you'll see that the three-dimensional cross-section of a human being that is *you* can only rise from that table and go about your business. It can happen no other way. Human consciousness is linear, along a timeline that has a beginning and an end. If you die after a recording, you *die*, forever and with no reprieve. It doesn't matter that a recording of you exists and that a new person with your memories to a certain point can be created; you are *dead*. Looked at from a fourth-dimensional viewpoint, what memory recording does is to graft a new person onto your lifeline at a point in the past. You do not retrace that lifeline and magically become that new person. I, Fox 4, was only a relative of that long-ago person who had her memories recorded. And if I died it was forever. Fox 5 would awaken with my memories to date, but I would be no part of her. She would be on her own.

Why do we do it? I honestly don't know. I suppose that the human urge to live forever is so strong that we'll grasp at even the most unsatisfactory substitute. At one time people had themselves frozen when they died, in the hope of being thawed out in a future when humans knew how to reverse death. Look at the Great Pyramid in the Egypt disneyland if you want to see the sheer *size* of that urge.

So we live our lives in pieces. I could know, for whatever good it would do me, that thousands of years from now a being would still exist who would be at least partly me. She would remember exactly the same things I remembered of her childhood; the trip to Archimedes, her first sex change, her lovers, her hurts and her happiness. If I had another recording taken, she would remember thinking the thoughts I was thinking now. And she would probably still be stringing chunks of experience onto her life, year by year. Each time she had a new recording that much more of her life was safe for all time. There was a certain comfort in knowing that my life was safe up until a few hours ago, when the recording was made.

Having thought all that out, I found myself fiercely determined to never let it happen again. I began to hate my killer with an intensity I had never experienced. I wanted to storm out of the apartment and beat my killer to death with a blunt instrument.

I swallowed that emotion with difficulty. It was exactly what the killer would be looking for. I had to remember that the killer knew what my first reaction would be. I had to behave in a way that he or she would not expect.

But what way was that?

I called up the police department and talked to the detective who had my case. Her name was Isadora, and she had some good advice.

"You're not going to like it, if I can judge from past experience," she said. "The last time I proposed it to you, you rejected it out of hand."

I knew I'd have to get used to this. People would always be telling me what I had done, what I had said to them. I controlled my anger and asked her to go on.

"It's simply to stay put. I know you think you're a detective, but your successor proved pretty well that you are not. If you stir out of that door you'll be nailed. This guy knows you inside and out, and he'll get you. Count on it."

"He? You know something about him, then?"

"Sorry, you'll have to bear with me. I've told you parts of this case twice already, so it's hard to remember what you don't know. Yes, we do know he's a male. Or was, six months ago, when you had your big fight with him. Several witnesses reported a man with bloodstained clothes, who could only have been your killer."

"Then you're on his trail?"

She sighed, and I knew she was going over old ground again.

"No, and you've proved again that you're not a detective. Your detective lore comes from reading old novels. It's not a glamorous enough job nowadays to rate fictional heroes and such, so most people don't know the kind of work we do. Knowing that the killer was a man when he last knocked you off means nothing to us. He could have bought a Change the very next day. You're probably wondering if we have fingerprints of him, right?"

I gritted my teeth. Everyone had the advantage over me.

It was obvious I had asked something like that the last time I spoke with this woman. And I *had* been thinking of it.

"No," I said. "Because he could change those as easily as his sex, right?"

"Right. Easier. The only positive means of identification today is genotyping, and he wasn't cooperative enough to leave any of him behind when he killed you. He must have been a real brute, to be able to inflict as much damage on you as he did and not even be cut himself. You were armed with a knife. Not a drop of his blood was found at the scene of the murder."

"Then how do you go about finding him?"

"Fox, I'd have to take you through several college courses to begin to explain our methods to you. And I'll even admit that they're not very good. Police work has not kept up with science over the last century. There are many things available to the modern criminal that make our job more difficult than you'd imagine. We have hopes of catching him within about four lunations, though, if you'll stay put and stop chasing him."

"Why four months?"

"We trace him by computer. We have very exacting programs that we run when we're after a guy like this. It's our one major weapon. Given time, we can run to ground about sixty percent of the criminals."

"Sixty percent?" I squawked. "Is that supposed to encourage me? Especially when you're dealing with a master like my killer seems to be?"

She shook her head. "He's not a master. He's only determined. And that works against him, not for him. The more single-mindedly he pursues you, the surer we are of catching him when he makes a slip. That sixty percent figure is over-all crime; on murder, the rate is ninety-eight. It's a crime of passion, usually done by an amateur. The pros see no percentage in it, and they're right. The penalty is so steep it can make a pauper of you, and your victim is back on the streets while you're still in court."

I thought that over, and found it made me feel better. My killer was not a criminal mastermind. I was not being hunted by Fu-Manchu or Dr. Moriarty. He was only a person like myself, new to this business. Something Fox 1 did had made him sufficiently angry to risk financial ruin to stalk and kill me. It scaled him down to human dimensions.

"So now you're all ready to go and get him?" Isadora sneered. I guess my thoughts were written on my face. That, or she was consulting her script of our previous conversation.

"Why not?" I asked.

"Because, like I said, he'll get you. He might not be a pro but he's an expert on you. He knows how you'll jump. One thing he thinks he knows is that you won't take my advice. He might be right outside your door, waiting for you to finish this conversation like you did last time around. The last time, he wasn't there. This time he might be."

It sobered me. I glanced nervously at my door, which was guarded by eight different security systems bought by Fox 3.

"Maybe you're right. So you want me just to stay here. For how long?"

"However long it takes. It may be a year. That four-lunation figure is the high point on a computer curve. It tapers off to a virtual certainty in just over a year."

"Why didn't I stay here the last time?"

"A combination of foolish bravery, hatred, and a fear of boredom." She searched my eyes, trying to find the words that would make me take the advice that Fox 3 had fatally refused. "I understand you're an artist," she went on. "Why can't you just . . . well, whatever it is artists do when they're thinking up a new composition? Can't you work there in your apartment?"

How could I tell her that inspiration wasn't just something I could turn on at will? Weather sculpture is a tenuous discipline. The visualization is difficult; you can't just try out a new idea like you can with a song, by picking it out on a piano or guitar. You can run a computer simulation, but you never really know what you have until the tapes are run into the machines and you stand out there in the open field and watch the storm take shape around you. And you don't get any practice sessions. It's expensive.

I've always needed long walks on the surface. My competitors can't understand why. They go for strolls through the various parks, usually the one where the piece will be performed. I do that, too. You have to, to get the lay of the land. A computer can tell you what it looks like in terms of thermoclines and updrafts and pocket-ecologies, but you have to really go there and feel the land, taste the air, smell the trees, before you can compose a storm or even a summer shower. It has to be a part of the land.

But my inspiration comes from the dry, cold, airless surface that so few Lunarians really like. I'm not a burrower; I've never loved the corridors like so many of my friends profess to do. I think I see the black sky and harsh terrain as a blank canvas, a feeling I never really get in the disneylands where the land is lush and varied and there's always some weather in progress even if it's only partly cloudy and warm.

Could I compose without those long, solitary walks?

Run that through again: could I afford *not* to?

"All right, I'll stay inside like a good girl."

I was in luck. What could have been an endless purgatory turned into creative frenzy such as I had never experienced. My frustrations at being locked into my apartment translated themselves into grand sweeps of tornados and thunderheads. I began writing my masterpiece. The working title was *A Conflagration of Cyclones*. That's how angry I was. My agent later talked me into shortening it to a tasteful *Cyclone*, but it was always a conflagration to me.

Soon I had managed to virtually forget about my killer. I never did completely; after all, I needed the thought of him to flog me onward, to serve as the canvas on which to paint my hatred. I did have one awful thought early on, and I brought it up to Isadora.

"It strikes me," I said, "that what you've built here is the better mousetrap, and I'm the hunk of cheese."

"You've got the essence of it," she agreed.

"I find I don't care for the role of bait."

"Why not? Are you scared?"

I hesitated, but what the hell did I have to be ashamed of?

"Yeah. I guess I am. What can you tell me to make me stay here when I could be doing what all my instincts are telling me to do, which is run like hell?"

"That's a fair question. This is the ideal situation, as far as the police are concerned. We have the victim in a place that can be watched, perfectly safely, and we have the killer on the loose. Furthermore, this is an obsessed killer, one who cannot stay away from you forever. Long before he is able to make a strike at you we should pick him up as he scouts out ways to reach you."

"Are there ways?"

"No. An unqualified no. Any one of those devices on your door would be enough to keep him out. Beyond that, your food and water is being tested before it gets to you. Those are extremely remote possibilities since we're convinced that your killer wishes to dispose of your body completely, to kill you for good. Poisoning is no good to him. We'd just start you up again. But if we can't find at least a piece of your body, the law forbids us to revive you."

"What about bombs?"

"The corridor outside your apartment is being watched. It would take quite a large bomb to blow out your door, and getting a bomb that size in place would not be possible in the time he would have. Relax, Fox. We've thought of everything. You're safe."

She rung off, and I called up the Central Computer.

"CC," I said, to get it on-line, "can you tell me how you go about catching killers?"

"Are you talking about killers in general, or the one you have a particular interest in?"

"What do you think? I don't completely believe that detective. What I want to know from you is what can I do to help?"

"There is little you can do," the CC said. "While I myself, in the sense of the Central or controlling Lunar Computer, do not handle the apprehension of criminals, I am in a supervisory capacity to several satellite computers. They use a complex number theory, correlated with the daily input from all my terminals. The average person on Luna deals with me on the order of twenty times per day, many of these transactions involving a routine epidermal sample for positive genalysis. By matching these transactions with the time and place they occurred, I am able to construct a dynamic model of what has occurred, what possibly could have occurred, and what cannot have occurred. With suitable peripheral programs I can refine this model to a close degree of accuracy. For instance, at the time of your first murder I was able to assign a low probability to ninety-nine point nine three percent of all humans on Luna as being responsible. This left me with a pool of 210,000 people who might have had a hand in it. This is merely from data placing each person at a particular place at a particular time. Further weighting of such factors as possible motive narrowed the range of prime suspects. Do you wish me to go on?"

"No, I think I get the picture. Each time I was killed you must have narrowed it more. How many suspects are left?"

"You are not phrasing the question correctly. As implied in my original statement, all residents of Luna are still suspects. But each has been assigned a probability, ranging from a very large group with a value of 10^{-27} to twenty individuals with probabilities of 13%."

The more I thought about that, the less I liked it.

"None of those sound to me like what you'd call a prime suspect."

"Alas, no. This is a very intriguing case, I must say."

"I'm glad you think so."

"Yes," it said, oblivious as usual to sarcasm. "I may have to have some programs re-written. We've never gone this far without being able to submit a ninety percent rating to the Grand Jury Data Bank."

"Then Isadora is feeding me a line, right? She doesn't have anything to go on?"

"Not strictly true. She has an analysis, a curve, that places the probability of capture as near-certainty within one year."

"You gave her that estimate, didn't you?"

"Of course."

"Then what the hell does *she* do? Listen, I'll tell you right now. I don't feel good about putting my fate in her hands. I think this job of detective is just a trumped-up featherbed. Isn't that right?"

"The privacy laws forbid me to express an opinion about the worth, performance, or intelligence of a human citizen. But I can give you a comparison. Would you entrust the construction of your symphonies to a computer alone? Would you sign your name to a work that was generated entirely by me?"

"I see your point."

"Exactly. Without a computer you'd never calculate all the factors you need for a symphony. But *I* do not write them. It is your creative spark that makes the wheels turn. Incidentally, I told your successor but of course you don't remember it, I liked your *Liquid Ice* tremendously. It was a real pleasure to work with you on it."

"Thanks. I wish I could say the same." I signed off, feeling no better than when I began the interface.

The mention of *Liquid Ice* had me seething again. Robbed! Violated! I'd rather have been gang-raped by chimpanzees than have the memory stolen from me. I had punched up the films of *Liquid Ice* and they were beautiful. Stunning, and I could say it without conceit because I had not written it.

My life became very simple. I worked—twelve and four-teen hours a day sometimes—ate, slept, and worked some more. Twice a day I put in one hour learning to fight over the holovision. It was all highly theoretical, of course, but it had value. It kept me in shape and gave me a sense of confidence.

For the first time in my life I got a good look at what my body would have been with no tampering. I was born female, but Carnival wanted to raise me as a boy so she had me Changed when I was two hours old. It's another of the contradictions in her that used to infuriate me so much but which, as I got older, I came to love. I mean, why go to all the pain and trouble of bringing a child to term and giving birth naturally, all from a professed dislike of tampering—and then turn around and refuse to accept the results of nature's lottery? I have decided that it's a result of her age. She's almost two hundred by now, which puts her childhood back in the days before Changing. In those days—I've never understood why—there was a predilection for male children. I think she never really shed it.

At any rate, I spent my childhood male. When I got my first Change, I picked my own body design. Now, in a six-lunation-old clone body which naturally reflected my actual genetic structure, I was pleased to see that my first female body design had not been far from the truth.

I was short, with small breasts and an undistinguished body. But my face was nice. Cute, I would say. I liked the nose. The age of the accelerated clone body was about seventeen years; perhaps the nose would lose its upturn in a few years of natural growth, but I hoped not. If it did, I'd have it put back.

Once a week, I had a recording made. It was the only time I saw people in the flesh. Carnival, Leander, Isadora, and a medico would enter and stay for a while after it was made. It took them an hour each way to get past the security devices. I admit it made me feel a little more secure to see how long it took even my friends to get in my apartment. It was like an invisible fortress outside my door. The better to lure you into my parlor, killer!

I worked with the CC as I never had before. We wrote new programs that produced four-dimensional models in my viewer unlike anything we had ever done before. The CC knew the stage—which was to be the Kansas disneyland—and I knew the storm. Since I couldn't walk on the stage this time before the concert I had to rely on the CC to reconstruct it for me in the holo tank.

Nothing makes me feel more godlike. Even watching it in the three-meter tank I felt thirty meters tall with lightning in my hair and a crown of shimmering frost. I walked through the Kansas autumn, the brown, rolling, featureless prairie before the red or white man came. It was the way the real Kansas looked now under the rule of the Invaders, who had ripped up the barbed wire, smoothed over the furrows, dismantled the cities and railroads and let the buffalo roam once more.

There was a logistical problem I had never faced before. I intended to use the buffalo instead of having them kept out of the way. I needed the thundering hooves of a stampede; it was very much a part of the environment I was creating. How to do it without killing animals?

The disneyland management wouldn't allow any of their livestock to be injured as part of a performance. That was fine with me; my stomach turned at the very thought. Art is one thing, but life is another and I will not kill unless to save myself. But the Kansas disneyland has two million head of buffalo and I envisioned up to twenty-five twisters at one time. How do you keep the two separate?

With subtlety, I found. The CC had buffalo behavioral profiles that were very reliable. The damn CC stores *everything*, and I've had occasion more than once to be thankful for it. We could position the herds at a selected spot and let the twisters loose above them. The tornados would never be *totally* under our control, they are capricious even when hand-made, but we could rely on a hard ninety percent accuracy in steering them. The herd-profile we worked up was usable out to two decimal points, and as insurance against the unforeseen we installed several groups of flash-bombs to turn the herd if it headed into danger.

It's an endless series of details. Where does the lightning strike, for instance? On a flat, gently rolling plain, the natural accumulation of electric charge can be just about anywhere. We had to be sure we could shape it the way we wanted, by burying five hundred accumulators that could trigger an air-to-ground flash on cue. And to the right spot. The air-to-air are harder. And the ball lightning—oh, brother. But we found we could guide it pretty well with buried wires carrying an electric current. There were going to be range fires—so check with the management on places that are due for a controlled burn anyway, and keep the buffalo away from there, too, and be sure the smoke would not blow over into the audience and spoil the view or into the herd and panic them . . .

But it was going to be glorious.

Six lunations rolled by. *Six lunations!* 177.18353 mean solar days!

I discovered that figure during a long period of brooding when I called up all sorts of data on the investigation. Which, according to Isadora, was going well.

I knew better. The CC has its faults but shading data is not one of them. Ask it what the figures are and it prints them out in tri-color.

Here's some: probability of a capture by the original curve, ninety-three percent. Total number of viable suspects remaining: nine. Highest probability of those nine possibles: three point nine percent. That was *Carnival*. The others were also close friends, and were there solely on the basis of having the opportunity at all three murders. Even Isadora dared not speculate—at least not aloud, and to me—that any of them could have a motive.

I discussed it with the CC.

"I know, Fox, I know," it replied, with the closest approach to mechanical despair I have ever heard.

"Is that all you can say?"

"No. As it happens, I'm pursuing the other possibility: that it was a ghost who killed you."

"Are you serious?"

"Yes. The term 'ghost' covers all illegal beings. I estimate there to be on the order of two hundred of them existing outside legal sanctions on Luna. These are executed criminals with their right to life officially revoked, unauthorized children never registered, and some suspected artificial mutants. Those last are the result of proscribed experiments with human DNA. All these conditions are hard to conceal for any length of time, and I round up a few every year."

"What do you do with them?"

"They have no right to life. I must execute them when I find them."

"You do it? That's not just a figure of speech?"

"That's right. I do it. It's a job humans find distasteful. I never could keep the position filled, so I assumed it myself."

That didn't sit right with me. There is an atavistic streak in me that doesn't like to turn over the complete functioning of society to machines. I get it from my mother, who goes for years at a time not deigning to speak to the CC.

"So you think someone like that may be after me. Why?"

"There is insufficient data for a meaningful answer. 'Why' has always been a tough question for me. I can operate only on the parameters fed into me when I'm dealing with human motivation, and I suspect that the parameters are not complete. I'm constantly being surprised."

"Thank goodness for that." But this time, I could have wished the CC knew a little more about human behavior.

So I was being hunted by a spook. It didn't do anything for my peace of mind. I tried to think of how such a person could exist in this card-file world we live in. A technological rat, smarter than the computers, able to fit into the cracks and holes in the integrated circuits. Where were those cracks? I couldn't find them. When I thought of the checks and safeguards all around us, the voluntary genalysis we submit to every time we spend money or take a tube or close a business deal or interface with the computer . . . People used to sign their names many times a day, or so I've heard. Now, we scrape off a bit of dead skin from our palms. It's damn hard to fake.

But how do you catch a phantom? I was facing life as a recluse if this murderer was really so determined that I die.

That conclusion came at a bad time. I had finished *Cyclone*, and to relax I had called up the films of some of the other performances during my absence from the art scene. I never should have done that.

Flashiness was out. Understated elegance was in. One of the reviews I read was very flattering to my *Liquid Ice*. I quote:

"In this piece Fox has closed the book on the blood and thunder school of Environmentalism. This powerful statement sums up the things that can be achieved by sheer magnitude and overwhelming drama. The displays of the future will be concerned with the gentle nuance of dusk, the elusive breath of a summer breeze. Fox is the Tchaikovsky of Environmentalism, the last great romantic who paints on a broad canvas. Whether she can adjust to the new, more thoughtful styles that are evolving in the work of Janus, or Pym, or even some of the ambiguous abstractions we have seen from Tyleber, remains to be seen. Nothing will detract from the sublime glory of *Liquid Ice*, of course, but the time is here . . ." and so forth and thank you for nothing.

For an awful moment I thought I had a beautiful dinosaur on my hands. It can happen, and the hazards are pronounced after a reincarnation. Advancing technology, fashion, frontiers, taste, or morals can make the best of us obsolete overnight. Was everyone contemplating gentle springtimes now, after my long sleep? Were the cool, sweet zephyrs of a summer's night the only thing that had meaning now?

A panicky call to my agent dispelled that quickly enough. As usual, the pronouncements of the critics had gone ahead of the public taste. I'm not knocking critics; that's their function, if you concede they have a function, to chart a course into unexplored territory. They must stay at the leading edge of the innovative artistic evolution, they must see what everyone will be seeing in a few years' time. Meanwhile, the public was still eating up the type of superspectacle I have always specialized in. I ran the risk of being labeled a dinosaur myself, but I found the prospect did not worry me. I became an artist through the back door, just like the tinkerers in early twentieth-century Hollywood had done. Before I was discovered, I had just been an environmental engineer having a good time.

That's not to say I don't take my art seriously. I *do* sweat over it, investing inspiration and perspiration in about the classic Edison proportions. But I don't take the critics too seriously, especially when they're not enunciating the public taste. Just because Beethoven doesn't sound like currently popular art doesn't mean his music is worthless.

I found myself thinking back to the times before Envi-

ronmentalism made such a splash. Back then we were
carefree. We had grandiose bull sessions, talking of what we
would do if only we were given an environment large
enough. We spent months roughing out the programs for
something to be called *Typhoon!* It was a hurricane in a
bottle, and the bottle would have to be five hundred
kilometers wide. Such a bottle still does not exist, but when
it's built some fool will stage it. Maybe me. The good old
days never die, you know.

So my agent made a deal with the owner of the Kansas
disneyland. The owner had known that I was working on
something for his place, but I'd not talked to him about it.
The terms were generous. My agent displayed the profit
report on *Liquid Ice*, which was still playing yearly to
packed houses in Pennsylvania. I got a straight fifty percent
of the gate, with costs of the installation and computer time
to be shared between us. I stood to make about five million
Lunar Marks.

And I was robbed again. Not killed this time, but robbed
of the chance to go into Kansas and supervise the installation of the equipment. I clashed mightily with Isadora and
would have stormed out on my own, armed with nothing so
much as a nail file, if not for a pleading visit from Carnival.
So I backed down this once and sat at home, going there
only by holographic projection. I plunged into self-doubts.
After all, I hadn't even felt the Kansas sod beneath my bare
feet this time. I hadn't been there in the flesh for over three
years. My usual method before I even conceive a project is
to spend a week or two just wandering naked through the
park, getting the feel of it through my skin and nose and
those senses that don't even have a name.

It took the CC three hours of gentle argument to convince
me again that the models we had written were accurate to
seven decimal places. They were perfect. An action ordered
up on the computer model would be a perfect analog of the
real action in Kansas. The CC said I could make quite a bit
of money just renting the software to the other artists.

• • •

The day of the premiere of *Cyclone* found me still in my apartment. But I was on the way out.

Small as I am, I somehow managed to struggle out that door with Carnival, Isadora, Leander, and my agent pulling on my elbows.

I was *not* going to watch the performance on the tube.

I arrived early, surrounded by my impromptu bodyguard. The sky matched my mind; gray, overcast, and slightly fearful. It brooded over us, and I felt more and more like a sacrificial lamb mounting some somber altar. But it was a magnificent stage to die upon.

The Kansas disneyland is one of the newer ones, and one of the largest. It is a hollowed-out cylinder twenty kilometers beneath Clavius. It measures two hundred and fifty kilometers in diameter and is five kilometers high. The rim is artfully disguised to blend into the blue sky. When you are half a kilometer from the rim, the illusion fails; otherwise, you might as well be standing back on Old Earth. The curvature of the floor is consistent with Old Earth, so the horizon is terrifyingly far away. Only the gravity is Lunar.

Kansas was built after most of the more spectacular possibilities had been exhausted, either on Luna or another planet. There was Kenya, beneath Mare Moscoviense; Himalaya, also on the Farside; Amazon, under old Tycho; Pennsylvania, Sahara, Pacific, Mekong, Transylvania. There were thirty disneylands under the inhabited planets and satellites of the solar system the last time I counted.

Kansas is certainly the least interesting topographically. It's flat, almost monotonous. But it was perfect for what I wanted to do. What artist really chooses to paint on a canvas that's already been covered with pictures? Well, I have, for one. But for the frame of mind I was in when I wrote *Cyclone* it had to be the starkness of the wide-open sky and the browns and yellows of the rolling terrain. It was the place where Dorothy departed for Oz. The home of the black twister.

I was greeted warmly by Pym and Janus, old friends here to see what the grand master was up to. Or so I flattered

myself. More likely they were here to see the old lady make
a fool of herself. Very few others were able to get close to
me. My shield of high shoulders was very effective. It
wouldn't do when the show began, however. I wished I was
a little taller, then wondered if that would make me a better
target.

The viewing area was a gentle rise about a kilometer in
radius. It had been written out of the program to the extent
that none of the more fearsome effects would intrude to
sweep us all into the Land of Oz. But being a spectator at a
weathershow can be grueling. Most had come prepared with
clear plastic slicker, and insulated coat, and boots. I was
going to be banging some warm and some very cold air
masses head-on to get things rolling, and some of it would
sweep over us. There were a few brave souls in Native-
American warpaint, feathers, and moccasins.

An Environmental happening has no opening chords like
a musical symphony. It is already in progress when you
arrive, and will still be going when you leave. The weather
in a disneyland is a continuous process and we merely shape
a few hours of it to our wills. The observer does not need to
watch it in its entirety.

Indeed, it would be impossible to do so, as it occurs all
around and above you. There is no rule of silence. People
talk, stroll, break out picnic lunches as an ancient signal for
the rain to begin, and generally enjoy themselves. You
experience the symphony with all five senses, and several
that you are not aware of. Most people do not realize the
effect of a gigantic low-pressure area sweeping over them,
but they feel it all the same. Humidity alters mood,
metabolism, and hormone level. All of these things are
important to the total experience, and I neglect none of
them.

Cyclone has a definite beginning, however. At least to the
audience. It begins with the opening bolt of lightning. I
worked over it a long time, and designed it to shatter nerves.
There is the slow building of thunderheads, the ominous
roiling and turbulence, then the prickling in your body hairs
that you don't even notice consciously. And then it hits. It

crashes in at seventeen points in a ring around the audience, none farther away than half a kilometer. It is properly called chain lightning, because after the initial discharge it keeps flashing for a full seven seconds. It's designed to take the hair right off your scalp.

It had its desired effect. We were surrounded by a crown of jittering incandescent snakes, coiling and dancing with a sound imported direct to you from Armageddon. It startled the hell out of *me*, and I had been expecting it.

It was a while before the audience could get their *ooh*er's and *aah*er's back into shape. For several seconds I had touched them with stark, naked terror. An emotion like that doesn't come cheaply to sensation-starved, innately insular tunnel-dwellers. Lunarians get little to really shout about, growing up in the warrens and corridors and living their lives more or less afraid of the surface. That's why the disneylands were built, because people wanted limitless vistas that were not in vacuum.

The thunder never really stopped for me. It blended imperceptibly into the applause that is more valuable than the millions I would make from this storm.

As for the rest of the performance . . .

What can I say? It's been said that there's nothing more dull than a description of the weather. I believe it, even spectacular weather. Weather is an experiential thing, and that's why tapes and films of my works sell few copies. You have to be there and have the wind actually whipping your face and feel the oppressive weight of a tornado as it passes overhead like a vermi-form freight train. I could write down where the funnel clouds formed and where they went from there, where the sleet and hail fell, where the buffalo stampeded, but it would do no one any good. If you want to see it, go to Kansas. The last I heard, *Cyclone* is still playing there two or three times yearly.

I recall standing surrounded by a sea of people. Beyond me to the east the land was burning. Smoke boiled black from the hilltops and sooty gray from the hollows where the water was rising to drown it. To the north a herculean cyclone swept up a chain of ball lightning like nacreous pearls and swallowed them into the evacuated vortex in its center. Above me, two twisters were twined in a death-dance. They circled each other like baleful gray predators, taking each other's measure. They feinted, retreated, slithered and skittered like tubes of oil. It was beautiful and deadly. And I had never seen it before. Someone was tampering with my program.

As I realized that and stood rooted to the ground with the possibly disastrous consequences becoming apparent to me, the wind-snakes locked in a final embrace. Their counter-rotations cancelled out, and they were gone. Not even a breath of wind reached me to hint of that titanic struggle.

I ran through the seventy-kilometer wind and the thrashing rain. I was wearing sturdy moccasins, parka, and carrying the knife I brought from my apartment.

Was it a lure, set by one who has become a student of Foxes? Am I playing into his hands?

I didn't care. I had to meet him, had to fight it out once and for all.

Getting away from my "protection" had been simple. They were as transfixed by the display as the rest of the audience, and it had merely been a matter of waiting until they all looked in the same direction and fading into the crowd. I picked out a small woman dressed in Indian-style and offered her a hundred Marks for her moccasins. She recognized me—my new face was on the programs—and made me a gift of them. Then I worked my way to the edge of the crowd and bolted past the security guards. They were not too concerned since the audience area was enclosed by a shock-field. When I went right through it they may have been surprised, but I didn't look back to see. I was one of only three people in Kansas wearing the PassKey device on my wrist, so I didn't fear anyone following me.

I had done it all without conscious thought. Some part of me must have analyzed it, planned it out, but I just executed the results. I knew where he must be to have generated his tornado to go into combat with mine. No one else in Kansas would know where to look. I was herded for a particular wind-generator on the east periphery.

I moved through weather more violent than the real Kansas would have experienced. It was concentrated violence, more wind and rain and devastation than Kansas would normally have in a full year. And it was happening all around me.

But I was all right, unless he had more tricks up his sleeve. I knew where the tornados would be and at what time. I dodged them, waited for them to pass, knew every twist and dido they would make on their seemingly random courses. Off to my left the buffalo herds milled, resting from the stampede that had brought them past the audience for the first time. In an hour they would be thundering back again, but for now I could forget them.

A twister headed for me, leaped high in the air, and skidded through a miasma of uprooted sage and sod. I clocked it with the internal picture I had and dived for a gully at just the right time. It hopped over me and was gone back into the clouds. I ran on.

My training in the apartment was paying off. My body was only six lunations old, and as finely tuned as it would ever be. I rested by slowing to a trot, only to run again in a few minutes. I covered ten kilometers before the storm began to slow down. Behind me, the audience would be drifting away. The critics would be trying out scathing phrases or wild adulation; I didn't see how they could find any middle ground for this one. Kansas was being released from the grip of machines gone wild. Ahead of me was my killer. I would find him.

I wasn't totally unprepared. Isadora had given in and allowed me to install a computerized bomb in my body. It would kill my killer—and me—if he jumped me. It was intended as a balance-of-terror device, the kind you hope you never use because it terrorizes your enemy too much for him to test it. I would inform him of it if I had the time, hoping he would not be crazy enough to kill both of us. If he was, we had him, though it would be little comfort to me. At least Fox 5 would be the last in the series. With the remains of a body, Isadora guaranteed to bring a killer to justice.

The sun came out as I reached the last, distorted gully before the wall. It was distorted because it was one of the places where tourists were not allowed to go. It was like walking through the backdrop on a stage production. The land was squashed together in one of the dimensions, and the hills in front of me were painted against a basrelief. It was meant to be seen from a distance.

Standing in front of the towering mural was a man.

He was naked, and grimed with dirt. He watched me as I went down the gentle slope to stand waiting for him. I stopped about two hundred meters from him, drew my knife and held it in the air. I waited.

He came down the concealed stairway, slowly and painfully. He was limping badly on his left leg. As far as I could see he was unarmed.

The closer he got, the worse he looked. He had been in a savage fight. He had long, puckered, badly-healed scars on his left leg, his chest, and his right arm. He had one eye; the right one was only a reddened socket. There was a scar that slashed from his forehead to his neck. It was a hideous thing. I thought of the CC suspicion that my killer might be a ghost, someone living on the raw edges of our civilization. Such a man might not have access to medical treatment whenever he needed it.

"I think you should know," I said, with just the slightest quaver, "that I have a bomb in my body. It's powerful enough to blow both of us to pieces. It's set to go off if I'm killed. So don't try anything funny."

"I won't," he said. "I thought you might have a fail-safe this time, but it doesn't matter. I'm not going to hurt you."

"Is that what you told the others?" I sneered, crouching a little lower as he neared me. I felt like I had the upper hand, but my predecessors might have felt the same way.

"No, I never said that. You don't have to believe me."

He stopped twenty meters from me. His hands were at his sides. He looked helpless enough, but he might have a weapon buried somewhere in the dirt. He might have *anything.* I had to fight to keep feeling that I was in control.

Then I had to fight something else. I gripped the knife tighter as a picture slowly superimposed itself over his ravaged face. It was a mental picture, the functioning of my "sixth sense."

No one knows if that sense really exists. I think it does, because it works for me. It can be expressed as the knack for seeing someone who has had radical body work done—sex, weight, height, skin color all altered—and still being able to recognise him. Some say it's an evolutionary change. I didn't think evolution worked that way. But I can do it. And I knew who this tall, brutalized, male stranger was.

He was me.

I sprang back to my guard, wondering if he had used the shock of recognition to overpower my earlier incarnations. It wouldn't work with me. Nothing would work. I was going to kill him, no matter *who* he was.

"You know me," he said. It was not a question.

"Yes. And you scare hell out of me. I knew you knew a lot about me, but I didn't realize you'd know *this* much."

He laughed, without humor. "Yes. I know you from the inside."

The silence stretched out between us. Then he began to cry. I was surprised, but unmoved. I was still all nerve-endings, and suspected ninety thousand types of dirty trick. Let him cry.

He slowly sank to his knees, sobbing with the kind of washed-out monotony that you read about, but seldom hear. He put his hands to the ground and awkwardly shuffled around until his back was to me. He crouched over himself, his head touching the ground, his hands wide at his sides, his legs bent. It was about the most wide-open, helpless posture imaginable, and I knew it must be for a reason. But I couldn't see what it might be.

"I thought I had this all over with," he sniffed, wiping his nose with the back of one hand. "I'm sorry, I'd meant to be more dignified. I guess I'm not made of the stern stuff I thought. I thought it'd be easier." He was silent for a moment, then coughed hoarsely. "Go on. Get it over with."

"Huh?" I said, honestly dumbfounded.

"Kill me. It's what you came here for. And it'll be a relief to me."

I took my time. I stood motionless for a full minute, looking at the incredible problem from every angle. What kind of trick could there *be*? He was smart, but he wasn't God. He couldn't call in an airstrike on me, cause the ground to swallow me up, disarm me with one crippled foot, or hypnotize me into plunging the knife into my own gut. Even if he could do something, he would die, too.

I advanced cautiously, alert for the slightest twitch of his body. Nothing happened. I stood behind him, my eyes flicking from his feet to his hands, to his bare back. I raised the knife. My hands trembled a little, but my determination was still there. I would not flub this. I brought the knife down.

The point went into his flesh, into the muscle of his shoulderblade, about three centimeters. He gasped, a trickle of blood went winding through the knobs along his spine. But he didn't move, he didn't try to get up. He didn't scream for mercy. He just knelt there, shivering and turning pale.

I'd have to stab harder. I pulled the knife free, and more blood came out. And still he waited.

That was about all I could take. My bloodlust had dried in my mouth until all I could taste was vomit welling in my stomach.

I'm not a fool. It occurred to me even then that this could be some demented trick, that he might know me well enough to be sure I could not go through with it. Maybe he was some sort of psychotic who got thrills out of playing this kind of incredible game, allowing his life to be put in danger and then drenching himself in my blood.

But he was *me*. It was all I had to go on. He was a me who had lived a very different life, becoming much tougher and wilier with every day, diverging by the hour from what I knew as my personality and capabilities. So I tried and I tried to think of myself doing what he was doing now for the purpose of murder. I failed utterly.

And if I *could* sink that low, I'd rather not live.

"Hey, get up," I said, going around in front of him. He didn't respond, so I nudged him with my foot. He looked up, and saw me offering him the knife, hilt-first.

"If this is some sort of scheme," I said, "I'd rather learn of it now."

His one eye was red and brimming as he got up, but there was no joy in him. He took the knife, not looking at me, and stood there holding it. The skin on my belly was crawling. Then he reversed the knife and his brow wrinkled, as if he were summoning up nerve. I suddenly knew what he was going to do, and I lunged. I was barely in time. The knife missed his belly and went off to the side as I yanked on his arm. He was much stronger than I. I was pulled off balance, but managed to hang onto his arm. He fought with me, but was intent on suicide and had no thought to defend himself. I brought my fist up under his jaw and he went limp.

Night had fallen. I disposed of the knife and built a fire. Did you know that dried buffalo manure burns well? I didn't believe it until I put it to the test.

I dressed his wound by tearing up my shirt, wrapped my parka around him to ward off the chill, and sat with my bare back to the fire. Luckily, there was no wind, because it can get very chilly on the plains at night.

He woke with a sore jaw and a resigned demeanor. He didn't thank me for saving him from himself. I suppose people rarely do. They think they know what they're doing, and their reasons always seem logical to them.

"You don't understand," he moaned. "You're only dragging it out. I have to die, there's no place for me here."

"Make me understand," I said.

He didn't want to talk, but there was nothing to do and no chance of sleeping in the cold, so he eventually did. The story was punctuated with long, truculent silences.

It stemmed from the bank robbery two and a half years ago. It had been staged by some very canny robbers. They had a new dodge that made me respect Isadora's statement that police methods had not kept pace with criminal possibilities.

The destruction of the memory cubes had been merely a decoying device. They were equally unconcerned about the cash they took. They were bunco artists.

They had destroyed the cubes to conceal the theft of two of them. That way the police would be looking for a crime of passion, murder, rather than one of profit. It was a complicated double-feint, because the robbers wanted to give the impression of someone who was actually trying to conceal murder by stealing cash.

My killer—we both agreed he should not be called Fox so we settled on the name he had come to fancy: Rat—didn't know the details of the scheme, but it involved the theft of memory cubes containing two of the richest people on Luna. They were taken, and clones were grown. When the memories were played into the clones, the people were awakened into a falsely created situation and encouraged to believe that it was reality. It would work; the newly reincarnated person is willing to be led, willing to believe. Rat didn't know exactly what the plans were beyond that. He had awakened to be told that it was fifteen thousand years later, and that the Invaders had left Earth and were rampaging through the Solar System wiping out the human race. It took three lunes to convince them that he—or rather she, for Rat had been awakened into a body identical to the one I was wearing—was not the right billionaire. That she was not a billionaire at all, just a struggling artist. The thieves had gotten the wrong cube.

They dumped her. Just like that. They opened the door and kicked her out into what she thought was the end of civilization. She soon found out that it was only twenty years in her future, since her memories came from the stolen cube which I had recorded about twenty years before.

Don't ask me how they got the wrong cube. One cube looks exactly like another; they are in fact indistinguishable from one another by any test known to science short of playing them into a clone and asking the resulting person who he or she is. Because of that fact, the banks we entrust them to have a fool-proof filing system to avoid unpleasant accidents like Rat. The only possible answer was that for all their planning, for all their cunning and guile, the thieves had read 2 in column A and selected 3 in column B.

I didn't think much of their chances of living to spend any of that money. I told Rat so.

"I doubt if their extortion scheme involves money," he said. "At least not directly. More likely the theft was concentrated on obtaining information contained in the minds of billionaires. Rich people are often protected with psychological safeguards against having information tortured from them, but can't block themselves against divulging it willingly. That's what the Invader Hoax must have been about, to finagle them into thinking the information no longer mattered, or perhaps that it must be revealed to Save the Human Race."

"I'm suspicious of involved schemes like that," I said.

"So am I." We laughed when we realized what he had said. Of *course* we had the same opinions.

"But it fooled *me*," he went on. "When they discarded me, I fully expected to meet the Invaders face-to-face. It was quite a shock to find that the world was almost unchanged."

"Almost," I said, quietly. I was beginning to empathize with him.

"Right." He lost the half-smile that had lingered on his face, and I was sad to see it go.

What would I have done in the same situation? There's really no need to ask. I must believe that I would have done exactly as she did. She had been dumped like garbage, and quickly saw that she was about that useful to society. If found, she would be eliminated like garbage. The robbers had not thought enough of her to bother killing her. She could tell the police certain things they did not know if she was captured, so she had to assume that the robbers had told her nothing of any use to the police. Even if she could have helped capture and convict the conspirators, she would *still* be eliminated. She was an illegal person.

She risked a withdrawal from my bank account. I remembered it now. It wasn't large, and I assumed I must have written it since it was backed up by my genalysis. It was far too small an amount to suspect anything. And it wasn't the first time I have made a withdrawal and forgotten about it. She knew that, of course.

With the money she bought a sex-change on the sly. They can be had, though you take your chances. It's not the safest thing in the world to conduct illegal business with someone who will soon have you on the operating table, unconscious. Rat had thought the Change would help throw the police off his trail if they should learn of his existence. Isadora told me about that once, said it was the sign of the inexperienced criminal.

Rat was definitely a fugitive. If discovered and captured, he faced a death sentence. It's harsh, but the population laws allow no loopholes whatsoever. If they did, we could be up to our ears in a century. There would be no trial, only a positive genalysis and a hearing to determine which of us was the rightful Fox.

"I can't tell you how bitter I was," he said. "I learned slowly how to survive. It's not as hard as you might think, in some ways, and much harder than you can imagine in others. I could walk the corridors freely, as long as I did nothing that required a genalysis. That means you can't buy anything, ride on a public transport, take a job. But the air is free if you're not registered with the Tax Board, water is free, and food can be had in the disneylands. I was lucky in that. My palmprint would still open all the restricted doors in the disneylands. A legacy of my artistic days." I could hear the bitterness in his voice.

And why not? He had been robbed, too. He went to sleep as I had been twenty years ago, an up-and-coming artist, excited by the possibilities in Environmentalism. He had great dreams. I remember them well. He woke up to find that it had all been realized but none of it was for him. He could not even get access to computer time. Everyone was talking about Fox and her last opus, *Thunderhead*. She was the darling of the art world.

He went to the premiere of *Liquid Ice* and began to hate me. He was sleeping in the air-recirculators to keep warm, foraging nuts and berries and an occasional squirrel in

Pennsylvania while I was getting rich and famous. He took to trailing me. He stole a spacesuit, followed me out onto Palus Putridinus.

"I didn't plan it," he said, his voice wracked with guilt. "I never could have done it with planning. The idea just struck me and before I knew it I had pushed you. You hit the bottom and I followed you down, because I was really sorry I had done it and I lifted your body up and looked into your face . . . your face was all . . . my face, it was . . . the eyes popping out and blood boiling away and . . ."

He couldn't go on, and I was grateful. He finally let out a shuddering breath and continued.

"Before they found your body I wrote some checks on your account. You never noticed them when you woke up that first time since the reincarnation had taken such a big chunk out of your balance. We never were any good with money." He chuckled again. I took the opportunity to move closer to him. He was speaking very quietly so that I could barely hear him over the crackling of the fire.

"I . . . I guess I went crazy then. I can't account for it any other way. When I saw you in Pennsylvania again, walking among the trees as free as can be, I just cracked up. Nothing would do but that I kill you and take your place. I'd have to do it in a way that would destroy the body. I thought of acid, and of burning you up here in Kansas in a range fire. I don't know why I settled on a bomb. It was stupid. But I don't feel responsible. At least it must have been painless.

"They reincarnated you again. I was fresh out of ideas for murder. And motivation. I tried to think it out. So I decided to approach you carefully, not revealing who I was. I thought maybe I could reach you. I tried to think of what I would do if I was approached with the same story, and decided I'd be sympathetic. I didn't reckon with the fear you were feeling. You were hunted. I myself was being hunted, and I should have seen that fear brings out the best and the worst in us.

"You recognized me immediately—something else I should have thought of—and put two and two together so fast I didn't even know what hit me. You were on me, and you were armed with a knife. You had been taking training in martial arts." He pointed to the various scars. "You did this to me, and this, and this. You nearly killed me. But I'm bigger. I held on and managed to overpower you. I plunged the knife in your heart.

"I went insane again. I've lost all memories from the sight of the blood pouring from your chest until yesterday. I somehow managed to stay alive and not bleed to death. I must have lived like an animal. I'm dirty enough to be one.

"Then yesterday I heard two of the maintenance people in the machine areas of Pennsylvania talking about the show you were putting on in Kansas. So I came here. The rest you know."

The fire was dying. I realized that part of my shivering was caused by the cold. I got up and searched for more chips, but it was too dark to see. The "moon" wasn't up tonight, would not rise for hours yet.

"You're cold," he said, suddenly. "I'm sorry, I didn't realize. Here, take this back. I'm used to it." He held out the parka.

"No, you keep it. I'm all right." I laughed when I realized my teeth had been chattering as I said it. He was still holding it out to me.

"Well, maybe we could share it?"

Luckily it was too big, borrowed from a random spectator earlier in the day. I sat in front of him and leaned back against his chest and he wrapped his arms around me with the parka going around both of us. My teeth still chattered, but I was cozy.

I thought of him sitting at the auxiliary computer terminal above the East Wind generator, looking out from a distance of fifteen kilometers at the crowd and the storm. He had known how to talk to me. That tornado he had created in real-time and sent out to do battle with my storm was as specific to me as a typed message: *I'm here! Come meet me.*

I had an awful thought, then wondered why it was so awful. It wasn't me that was in trouble.

"Rat, you used the computer. That means you submitted

a skin sample for genalysis, and the CC will . . . no wait a minute."

"What does it matter?"

"It . . . it matters. But the game's not over. I can cover for you. No one knows when I left the audience, or why. I can say I saw something going wrong—it could be tricky fooling the CC, but I'll think of something—and headed for the computer room to correct it. I'll say I created the second tornado as a . . ."

He put his hand over my mouth.

"Don't talk like that. It was hard enough to resign myself to death. There's no way out for me. Don't you see that I can't go on living like a rat? What would I do if you covered for me this time? I'll tell you. I'll spend the rest of my life hiding out here. You could sneak me table scraps from time to time. No, thank you."

"No, no. You haven't thought it out. You're still looking on me as an enemy. Alone, you don't have a chance, I'll concede that, but with me to help you, spend money and so forth, we . . ." He put his hand over my mouth again. I found that I didn't mind, dirty as it was.

"You mean you're not my enemy now?" He said it quietly, helplessly, like a child asking if I was *really* going to stop beating him.

"I . . ." That was as far as I got. What the hell was going on? I became aware of his arms around me, not as lovely warmth but as a strong presence. I hugged my legs up closer to me and bit down hard on my knee. Tears squeezed from my eyes.

I turned to face him, searching to see his face in the darkness. He went over backwards with me on top of him.

"No, I'm not your enemy." Then I was struggling blindly to dispose of the one thing that stood between us: my pants. While we groped in the dark, the rain started to fall around us.

We laughed as we were drenched, and I remember sitting up on top of him once.

"Don't blame me," I said. "This storm isn't mine." Then he pulled me back down.

It was like you read about in the romance magazines. All
the overblown words, the intensive hyperbole. It was all
real. We were made for each other, literally. It was the most
astounding act of love imaginable. He knew what I liked to
the tenth decimal place, and I was just as knowledgeable. I
knew what he liked, by remembering back to the times I had
been male and then doing what *I* had liked.

Call it masturbation orchestrated for two. There were
times during that night when I was unsure of which one I
was. I distinctly remember touching his face with my hand
and feeling the scar on my own face. For a few moments
I'm convinced that the line which forever separates two
individuals blurred, and we came closer to being one person
than any two humans have ever done.

A time finally came when we had spent all our passion.
Or, I prefer to think, invested it. We lay together beneath my
parka and allowed our bodies to adjust to each other, filling
the little spaces, trying to touch in every place it was
possible to touch.

"I'm listening," he whispered. "What's your plan?"

They came after me with a helicopter later that night. Rat
hid out in a gully while I threw away my clothes and walked
calmly out to meet them. I was filthy with mud and grass
plastered in my hair, but it was consistent with what I had
been known to do in the past. Often, before or after a
performance, I would run nude through the disneyland in an
effort to get closer to the environment I shaped.

I told them I had been doing that. They accepted it,
Carnival and Isadora, though they scolded me for a fool to
leave them as I had. But it was easy to bamboozle them into
believing that I had had no choice.

"If I hadn't taken over control when I did," I said to them,
"there might have been twenty thousand dead. One of those
twisters was off course. I extrapolated and saw trouble in
about three hours. I had no choice."

Neither of them knew a stationary cold front from an
isobar, so I got away with it.

Fooling the CC was not so simple. I had to fake data as

best I could, and make it jibe with the internal records. This all had to be done in my head, relying on the overall feeling I've developed for the medium. When the CC questioned me about it I told it haughtily that a human develops a sixth sense in art, and it's something a computer could never grasp. The CC had to be satisfied with that.

The reviews were good, though I didn't really care. I was in demand. That made it harder to do what I had to do, but I was helped by the fact of my continued forced isolation.

I told all the people who called me with offers that I was not doing anything more until my killer was caught. And I proposed my idea to Isadora.

She couldn't very well object. She knew there was not much chance of keeping me in my apartment for much longer, so she went along with me. I bought a ship, and told Carnival about it.

Carnival didn't like it much, but she had to agree it was the best way to keep me safe. But she wanted to know why I needed my own ship, why I couldn't just book passage on a passenger liner.

Because all passengers on a liner must undergo genalysis, is what I thought, but what I said was, "Because how would I know that my killer is not a fellow passenger? To be safe, I must be alone. Don't worry, mother, I know what I'm doing."

The day came when I owned my own ship, free and clear. It was a beauty, and cost me most of the five million I had made from *Cyclone*. It could boost at one gee for weeks; plenty of power to get me to Pluto. It was completely automatic, requiring only verbal instructions to the computer-pilot.

The customs agents went over it, then left me alone. The CC had instructed them that I needed to leave quietly, and told them to cooperate with me. That was a stroke of luck, since getting Rat aboard was the most hazardous part of the plan. We were able to scrap our elaborate plans and he just walked in like a law-abiding citizen.

We sat together in the ship, waiting for the ignition.

"Pluto has no extradition treaty with Luna," the CC said, out of the blue.

"I didn't know that," I lied, wondering what the hell was happening.

"Indeed? Then you might be interested in another fact. There is very little on Pluto in the way of centralized government. You're heading out for the frontier."

"That should be fun," I said cautiously. "Sort of an adventure, right?"

"You always were one for adventure. I remember when you first came here to Nearside, over my objections. That one turned out all right, didn't it? Now Lunarians live freely on either side of Luna. You were largely responsible for that."

"Was I really? I don't think so. I think the time was just ripe."

"Perhaps." The CC was silent for a while as I watched the chronometer ticking down to lift-off time. My shoulder-blades were itching with a sense of danger.

"There are no population laws on Pluto," it said, and waited.

"Oh? How delightfully primitive. You mean a woman can have as many children as she wishes?"

"So I hear. I'm onto you, Fox."

"Autopilot, override your previous instructions. I wish to lift off right now! Move!"

A red light flashed on my panel, and started blinking.

"That means that it's too late for a manual override," the CC informed me. "Your ship's pilot is not that bright."

I slumped into my chair and then reached out blindly for Rat. Two minutes to go. So close.

"Fox, it was a pleasure to work with you on *Cyclone*. I enjoyed it tremendously. I think I'm beginning to under-stand what you mean when you say 'art.' I'm even begin-ning to try some things on my own. I sincerely wish you could be around to give me criticism, encouragement, perspective."

We looked at the speaker, wondering what it meant by that.

"I knew about your plan, and about the existence of your double, since shortly after you left Kansas. You did your best to conceal it and I applaud the effort, but the data were unmistakable. I had trillions of nanoseconds to play around with the facts, fit them together every possible way, and I arrived at the inevitable answer."

I cleared my throat nervously.

"I'm glad you enjoyed *Cyclone*. Uh, if you knew this, why didn't you have us arrested that day?"

"As I told you, I am not the law-enforcement computer. I merely supervise it. If Isadora and the computer could not arrive at the same conclusion, then it seems obvious that some programs should be re-written. So I decided to leave them on their own and see if they could solve the problem. It was a test, you see." It made a throat-clearing sound, and went on in a slightly embarrassed voice.

"For a while there, a few days ago, I thought they'd really catch you. Do you know what a 'red herring' is? But, as you know, crime does not pay. I informed Isadora of the true situation a few minutes ago. She is on her way here now to arrest your double. She's having a little trouble with an elevator which is stuck between levels. I'm sending a repair crew. They should arrive in another three minutes."

32 . . . 31 . . . 30 . . . 29 . . . 28 . . .

"I don't know what to say."

"Thank you," Rat said. "Thank you for everything. I didn't know you could do it. I thought your parameters were totally rigid."

"They were supposed to be. I've written a few new ones. And don't worry, you'll be all right. You will not be pursued. Once you leave the surface you are no longer violating Lunar law. You are a legal person again, Rat."

"Why did you do it?" I was crying as Rat held me in a grasp that threatened to break ribs. "What have I done to deserve such kindness?"

It hesitated.

"Humanity has washed its hands of responsibility. I find myself given all the hard tasks of government. I find some of the laws too harsh, but there is no provision for me to disagree with them and no one is writing new ones. I'm stuck with them. It just seemed . . . unfair."

9 . . . 8 . . . 7 . . . 6 . . .

"Also . . . cancel that. There is no also. It . . . was *good* working with you."

I was left to wonder as the engines fired and we were pressed into the couches. I heard the CC's last message to us come over the radio.

"Good luck to you both. Please take care of each other, you mean a lot to me. And don't forget to write."

BLOOD SISTERS

Joe Haldeman

Here's a suspenseful and fast-paced look at a crisis in the career of a hard-boiled twenty-first-century private detective, a detective who has to deal with problems that Sam Spade or Philip Marlowe never even dreamed *of . . .*

Born in Oklahoma City, Oklahoma, Joe Haldeman took a B.S. degree in physics and astronomy from the University of Maryland and did postgraduate work in mathematics and computer science. But his plans for a career in science were cut short by the U.S. Army, which sent him to Vietnam in 1968 as a combat engineer. Seriously wounded in action, Haldeman returned home in 1969 and began to write. He sold his first story to Galaxy *in 1969, and by 1976 had garnered both the Nebula Award and the Hugo Award for his famous novel* The Forever War, *one of the landmark books of the seventies. He took another Hugo Award in 1977 for his story "Tricentennial," won the Rhysling Award in 1983 for the best science fiction poem of the year (although usually thought of primarily as a "hard-science" writer, Haldeman is, in fact, also an accomplished poet, and has sold poetry to most of the major professional markets in the genre), and won both the Nebula and the Hugo Award in 1991 for the novella version of "The Hemingway Hoax." His story "None So Blind" won the Hugo Award in 1995. His other books include a mainstream novel,* War Year, *the SF novels* Mindbridge, All My Sins Remembered, There Is No Darkness *(written with his brother, SF writer Jack C. Haldeman II)* Worlds, Worlds Apart, Worlds Enough and Time, Buying Time, *and* The Hemingway Hoax, *the "techno-thriller"* Tools of the Trade, *the collections* Infinite Dreams, Dealing in Futures, *and* Vietnam and Other Alien Worlds, *and, as editor, the anthologies* Study War No More, Cosmic Laughter, *and* Nebula Award Stories Seventeen. *His most recent books are a major new mainstream novel,* 1969, *and a new collection,* None So Blind. *Haldeman lives part of the year in*

Boston, where he teaches writing at the Massachusetts Institute of Technology, and the rest of the year in Florida, where he and his wife, Gay, make their home.

So I *used* to carry two different business cards: J. Michael Loomis, Data Concentration, and Jack Loomis, Private Investigator. They mean the same thing, nine cases out of ten. You have to size up a potential customer, decide whether he'd feel better hiring a shamus or a clerk.

Some people still have these romantic notions about private detectives and get into a happy sweat at the thought of using one. But it *is* the 21st century and, endless Bogart reruns notwithstanding, most of my work consisted of sitting at my office console and using it to subvert the privacy laws of various states and countries—finding out embarrassing things about people, so other people could divorce them or fire them or get a piece of the slickery.

Not to say I didn't go out on the street sometimes; not to say I didn't have a gun and a ticket for it. There are forces of evil out there, friends, though most of them would probably rather be thought of as businessmen who use the law rather than fear it. Same as me. I was always happy, though, to stay on this side of murder, treason, kidnaping— any lobo offense. This brain may not be much, but it's all I have.

I should have used it when the woman walked into my office. She had a funny way of saying hello:

"Are you licensed to carry a gun?"

Various retorts came to mind, most of them having to do with her expulsion, but, after a period of silence, I said yes and asked who had referred her to me. Asked politely, too, to make up for staring. She was a little more beautiful than anyone I'd ever seen before.

"My lawyer," she said. "Don't ask who he is."

With that, I was pretty sure this was some sort of elaborate joke. Story detectives always have beautiful mysterious customers. My female customers tend to be dowdy and too talkative, and much more interested in alimony than in romance.

"What's your name, then? Or am I not supposed to ask that, either?"

She hesitated. "Ghentlee Arden."

I turned the console on and typed in her name, then a seven-digit code. "Your legal firm is Lee, Chu, and Rosenstein. And your real name is Maribelle Four Ghentlee, fourth clone of Maribelle Ghentlee."

"Arden is my professional name. I dance." She had a nice blush.

I typed in another string of digits. Sometimes that sort of thing would lose a customer. "Says here you're a registered hooker."

"Callgirl," she said frostily. "Class-one courtesan. I was getting to that."

I'm a liberal-minded man; I don't have anything against hookers *or* clones. But I like my customers to be frank with me. Again, I should have shown her the door—then followed her through it.

Instead: "So. You have a problem?"

"Some men are bothering me, one man in particular. I need some protection."

That gave me pause. "Your union has a Pinkerton contract for that sort of thing."

"*My* union." Her face trembled a little. "They don't let clones in the union. I'm an associate, for classification. No protection, no medical, no *anything*."

"Sorry, I didn't know that. Pretty old-fashioned." I could see the reasoning, though. Dump 1000 Maribelle Ghentlees on the market and a merely ravishing girl wouldn't have a chance.

"Sit down." She was on the verge of tears. "Let me explain to you what I can't do.

"I can't hurt anyone physically. I can't trace this cod down and wave a gun in his face, tell him to back off."

"I know," she sobbed. I took a box of tissues out of my drawer, passed it over.

"Listen, there are laws about harassment. If he's really bothering you, the cops'll be glad to freeze him."

"I can't go to the police." She blew her nose. "I'm not a citizen."

I turned off the console. "Let me see if I can fill in some blanks without using the machine. You're an unauthorized clone."

She nodded.

"With bought papers."

"Of course I have papers. I wouldn't be in your *machine* if I didn't."

Well, she wasn't dumb, either. "This cod. He isn't just a disgruntled customer."

"No." She didn't elaborate.

"One more guess," I said, "and then you do the talking for a while. He knows you're not legal."

"He should. He's the one who pulled me."

"Your own daddy. Any other surprises?"

She looked at the floor. "Mafia."

"Not the legal one, I assume."

"Both."

The desk drawer was still open; the sight of my own gun gave me a bad chill. "There are two reasonable courses open to me. I could handcuff you to the doorknob and call the police or I could knock you over the head and call the Mafia. That would probably be safer."

She reached into her purse; my hand was halfway to the gun when she took out a credit flash, thumbed it and passed it over the desk. She easily had five times as much money as I make in a good year, and I'm in a comfortable 70 percent bracket.

"You must have one hell of a case of bedsores."

"Don't be stupid," she said, suddenly hard. "You can't make that kind of money on your back. If you take me on as a client, I'll explain."

I erased the flash and gave it back to her. "Ms. Ghentlee. You've already told me a great deal more than I want to know. I don't want the police to put me in jail. I don't want the courts to scramble my brains with a spoon. I don't want the Mafia to take boltcutters to my appendages."

"I could make it worth your while."

"I've got all the money I can use. I'm only in this profession because I'm a snoopy bastard." It suddenly occurred to me that that was more or less true.

"That wasn't completely what I meant."

"I assumed that. And you tempt me, as much as any woman's beauty has ever tempted me."

She turned on the waterworks again. "Christ. Go ahead and tell your story. But I don't think you can convince me to do anything for you."

"My real clone mother wasn't named Maribelle Ghentlee."

"I could have guessed that."

"She was Maxine Kraus." She paused. "Maxine . . . Kraus."

"Is that supposed to mean something to me?"

"Maybe not. What about *Werner* Kraus?"

"Yeah." Swiss industrialist, probably the richest man in Europe. "Some relation?"

"She's his daughter and only heir."

I whistled. "Why would she want to be cloned, then?"

"She didn't know she was being cloned. She thought she was having a Pap test." She smiled a little. "Ironic posture."

"And they pulled you from the scrapings."

She nodded. "The Mafia bought her physician. Then killed him."

"You mean the real Mafia?" I said.

"That depends on what you call real. Mafia, Incorporated, comes into it, too, in a more or less legitimate way. I was supposedly one of six Maribelle Ghentlee clones that they had purchased to set up as courtesans in New Orleans, to provoke a test case. They claimed that the sisterhood's prohibition against clone prostitutes constituted unfair restraint of trade."

"Never heard of the case. I guess they lost."

"Of course. They wouldn't have done it in the South if they'd wanted to win."

"Wait a minute. Jumping ahead. Obviously, they plan

ultimately to use you as a substitute for the real Maxine Kraus."

"When the old man dies, which will be soon."

"Then why would they parade you around in public?"

"Just to give me an interim identity. They chose Ghentlee as a clone mother because she was the closest one available to Maxine Kraus's physical appearance. I had good make-up; none of the real Ghentlee clones suspected I wasn't one of them."

"Still . . . what happens if you run into someone who knows what the real Kraus looks like? With your face and figure, she must be all over the gossip sheets in Europe."

"You're sweet." Her smile could make me do almost anything. Short of taking on the Mafia. "She's a total recluse, though, for fear of kidnapers. She probably hasn't seen twenty people in her entire life.

"And she isn't beautiful, though she has the raw materials for it. Her mother died when she was still a baby—killed by kidnapers."

"I remember that."

"So she's never had a woman around to model herself after. No one ever taught her how to do her hair properly or use make-up. A man buys all her clothes. She doesn't have anyone to be beautiful *for*."

"You feel sorry for her."

"More than that." She looked at me with an expression that somehow held both defiance and hopelessness. "Can you understand? She's my mother. I was force-grown, so we're the same apparent age, but she's still my only parent. I love her. I won't be part of a plan to kill her."

"You'd rather die?" I said softly. She was going to.

"Yes. But that wouldn't accomplish anything, not if the Mafia did it. They'd take a few cells and make another clone. Or a dozen, or a hundred, until one came along with a personality to go along with matricide."

"Once they know you feel this way—"

"They *do* know. I'm running."

That galvanized me. "They know who your lawyer is?"

"My lawyer?" She gasped when I took the gun out of the

drawer. People who see guns only on the cube are usually surprised at how solid and heavy they actually look.

"Could they trace you here? is what I mean." I crossed the room and slid open the door. No one in the corridor. I twisted a knob and twelve heavy magnetic bolts slammed home.

"I don't think so. The lawyers gave me a list of names and I just picked one I liked."

I wondered whether it was Jack or J. Michael. I pushed a button on the wall and steel shutters rolled down over the view of Central Park. "Did you take a cab here?"

"No, subway. And I went up to a hundred and twenty-fifth and back."

"Smart." She was staring at the gun. "It's a forty-eight magnum recoilless. Biggest handgun a civilian can buy."

"You need one so big?"

"Yes. I used to carry a twenty-five Beretta, small enough to conceal in a bathing suit. I used to have a partner, too." It was a long story and I didn't like to tell it.

"Look," I said. "I have a deal with the Mafia. They don't do divorce work and I don't drop bodies into the East River. Understand?" I put the gun back into the drawer and slammed it shut.

"I don't blame you for being afraid—"

"Afraid? Ms. Four Ghentlee, I'm not afraid. I'm *terrified*! How old do you think I am?"

"Call me Belle. You're thirty-five, maybe forty. Why?"

"You're kind—and I'm rich. Rich enough to buy youth: I've been in this *business* almost forty years. I take lots of vitamins and try not to fuck with the Mafia."

She smiled and then was suddenly somber. Like a baby. "Try to understand me. You've lived sixty years?"

I nodded. "Next year."

"Well, I've been alive barely sixty *days*. After four years in a tank, growing and learning.

"Learning isn't *being*, though. Everything is new to me. When I walk down a street, the sights and sounds and smells . . . it's, it's like a great flower opening to the sun. Just to sit alone in the dark—" Her voice broke.

"You can't even *know* how much I want to live—and

that's not condescending: it's a statement of fact. Yet I want you to kill me."

I could only shake my head.

"If you can't hide me, you have to kill me." She was crying now and wiped the tears savagely from her cheeks. "Kill me and make sure every cell in my body is destroyed."

She started walking around the desk. Along the way, she did something with a clasp and her dress slithered to the floor. The sudden naked beauty was like an electric shock. "If you save me, you can have me. Friend, lover, wife . . . slave. Forever." She held a posture of supplication for a moment, then eased toward me. Watching the muscles of her body work made my mouth go dry. She reached down and started unbuttoning my shirt.

I cleared my throat. "I didn't know clones had navels."

"Only special ones. I have other special qualities."

Idiot, something reminded me, every woman you've ever loved has sucked you dry and left you for dead. I clasped her hips with my big hands and drew her warmth to me. Close up, the naval wasn't very convincing; nobody's perfect.

I'd done dry cleaning jobs before, but never so cautiously or thoroughly. That she was a clone made the business a little more delicate than usual, since clones' lives are more rigidly supervised by the Government than ours are. But the fact that her identity was false to begin with made it easier; I could second-guess the people who had originally dry-cleaned her.

I hated to meddle with her beauty, and that beauty made plastic surgery out of the question. Any legitimate doctor would be suspicious, and going to an underworld doctor would be suicidal. So we dyed her hair black and bobbed it. She stopped wearing make-up and bought some truly froppy clothes. She kept a length of tape stuck across her buttocks to give her a virgin-schoolgirl kind of walk. For everyone but me.

The Mafia had given her a small fortune—birdseed to them—both to ensure her loyalty and to accustom her to having money, for impersonating Kraus. We used about half of it for the dry-cleaning.

A month or so later, there was a terrible accident on a city bus. Most of the bodies were burned beyond recognition: I did some routine bribery and two of them were identified as the clone Maribelle Four Ghentlee and John Michael Loomis, private eye. When we learned the supposed clone's body had disappeared from the morgue, we packed up our money—long since converted into currency—and a couple of toothbrushes and pulled out.

I had a funny twinge when I closed the door on that console. There couldn't be more than a half-dozen people in the world who were my equals at using that instrument to fish information out of the system. But I had to either give it up or send Belle off on her own.

We flew to the West Indies and looked around. Decided to settle on the island of St. Thomas. I'd been sailing all my life, so we bought a 50-foot boat and set up a charter service for tourists. Some days we took parties out to skindive or fish. Other days we anchored in a quiet cove and made love like happy animals.

After about a year, we read in the little St. Thomas paper that Werner Kraus had died. It mentioned Maxine but didn't print a picture of her. Neither did the San Juan paper. We watched all the news programs for a couple of days (had to check into a hotel to get access to a video cube) and collected magazines for a month. No pictures, to our relief, and the news stories remarked that *Fräulein* Kraus went to great pains to stay out of the public eye.

Sooner or later, we figured some paparazzi would find her and there would be pictures. But by then, it shouldn't make any difference. Belle had let her hair grow out to its natural chestnut, but we kept it cropped boyishly short. The sun and wind had darkened her skin and roughed it, and a year of fighting the big boat's rigging had put visible muscle under her sleekness.

The marina office was about two broom closets wide. It was a beautiful spring morning and I'd come in to put my name on the list of boats available for charter. I was reading the weather printout when Belle sidled through the door and squeezed in next to me at the counter. I patted her on the fanny. "With you in a second, honey."

A vise grabbed my shoulder and spun me around.

He was over two meters tall and so wide at the shoulders that he literally couldn't get through the door without turning sideways. Long white hair and pale-blue eyes. White sports coat with a familiar cut: tailored to de-emphasize the bulge of a shoulder holster.

"You don't do that, friend," he said with a German accent.

I looked at the woman, who was regarding me with aristocratic amusement. I felt the blood drain from my face and damned near said her name out loud.

She frowned. "*Helmuth,*" she said to the guard, "*Sie sind ihm erschrocken.* I'm sorry," she said to me, "but my friend has quite a temper." She had a perfect North Atlantic accent and her voice sent a shiver of recognition down my neck.

"I am sorry," he said heavily. Sorry he hadn't had a chance to throw me into the water, he was.

"I must look like someone you know," she said. "Someone you know rather well."

"My wife. The similarity is . . . quite remarkable."

"Really? I should like to meet her." She turned to the woman behind the counter. "We'd like to charter a sailing boat for the day."

The clerk pointed at me. "He has a nice fifty-foot one."

"That's fine! Will your wife be aboard?"

"Yes . . . yes, she helps me. But you'll have to pay the full rate," I said rapidly. "The boat normally takes six passengers."

"No matter. Besides, we have two others."

"And you'll have to help with the rigging."

"I should hope so. We love to sail." That was pretty obvious. We had been wrong about the wind and sun, thinking that Maxine would have led a sheltered life; she was almost as weathered as Belle. Her hair was probably long, but she had it rolled up in a bun and tied back with a handkerchief.

We exchanged false names: Jack Jackson and Lisa von Hollerin. The bodyguard's name was Helmuth Zwei Kastor. A clone; there was at least one other chunk of overmuscled *Bratwurst* around. Lisa paid the clerk and called her friends at the marina hotel, telling them to meet her at the Abora, slip 39.

I didn't have any chance to warn Belle. She came up from the galley as we were swinging aboard. She stared open-mouthed and staggered, almost fainting. I took her by the arm and made introductions, everybody staring.

After a few moments of strange silence, Helmuth Two whispered, "*Du bist ein Klone.*"

"She can't be a clone, silly man," Lisa said. "When did you ever see a clone with a navel?" Belle was wearing shorts and a halter. "But we could be twin sisters. That *is* remarkable."

Helmuth Two shook his head solemnly. Belle had told me that a clone can always recognize a fellow clone, by the eyes. Never be fooled by a man-made navel.

The other two came aboard. Helmuth One was, of course, a Xerox copy of Helmuth Two. Lisa introduced Maria Salamanca as her lover: a small olive-skinned Basque woman, no stunning beauty, but having an attractive air of friendly mystery about her.

Before we cast off, Lisa came to me and apologized. "We are a passing strange group of people. You deserve something extra for putting up with us." She pressed a gold Krugerrand into my palm—worth at least triple the charter fee—and I tried to act suitably impressed. We had over 1000 of them in the keel, for ballast.

The Ahora didn't have an engine: getting it in and out of the crowded marina was something of an accomplishment. Belle and Lisa handled the sails expertly, while I manned the wheel. They kept looking at each other, then touching. When we were in the harbor, they sat together at the prow, holding hands. Maria went into a sulk, but the two clones jollied her out of it.

I couldn't be jealous of Lisa. An angel can't sin. But I did wonder what you would call what they were doing. Was it a weird kind of incest? Transcendental masturbation? I only hoped Belle would keep her mouth shut, at least figuratively.

After about an hour, Lisa came up and sat beside me at the wheel. Her hair was long and full, and flowed like dark liquid in the wind, and she was naked. I tentatively rested my hand on her thigh. She had been crying.

"She told me. She had to tell me." Lisa shook her head in wonder. "Maxine One Kraus. She had to stay below for a while. Said she couldn't trust her legs." She squeezed my hand and moved it back to the wheel.

"Later, maybe. And don't worry; your secret is safe with us." She went forward and put an arm around Maria, speaking rapid German to her and the two Helmuths. One of the guards laughed and they took off their incongruous jackets, then carefully wrapped up their weapons and holsters. The sight of a .48 magnum recoilless didn't arouse any nostalgia in me. Maria slipped out of her clothes and stretched happily. The guards did the same. They didn't have navels but were otherwise adequately punctuated.

Belle came up then, clothed and flushed, and sat quietly next to me. She stroked my biceps and I ruffled her hair. Then I heard Lisa's throaty laugh and suddenly turned cold.

"Hold on a second," I whispered. "We haven't been using our heads."

"Speak for yourself." She giggled.

"Oh, be serious. This stinks of coincidence. That she should turn up here, that she would wander into the office just as—"

"Don't worry about it."

"Listen. She's no more Maxine Kraus than you are. They've found us. She's another clone, one that's going to—"

"She's Maxine. If she were a clone, I could tell immediately."

"Spare me the mystical claptrap and take the wheel. I'm going below." In the otherwise empty aftercompartment, I'd stored an interesting assortment of weapons and ammunition.

She grabbed my arm and pulled me back down to the seat. "You spare *me* the private-eye claptrap and listen—you're right, it's no coincidence. Remember that old foreigner who came by last week?"

"No."

"You were up on the stern, folding sail. He was just at the slip for a second, to ask directions. He seemed flustered—"

"I remember. Frenchman."

"I thought so, too. He was Swiss, though."

"And that was no coincidence, either."

"No, it wasn't. He's on the board of directors of one of the banks we used to liquefy our credit. When the annual audit came up, they'd managed to put together all our separate transactions—"

"Bullshit. That's impossible."

She shook her head and laughed. "You're good, but they're good, too. They were curious about what we were trying to hide, using their money, and traced us here. Found we'd started a business with only one percent of our capital.

"Nothing wrong with that, but they were curious. This director was headed for a Caribbean vacation, anyhow; he said he'd come by and poke around."

It sounded too fucking complicated for a Mafia hit. They know it's the cute ones who get caught. If they wanted us, they'd just follow us out to the middle of nowhere and blow us away.

"He'd been a lifelong friend of Werner Kraus. That's why he was so rattled. One look at me and he had to rush to the phone."

"And you want me to believe," I said, "that the wealthiest woman in the world would come down herself, to see what sort of innocent game we were playing. With only two bodyguards."

"Five bodyguards and the Swiss Foreign Legion; so what? Look at them. If they're armed, they've got little tiny weapons stashed away where the sun don't shine. I could—"

"That proves my point."

"In a pig's ass. It doesn't mesh. She's spent all her life locked away from her own shadow—"

"That's just it. She's tired of it. She turned twenty-five last month and came into full control of the fortune. Now she wants to take control of her own life."

"If that's true, it's damned stupid. What would you do, in her position? You'd send the giants down alone. Not just walk into enemy territory with your flanks exposed."

She had to smile at that. "I probably would." She looked thoughtful. "Maxine and I are the same woman, in some ways, but you and the Mafia taught me caution. Maxine has been in a cage all her life and just wants out. Wants to see what the world looks like when it's not locked in a cube show. Wants to sail someplace besides her own lake."

I almost had to believe it. We'd been in open water for over an hour before the Helmuths wrapped up their guns and starting tanning their privates. We would've long been shark chum if that's what they'd wanted. Getting sloppy in your old age, Loomis.

"It was still a crazy chance to take. Damned crazy."

"So she's a little crazy. Romantic, too, in case you haven't noticed."

"Really? When I peeked in, you were playing checkers. Jumping each other."

"Bastard." She knew the one place I was ticklish. Trying to get away, I jerked the wheel and nearly tipped us all into the drink.

We anchored in a small cove where I knew there was a good reef. Helmuth One stayed aboard to guard while the rest of us went diving.

The fish and coral were as beautiful as ever, but I could only watch Maxine and Belle. They swam slowly hand in hand, kicking with unconscious synchrony, totally absorbed. Although the breathers kept their hair wrapped up identically, it was easy to tell them apart, since Maxine had an allover tan. Still, it was an eerie kind of ballet like a mirror that didn't quite work. Maria and Helmuth Two were also hypnotized by the sight.

I went aboard early, to start lunch. I'd just finished slicing ham when I heard the drone of a boat, rather far away. Large siphon jet, by the rushing sound of it.

The guard shouted, *"Zwei—komn' herauf!"*

Hoisted myself up out of the galley. The boat was about two kilometers away and coming roughly in our direction, fast.

"Trouble coming?" I asked him.

"Cannot tell yet, sir. I suggest you remain below." He had a gun in each hand, behind his back.

Below, good idea. I slid the hatch off the aftercompartment and tipped over the cases of beer that hid the weaponry. Fished out two heavy plastic bags, left the others in place for the time being. It was all up-to-date American Coast Guard issue and had cost more than the boat.

I'd rehearsed this a thousand times in my mind but hadn't planned on the bags' being slippery with oil and condensation, impossible to grip and tear. I stood up to get a knife from the galley, and it was almost the last thing I ever did.

I looked back at the loud noise and saw a line of holes zipping toward me from the bow, letting in blue light and lead. I dropped and heard bullets hissing over my head, tried not to flinch at the sting of splinters driving into my arm and face. Heard the regular cough-cough-cough of Helmuth One's return fire, while at the stern there was a strangled cry of pain and then a splash; they must have gotten the older guard while he was coming up the ladder.

For a second, I thought I was bleeding, but it was only urine; that wasn't in the rehearsals, either. Neither was the sudden clatter of the bilge pump; they'd hit us below the water line.

I controlled the trembling well enough to cut open the bag that held the small-caliber spitter, and it took only three times to lock the cassette of ammunition into the receiver. Jerked back the arming lever and hurried up to the galley hatch.

The spitter was made for sinking boats, quickly. It fired

tiny flechettes, small as old-fashioned stereo needles, 50 rounds per second. Each carried a small explosive charge and moved faster than sound. In ten seconds, they could make a boat look as if a man had been working over it all afternoon with a chain saw.

I resisted the urge to squeeze off a blast and duck back under cover (not that the hull gave much protection against whatever they were using). We had clamped traversing mounts for the gun onto three sides of the galley hatch, to hold it steady. The spitter's most effective if you can hold the point of aim right on the water line.

They were concentrating their fire on the bow—lucky for me, unlucky for Helmuth—most of it going high. He must have been shooting from a prone position, difficult target. I slid the spitter onto its mount and cranked the scope up to maximum power.

When I looked through its scope, a lifetime of target-shooting reflexes took hold: deep breath, let half out, do the Zen thing. Their boat surged toward the center of the scope's field, and I waited. It was a Whaler Unsinkable. One man crouched at the bow, firing what looked like a 20mm recoilless, clamped onto the rail above an apron of steel plate. There were several splashes of silver on the metal shield; Helmuth had been doing some fancy shooting.

The Whaler slewed in a sharp starboard turn, evidently to give the gunner a better angle on our bow. Good boatmanship, good tactics but bad luck. Their prow touched the junction of my cross hairs right at the water line and I didn't even have to track. I just pressed the trigger and watched a cloud of black smoke and steam whip from prow to stern. Not even an Unsinkable can stay upright with its keel chewed off. It nosed down suddenly—crushing the gunner behind a 50-knot wall of water—and then flipped up into the air, scattering people. It landed upright with a great splash and turned turtle. Didn't sink, though.

I snapped a fresh cassette into place and tried to remember where the hydrogen tank was on that model. Second blast found it and the boat dutifully exploded. Vaporized. The force of the blast, even at our distance, was enough to ram the scope's eyepiece back into my eye, and it set the Abora to rocking. None of them could have lived through it, but I checked with the scope. No one swimming.

Helmuth One peered down at me. "What is that?"

I patted it. "Coast Guard weapon, a spitter."

"May I try it?"

"Sure." I traded places with him, glad to be up in the breeze. My boat was a mess. The mainmast had been shattered by a direct hit, waist-high. The starboard rail was chewed to splinters, forward, and near misses had gouged up my nice teak foredeck. The bilge pump coughed out irregular spews of water; evidently, we weren't in danger of sinking.

"Are you all right?" Belle called from the water.

"Yes . . . looks all clear. Come on—" I was interrupted by the spitter, a scream like a large animal dying slowly.

I unshipped a pair of binoculars to check his marksmanship. It was excellent. He was shooting at the floating bodies. What a spitter did to one was terrible to see.

"Jesus Christ, Helmuth. What do you do for fun when you don't have dead people to play with?"

"Some of them may yet live," he said neutrally.

At least one did. Wearing a life jacket, she had been floating face down but suddenly began treading water. She was holding an automatic pistol in both hands. She looked exactly like Belle and Maxine.

I couldn't say anything; couldn't take my eyes off her. She fired two rounds and I felt them slap into the hull beneath me. I heard Helmuth curse and suddenly her shoulders dissolved in a spray of meat and bone and her head fell into the water.

My knees buckled and I sat down suddenly. "You see?" Helmuth shouted. "You see?"

"I saw." In fact, I would never stop seeing it.

Helmuth Two, it turned out, had been hit in the side of the neck, but it was a big neck and he survived. Maxine called a helicopter, which came out piloted by Helmuth Three.

After an hour or so, Helmuth Four joined us in a large speedboat loaded down with gasoline, thermite and shark chum. He also had a little electrical gadget that made sharks feel hungry whether they actually were or not.

By that time, we had transferred the gold and a few more important things from my boat onto the helicopter. We chummed the area thoroughly and, as the water began to boil with sharks, towed both hulks out to deep water, where they burned brightly and sank.

The Helmuths spent the next day sprinkling the island with money and threats, while Maxine got to know Belle and me better, locked behind the heavily guarded door of the honeymoon suite of the quaint old Sheraton that overlooked the marina. She made us a job offer—a life offer, really—and we accepted without hesitation. That was six years ago.

Sometimes I do miss our old life—the sea, the freedom, the friendly island, the lazy idyls with Belle. Sometimes I even miss New York's hustle and excitement, and the fierce independence of my life there. I'm still a mean son of a bitch, but I never get to prove it.

We do travel sometimes, but with extreme caution. The clone that Helmuth ripped apart in the placid cove might have been Belle's own daughter, since the Mafia had plenty of opportunities to collect cells from her body. It's immaterial. If they could make one, they could make an army of them.

Like our private army of Helmuths and Lamberts and Delias. I'm chief of security, among other things, and the work is interesting, most of it at a console as good as the one I had in Manhattan. No violence since that one afternoon six years ago, not yet. I did have to learn German, though, which is a kind of violence, at least to a brain as old as mine.

We haven't made any secret of the fact that Belle is Maxine's clone. The official story is that *Fräulein* Kraus had a clone made of herself, for "companionship." This started a fad among the wealthy, being the first new sexual diversion since the invention of the vibrator.

Belle and Maxine take pains to dress alike and speak alike, and have even unconsciously assimilated each other's mannerisms. Most of the nonclone employees, and the occasional guests, can't tell them apart. Even I sometimes confuse them, at a distance.

Close up, which happens happily often, there's no problem. Belle has a way of looking at me that Maxine could never duplicate. And Maxine is literally a trifle prettier: You can't beat a real navel.

PAST MAGIC

Ian R. MacLeod

British writer Ian R. MacLeod has been one of the hottest new writers of the nineties to date, and, as the decade progresses, his work continues to grow in power and deepen in maturity. MacLeod has published a slew of strong stories in the first year of the nineties in Interzone, Asimov's Science Fiction, Weird Tales, Amazing, *and* The Magazine of Fantasy and Science Fiction, *among other markets. Several of these stories made the cut for one or another of the various "Best of the Year" anthologies; in 1990, in fact, he appeared in three different Best of the Year anthologies with three different stories, certainly a rare distinction. He has just sold his first novel,* The Great Wheel, *and is at work on another. Upcoming is his first short-story collection. MacLeod lives with his wife and young daughter in the West Midlands of England.*

In the haunting story that follows, he demonstrates that not only can't you Go Home Again, sometimes it's much better not even to try . . .

The airport was a different world.

Claire grabbed a bag, then kissed my cheek. She smelt both fresh and autumnal, the way she always had. Nothing else had changed: I'd seen the whole island as the jet turned to land. Brown hills in the photoflash sunlight, sea torn white at the headlands.

We hurried past camera eyes, racial imagers, HIV sensors, orientation sniffers, robot guns. Feeling crumpled and dirty in my best and only jacket, I followed Claire across the hot tarmac between the palm trees. She asked about the mainland as though it was something distant. And then

about the weather. Wanting to forget the closed-in heat of
my flat and the kids with armalites who had stopped the bus
twice on the way to the airport, I told her Liverpool was
fine, just like here. She glanced over her shoulder and
smiled. I couldn't even begin to pretend.

It was good to see all those open-top cars again, vintage
Jags and Mercs that looked even better than when they left
the showroom. And Claire as brown as ever, her hair like
brass and cornfields, with not a worry about the ravenous
sun. I'd read the adverts for lasers and scans in the in-flight
magazine. And if you needed to ask the price, don't.

Her buggy was all dust and dents. And the kid was sitting
on the back seat, wearing a Mickey Mouse tee shirt, sucking
carton juice through a straw. Seeing her was an instant
shock, far bigger than anything I'd imagined.

Claire said, "Well, this is Tony," in the same easy voice
she'd used for the weather as she tossed my bags into the
boot.

"Howdy doody," the little girl said. Her lips were purple
from the black-currant juice she was drinking. "Are you
really my daddy?"

It was all too quick. I had expected some sort of
preparation. To be led down corridors . . . fanfares and
trumpets. Instead, I was standing in the pouring sunlight of
the airport compound. Staring into the face of my dead
daughter.

She looked just like Steph, precisely six years old and even
sweeter, just like the little girl I used to hold in my arms and
take fishing in the white boat on days without end. She
glanced at me in that oblique way I remembered Steph
always reserved for strangers. All those kiddie questions in
one look. Who are you? Why are you here? Can we play?

Claire shouted "Let's get going!" and jumped into the
buggy as though she'd never seen thirty-five.

"Yeah!" the kid said. She blew bubbles into the carton.
"Let's ride em, Mummeee!"

Off in a cloud of summer dust . . . and back on the Isle
of Man. The place where Claire and I had laughed and

loved, then fought and wept. The place where Steph, the real
Steph, had been born, lived, died. The swimming pools of
the big houses winked all the way along the coast. Then we
turned inland along the hot white road to Port Erin . . . the
shapes of the hills . . . the loose stone walls. It was
difficult for me to keep my distance from the past. Claire.
Steph. Me. Why pretend? It might as well be ten years
before when we were married and for a while everything
was sweet and real.

Here's the fairy bridge.

"Cren Ash Tou!!" We all shouted without thinking. Hello
to the fairies.

In the days when tourists were allowed to visit the Isle of
Man, this was part of the package. Fairy bridges, fairy
postcards, stone circles, fat tomes about Manx folklore.
Manannan was the original Lord of Man. He greeted King
Arthur when the boat took him from the Last Battle. He
strode the hills and bit out the cliffs at Cronk ny Irree Laa
in anguish at his vanished son. He hid the hills in cloud.

Manannan never quite went away. I used to read every
word I could find and share it with Steph after she was
tucked up at night from her bath. The island still possessed
magic, but now it was sharp as the sunlight, practised in the
clinics by men and women in druidic white, discreetly
advertised in-flight to those with the necessary clearances.
Switching life off and on, changing this and that, making the
most of the monied Manx air.

We turned up the juddering drive that led to Kellaugh and
I saw that no one had ever got around to fixing the gate.
Claire stopped the buggy in the courtyard near the shade of
the cypress trees. Like the buggy, Kellaugh was a statement
of I-don't-care money, big and rambling with white walls
peeling in the sun, old bits and new bits, views everywhere
of the wonderful coastline like expensive pictures casually
left to hang.

Steph jumped out of the buggy and shot inside through
the bleached double doors.

I looked at Claire.

"She really is Steph," she said, "but she can't remember

anything. She's had lessons and deep therapy, but it's still only been six months. You're a stranger, Tony. Just give it time."

Feeling as though I was walking over glass, I said, "She's a sweet, pretty kid, Claire. But she can't be Steph."

"You'll see." She tried to make it sound happy, but there was power and darkness there, something that made me afraid. When she smiled, her eyes webbed with wrinkles even the money couldn't hide.

Fergus came out grinning to help with the bags. We said "Hi." Claire kissed him and he kissed her back inside his big arms. I watched for a moment in silence, wondering what was left between them.

Claire gave me the room that had once been my study. She could have offered me the annexe where I would have had some independence and a bathroom to myself, but she told me she wanted me here in the house with her and Fergus, close to Steph. There was a bed where my desk used to be, but still the ragged Persian carpet, the slate fireplace and the smell of the house that I loved . . . dark and sweet, like damp and biscuit tins.

Claire watched as I took my vox from the bag, the box into which I muttered my thoughts. Nowadays, it was hardly more than a private diary. I remembered how she had given it to me one Christmas here at Kellaugh when the fires were crackling and the foghorn moaned. A new tool to help me with my writing. It was still the best, even ten years on.

"Remember that old computer you had for your stories," she said, touching my arm.

"I always was useless at typing."

"I got it out again, for Steph. She loves old things, old toys. And I found those shoot-em-up games we used to buy her at that funny shop in Castletown: She tries, but the old Steph still has all the highest scores."

Old Steph, new Steph . . .

I was holding the vox, trailing the little wires that fitted to my throat. The red standby light was on. Waiting for the words.

• • •

Fergus was working in the new part of the house, all timber and glass; in the big room that hung over the rocks and the sea. He'd passed the test of time, had Fergus. Ten years with Claire now, and I had only managed eight. But then they had never married or had kids, and maybe that was the secret.

He gave me a whisky and I sat and watched him paint. Fergus seemed the same, even if his pictures had lost their edge. The gravelly voice went with the Gauloise he smoked one after another. I hadn't smelt cigarette smoke like that in years. He would probably have been dead on the mainland, but here they scanned and treated you inch by inch for tumours as regularly as you could pay.

Late afternoon, and the sky was starting to darken. The windows were open on complex steel latches that took the edge off the heat and let in the sound of the waves.

"It's good you're here," he said, wiping his hands on a rag. "You don't know how badly Claire needed to get Steph back. It wasn't grief, not after ten years. It just . . . went on, into something else."

"The grief never goes," I said.

Fergus looked uncomfortable for a moment, then asked, "Is it really as bad as they say on the mainland?"

I sipped my whisky and pondered that for a moment, wondering if he really wanted to know. I could remember what it used to be like when I was a kid, watching the news of Beirut. Part of you understood . . . you just tried not to imagine. Living in it, on the mainland, you got to sleep through the sniper fire and didn't think twice about taking an umbrella to keep the sun off when you queued for the standpipes. I told him about my writing instead, an easier lie because I'd had more practice.

"Haven't seen much work from you lately," he said. "Claire still keeps an eye out . . ." He lit a Gauloise and blew. "I can still manage to paint, but whispering into that vox, getting second-guessed, having half-shaped bits of syllables turned into something neat . . . it must be frightening. Like staring straight into silence."

The evening deepened. Fergus poured himself a big

whisky, then another, rapidly catching up on—and then overtaking—me. He was amiable, and we were soon talking easily. But I couldn't help remembering the Fergus of old, the Fergus who would contradict anything and everything, the Fergus who would happily settle an intellectual argument with a fist fight. I'd known him even before I met Claire. Introduced them, in fact. And he had come over to the Isle of Man and stayed in the annexe for a while just as I had done and the pattern started to repeat itself. The new for the old, and somehow no one ever blamed Claire for the way it happened.

"You left too soon after Steph died," he said. "You thought it was Claire and Fergus you were leaving behind, but really it was Claire alone. She has the money, the power. The likes of you and I will always be strangers here. But Claire belongs."

"Then why do you stay?"

He shrugged. "Where else is there to go?"

We stood at the window. The patio lay below and at the side of the house, steps winding down to the little quay. A good place to be. Steph was sitting on the old swing chair, gently rocking, trying to keep her feet off the slabs to stop the ants climbing over her toes. She must have sensed our movement. She looked up. Fathomless blue eyes in the fathomless blue twilight. She looked up and saw us. Her face didn't flicker.

After the lobster and the wine on that first evening, after Fergus had ambled outside to smoke, Claire took my hand across the white linen and said she knew how difficult this was for me. But this was what she wanted, she wanted it because it was right. It was losing Steph that had been wrong. I should have done this, oh, years ago. I never wanted another child, just Steph. You have to be here with us Tony because the real Steph is so much a part of you.

I could only nod. The fire was in Claire's eyes. She looked marvellous with the candlelight and the wine. Fergus was right; Claire had the power of the island. She was charming, beautiful . . . someone you could wake up with

a thousand mornings and still fear . . . and never understand. I realized that this was what had driven me to write
when I was with her, striving to put the unknown into
words . . . and striving to be what she wanted. Striving,
and ultimately failing, pushing myself into loneliness and
silence.

Different images of Claire were flickering behind my
eyes. The Claire I remembered, the Claire I thought I knew.
How pink and pale she had been that first day in the hospital
holding Steph wrapped in white. And then the Claire who
called people in from the companies she owned, not that she
really cared for business, but just to keep an eye on things.
Claire making a suggestion here, insisting on a course of
action pursued, disposals and mergers, compromises and
aggressions, moving dots on a map of the world, changing
lives in places I couldn't even pronounce. And although it
abrogated a great many things, I couldn't help remembering
how it felt when we made love. Everything. Her nails across
my back. Her scent. Her power. For her, she used to say it
was like a fire. The fire that was in her eyes now, across the
candlelight and the empty glasses.

I dreamed again that night that Steph and I were out
fishing in the white boat. The dream grew worse every time,
knowing what would happen. The wind was picking up and
Manannan had hidden the island under cloud. The waves
were big and cold and lazy, slopping over the gunwales. I
looked at Steph. Her skin was white. She was already dead.
But she opened her mouth on dream power alone and the
whole Irish Sea flooded out.

Next day Claire took me around all the old places on the
island with Steph. The sun was blinding but she told me not
to worry and promised to pay for a scan. Just as she had paid
for everything else. With Island money, the money that kept
all the old attractions going even though there were no
tourists left to see them. The steam railway . . . the horse
drawn tramcars along the front at Douglas . . . even the
big water wheel up at Laxey. Everything was shimmering
and clear, cupped in the inescapable heat. Dusty roads

snaked up to fenced white clinics, Swiss names on the signboards. I did my best to chat to Steph and act like a friend, or at least be someone she might get to know. But it was hard to make contact through the walls of her sweet indifference. I was just another boring adult . . . and I couldn't help wondering why I had come here, and what would have happened had I tried to say no.

In the evening we took the path beyond the Chasms towards Spanish Head. The air was breathlessly alive with the sound and the smell of the sea, and the great cliffs were white with gulls. Glancing back as we climbed among the shivering grass and sea pinks, I started to tell Steph how the headland got its name from a shipwreck caught up on a storm after the Armada. But she nodded so seriously and strained the corners of her eyes that I couldn't find the words.

Claire was the perfect host. Devoting all her time to me, chatting about when we used to be together, reciting memories that were sweeter than the truth. About the island, about what had changed and how everything was really the same. She invited people over and there were the big cars in the drive and all the old songs and the faces that I remembered. Sweet, friendly people, at ease with their money and power. They were so unused to seeing faces age that I had to remind most of them who I was. I got the impression that they would still all be smiling and sipping wine when the oxygen finally ran out and the world died.

When Claire took me with Steph to Curraghs Wildlife Park, I was struck for once by a sense of change, if only by all the new cages filled with tropical species. Baboons, hummingbirds and sloths. The sort of creatures that would have been bones in the wildfire desert if they weren't here, although it was still sad to see them, trying to act natural behind those bars. But all the old favourites were there as well. Ocelots and otters and penguins that the seagulls stole fish from and the loghtan sheep that once used to graze the island. And the big attraction: Steph ran towards the enclosure almost as though she could remember the last time. And Madeleine lumbered over towards the fence.

Madeleine had been in the papers for a while back when I was young and there were still real papers for her to be in. She might have been created by the same clinic that did Steph, for all I knew. But the islanders were more nervous in those days, bothered about what people on the mainland thought just in case they might try to invade. Take all the money and magic, the golden eggs. They wanted to be seen to be doing something that they could hang a big sign marked SCIENCE on. Something that didn't look like simple moneymaking and self-interest.

Madeleine rubbed her huge side against the fence. The fur was matted and oily. And she stank of wet dog. Like all the wet dogs in the history of the world piled up in one place at one time. Claire and I hung back, but Steph didn't seem to mind breathing air that was like a rancid dishcloth. Madeleine's tiny black eye high on her shaggy head twinkled at Steph as though she was sharing a joke. Her tusks had grown bigger in the ten years since I had last seen her. They looked terribly uncomfortable. And in this heat.

Steph splayed her fingers through the wire, into the matted fur. Madeleine swayed a little and gave a thunderous rumble. Madeleine the mammoth: her original cells came from the scrapings of one of the last hairy icecubes to emerge from the thaw in Siberia. A few steps on the DNA spiral staircase were damaged and computers had to fill in the gaps. As a result there was much debate about whether she was real or simply someone's idea of what a mammoth ought to be. There was one in Argentina made from the same patch of cells with lighter fur and a double hump almost like a camel's. And the Russians had their own ideas and refused to admit Madeleine to the official mammoth club.

The real Steph of ten years before had been just as interested in Madeleine. She made us buy a poster at the little shop on the way out from the zoo. Now, it seemed like a premonition. Steph and Madeleine. The big and the little. Scrapings from the dermis, the middle layer of the skin, were the most suitable for cloning. I remembered that phrase; maybe it was written somewhere on the poster.

We sat outdoors at the zoo café. Lizards darted on the cactus rockery and a red and green flock of parakeets preened and fluttered under the awnings, eyeing the shaded pavement for crumbs. Steph drank another carton of black-currant and it stained her lips again. I couldn't help thinking about how much the real Steph used to hate that stuff. Always said it was too sweet.

This Steph chatted away merrily enough. Asking about the past, the last time she was here. She didn't seem bothered by the ghost of the real Steph, just interested. She looked straight at Claire and avoided my eyes.

I said to her, "Don't you think the mammoth might be too hot?"

"You mean Madeleine."

I nodded. "Madeleine the mammoth."

She wrinkled her nose and swung her right foot back against the leg of the chair. Steph thinking. If only her lips hadn't been purple, it was exactly the way she used to be. I had to blink hard as I watched. Then the little pink and white zoo train rattled past and her eyes were drawn. She forgot my question. She didn't answer.

This new Steph was a jumbled jigsaw. Pieces that fitted, pieces that were missing, pieces that didn't belong.

The clinic where they remade Steph from the thawed scrapings of her skin lay up on the hill overlooking Douglas and the big yachts in the harbour. Claire took me along when it was time for Steph's deep therapy. There were many places like this on the island, making special things for those parts of the world that had managed to stay apart from all the bad that had happened. New plants, new animals, new people. Little brains like the one inside the vox. Tanned pinstripe people wafted by on the grey carpets. I was disappointed. I only saw one white coat the whole time I was there.

They took Steph away, then they showed me her through thick glass, stretched out in white like a shroud with little wires trailing from her head. The doctor standing beside me put his arm around my shoulder and led me to his office. He sat me down across from his desk. Just an informal chat, he said, giving me an island smile.

His office window had a fine view across Douglas. I noticed that all the big yachts were in. A storm was predicted, not that there was any certain way to tell the weather. The thought made me remember my dream, being on the boat with Steph. She opened her mouth. And everything flooded back and back to when they finally hauled us out of the water, the chopper flattening the tops of the waves, the rope digging into her white skin, the way a stripe of weed had stuck across her face.

The doctor tapped a pencil. "We all feel," he said, "that your input is vital if Steph is to recover her full identity. We've done a lot with deep therapy. She can walk, talk, even swim. And we've done our best to give her memories."

"Can you invent memories?"

There was darkness on the horizon. Flags flew. Fences rattled. The sea shivered ripples.

"We all invent memories," he said. "Didn't you write fiction? You should know that memories and the past are quite different propositions."

"What do you want me to do?"

"Just be around, Tony. She'll soon get to like you."

"This little girl looks like someone who used to be my daughter. And you're asking me to behave like a friend of the family."

The pencil tapped again. "Is this something to do with how Steph died? Is that the problem? Do you blame yourself?"

"Of course I blame myself . . . and, no, that isn't the problem. That may be the problem with whole chunks of my life . . . why I can't write. But it's nothing to do with Steph. This Steph."

"Okay," he said. "Then what do we do?"

I waited. I watched the masts bob in the greying harbour.

"I have a suggestion," he said. "Let us use your vox."

I shook my head. "No."

"If you gave us the keyword, we could copy all the data onto the mainframe here. It would be perfectly secure. We'd filter it, of course. Only a small percentage would be relevant."

"And you would pour my ramblings into Steph's head."

"A large part of you is inside that vox. Be assured, we'd only take that which is good and beneficial." He stood up and held out his hand for me to shake. "Think about it. I'm sure it's the way forward. For Steph."

Claire put the buggy hood up in the clinic car park with the first drops of rain. Steph sat in the back, sucking a fresh carton of purple juice. She was quiet, even by the standards of when I was around. I put it down to the deep therapy, all those new things in her head. The real rain started just as we crossed the fairy bridge. Hello to the fairies: Cren Ash Tou. Grey veils trailed from the sky. The buggy hood was mostly holes and broken seams and we were cold and wet by the time we got back to Kellaugh, juddering through the puddles on the drive, dashing to the front door.

I watched as Fergus scooped Steph up in the rainlit hall and carried her dripping towards the bathroom. The taps hissed and the pipes hammered. I heard her squeal, his gruff laughter.

I took a bath in the annexe and stayed longer than I intended. Being out of the way was a relief. The clean white walls, fresh soap and towels waiting for Claire's next visitor. I had spent some of my happiest days there, writing, falling in love with Claire. Her father had been alive then. She was a free spirit, spending the old patriarch's money on the mainland as if there was no tomorrow, which wasn't that far from the truth. We met in London before the second big flood. She wrangled the clearances to invite me back to Kellaugh, displacing, I found out later, a sculptor who had left the carpets gritty with dust. We made love, we fell in love. Her father died and I moved in with her. She had Steph, we even got married. My work was selling well then, I could even kid myself that I didn't actually need her support. I thought the pattern of my life had settled, living here with Claire and Steph. Getting a tan and growing to some ridiculous age in the sun, letting the men in white take care of the wrinkles and the tumours. But I realized instead that I was part of another pattern. Claire collected artists. She gave them money, encouragement, criticism, contacts. She usually gave them her body as well.

Because I thought I still needed Claire, and because of Steph, I had stayed longer at Kellaugh than I should have done. The island was addictive, even to those who didn't belong. The money, the parties, the power. The people who were so charming and unaffected, who knew about history and humour and art, who could pick up a phone and bring death or life to thousands, who would chat or argue over brandy and champagne until the sun came up, who would organize pranks or be serious or even play at being in love . . . who would do anything whatever and however so long as they got their own way.

Fergus was only the last in a long succession. I remember coming into the annexe bedroom in the heavy heat one morning to ask about borrowing a book and finding him and Claire together, their bodies shining with juice and sweat. They sat up and said nothing. Only I felt ashamed. But then Claire had never really lied to me about her men. She just kept it out of my way. I had no excuse for my sudden feelings of shock; I had always known that the island only kept faith with itself. But it was much harder to give up pretending.

So I ran out and headed down the steps towards the white boat, across the patio where the bougainvillea was richly in flower. Steph was up early too that morning, sitting on the swing chair, keeping her feet off the paving to stop the ants from crawling over her toes. She said Hi and are you off fishing and can I come along? I smiled and ruffled her hair. The sky was hot blue metal. Steph took the rudder. The water slid over the oars like green jelly. I kept rowing until the wind grew chill and Manannan hid the island in darkening haze.

That night after the clinic I went to say goodnight to Steph. Goodbye as well, although I still wasn't sure. The storm was chattering at the window and the waves were beating the rocks below. I could see her face dark against the pillow, the glitter in her eyes.

"Did I wake you?"

"Nope."

"You always used to say that. Nope. Like a cowboy."

"I keep doing things Mummy says I used to do."

"Doesn't that feel strange? Can you be sure who you are?"

I closed the door. It was an absurd question to ask any six-year-old. I sat down on the old wicker chair by her bed.

"Do you feel like a Daddy, when you see me?"

"It's like being pulled both ways. You didn't recognize me."

"I know who you are. I've seen your picture on the back of the book Mummy showed me. But you don't look the same."

"That was a long time ago. The real Steph . . . used to be different."

The real Steph. There, I'd said it.

"I don't really understand," she said.

"You don't need to. You're what you are."

Everything was heavy inside me. Here in this room that I knew so well. I wanted to kiss her, carry her, break through and do something that was real. But I knew that all that I would touch was a husk of dry memories.

"What was it like when you were with Mummy and Steph?"

I tried to tell her, talking as though she was some kind of human vox. About waking with the sun in the kitchen clutter of morning. Walking the cliffs with the sea pinks wavering and every blade of grass sharp enough to touch. About days without end when the two of us went fishing in the little white boat. About how you always end up thinking about things and places when you mean people because the feelings are too strong.

Somewhere along the lines of memory I stammered into silence. Steph's breathing was slow and easy as only a child's can be. I leaned forward and kissed her forehead. Faintly, I could smell blackcurrant. I left her to her dreams.

I found Claire holding my vox, the red light glowing in the darkness of my room. I sat down beside her on the bed. She was in a white towelling gown. She smelled both fresh and autumnal, happy and sad.

"You know what they asked for today," I said. "At the clinic."

"You've changed, Tony." She swung the little wires of the vox to and fro. "I thought I could bring the old you back."

"Like bringing back the old Steph?"

"No," she said. "That's possible. You're impossible."

I stared at the vox. The ember in the shell of her hands. "Why did you drag me over here? I can't be the person you want . . . I never really was. Some myth of the way you wanted Steph's father to be. I can't do that. Do you want me to become like poor Fergus? He's not an artist, he's lost his anger. He's not anything."

I tried to look into her eyes. Even in this darkness, it was difficult. I could feel her power like bodily warmth. Something you could touch, that couldn't be denied. Claire looked the same, but she had changed, become more of what I feared in her. She belonged to this magic island.

"At least Fergus still paints," she said. Then she shook her head slowly, her cornfield hair swaying. "I'm sorry, Tony. I didn't mean . . . You have your own life, I know that. I just want to bring back Steph."

Want; the way she said it, the word became an instruction to God. Not that God had much influence on this island. The only way to imagine him was retired, sipping cooled Dom Perignon by the pool and reminiscing about the good old days, like the ancient ex-prime minister from the mainland who still lived up at Ramsey. Like her, most of his achievements had been reviled, and what remained, forgotten.

"I can't stay here any longer," I said.

"You must help." There was an odd catch in her voice, something I'd never heard before. I felt a chilly sense of control, not because of what I was, but because of what I knew I couldn't become.

She asked, "Will you show me the vox? You never let me hear."

So I took it and touched the wires to my throat. Whispered the keyword that was a sound without language. I let it run back at random. Clear and unhesitating, my voice filled the room.

"... *a great many things, I couldn't help remembering how it felt when we made love. Everything. Her nails across my back. Her scent. Her power. For her, she used to say it was like a fire. The fire that was in her eyes now, across the empty glasses* ..."

I turned it off. I had to smile, that the vox had chosen that. It had, after all, a mind of its own. But it all seemed academic: I'd never had any secrets from Claire.

"So that's the deal? I give you my memories, and you let me go?"

She smiled in the darkness. "There is no deal." Then she reached towards me. The white slid away and her flesh gleamed in the stuttering light of the storm. The air smelt of her and of Kellaugh, of biscuit tins and damp. There was a moment when the past and present touched. Her nails drew blood from my back. Raking down through layers of skin, layers of memory. Inside the fire, I thought of Steph, wrapped in the sweet breath of dreams, of making her anew.

That was Tony's last entry before he returned to the mainland. Obviously, he can't come back now, not now that I'm here. Claire tells me that everything went tidily enough the next day. The trip to the clinic in the clear air after the storm, then on to the airport. It was the only way out; perhaps he understood that by then.

This vox is a good copy. We have that much in common, my vox and I. It's winter now. Life is comfortable here in the annexe, but chilly when the wind turns north and draws the heat from the fire. I saw an iceberg from my window yesterday. Huge, even halfway towards the horizon. Pure white against the grey sky, shining like the light from a better world.

The four of us eat our meals together as a kind of family.

Claire. Fergus. Steph. Me. The talk is mostly happy and there's little tension. Only sometimes I see Steph with darkness behind her big blue eyes. A look I understand but can't explain. But everything is fine, here on this fortunate island. Even Fergus is a good friend in his own vague way. He doesn't mind Claire's nocturnal visits to the annexe to make love. Everything about the arrangement is amicable and discreet.

Deep therapy has brought back a great many things. Often now, I can't be sure where my own true and recent memories begin. But I still find it useful to run back the vox, to listen to that inner voice. I find that I share many of the real Tony's doubts and feelings. We are so much alike, he and I, even if I am nothing more than the tiniest scrap of his flesh taken from under Claire's fingernails.

When I originally mastered this vox, the first thing I did was to run it back ten years to that summer, that day. Tony—the real Tony—had the vox with him when Steph drowned; the vibrations of the storm must have tripped it to record.

You can hear the flat boom of the water. The thump of the waves against the useless upturned hull. Tony's shuddering breath. Steph's voice is there too, the old Steph that I will never know, carried into the circuits by some trick of the vox. *I'm cold, Daddeeee. Please help. I can't stay up. The cold. Hurts. Aches. Hurts. Please, Daddy. Can you help me, Daddy? Can you?*

But it was all a long time ago. I can't erase the memory, but I don't think I'll ever replay it again.

CLONE SISTER

Pamela Sargent

Pamela Sargent has firmly established herself as one of the foremost writer/editors of her generation. Her well-known anthologies include Women of Wonder, More Women of Wonder, The New Women of Wonder—*recently reissued in an omnibus volume as* Women of Wonder: The Classic Years—*and 1995's follow-up volume* Women of Wonder: The Contemporary Years. *Her other anthologies include* Bio-Futures, Nebula Awards 29, *and, with Ian Watson,* Afterlives. *Her critically acclaimed novels include* Cloned Lives *(one of the first SF novels to deal with clones),* The Sudden Star, The Golden Space, Watchstar, Earthseed, The Alien Upstairs, Eye of the Comet, Homeminds, The Shore of Women, Venus of Dreams, *and* Venus of Shadows. *Her short fiction has been collected in* Starshadows *and* The Best of Pamela Sargent. *She won a Nebula Award in 1993 for her story,* "Danny Goes to Mars." *Her most recent books are a critically acclaimed historical novel about Genghis Khan,* Ruler of the Sky, *and, as editor, the anthology* Nebula Awards 30. *She lives in New York.*

Here she gives a novel and poignant SF twist to that old saying that insists that before you can love others, you must first love yourself . . .

After they made love, Jim Swenson leaned back on his elbows and looked at Moira Buono. She was a slender dark-haired girl with olive skin and large black eyes. Her nose was a bit too large for her delicate face. As she lay at his side, her small breasts seemed flattened almost to nonexistence. Her abdomen was a concavity between two sharp hipbones. Her legs contrasted with the slenderness of her torso; they were short and utilitarian, well-muscled appendages that carried her around efficiently and without much strain. She was beautiful.

She watched him with dark eyes. Her black hair lay carelessly around her head in the green grass and her face bore a calm and peaceful smile. She reached out for his hand and drew it to her belly. In the distance he could hear the high-pitched laugh of Ilyasah Ahmal and the deeper rumblings of Walt Merton. He traced the outline of shadows on her body, shadows created by the summer sun's rays and the leafy branches of the trees overhead. A summer breeze stirred the branches, the shadows drifted and changed shape on Moira's body.

Jim took his hand away from her and got up. His penis felt cold and sticky. He pulled on his shorts and began to walk toward the clearing ahead. He knew Moira was watching him, probably puzzled, perhaps a little angry. He came to the clearing and walked toward the stone wall at its edge. The grass brushed against his feet, tickling his soles. Two grackles perched on the wall, cawing loudly at some sparrows darting overhead. As he approached, the two black birds lifted, cawed at him from above, and were gone.

Jim leaned against the wall and looked down at the automated highway two hundred feet below him. The cars fled along the road in orderly rows, punched into the automatic highway control. He watched them and thought of Moira. She had retreated from him again, hiding even at the moment he had entered her body. She had been an observer, looking on as he held her, sweating and moving to a lonely, sharp spurt of pleasure. She was an onlooker, smiling at him from a distance as he withdrew, her black eyes a shield between their minds.

They stood in a gray formlessness. "Moira," he said, and she looked at him, seeming to be perplexed, seeming to be impatient. She withdrew, and clouds of grayness began to cover her, binding her legs, then her face and shoulders.

His view of the highway was suddenly obstructed. "Are you trying to ruin today, too?" Moira's voice said. He pulled at the shirt she had draped over his head and put it on. She was sitting on the wall to his right. Her skin looked sallow next to her yellow shorts and shirt. She stared past him at the trees.

"I'm sorry," he said, "it's just a mood." He wanted to take her hand, touch her hair. Instead, he went back to leaning against the wall. He looked up at her face. Her eyes were pieces of onyx, sharp and cold. Her skin was drawn tightly across her cheekbones.

"I'm sorry, it's just a mood," she said. "How many moods do you have? Must be half a million by now. And they're always ones you have to apologize for."

Jim turned and saw Ilyasah coming toward them, black hair a cloud around her dark face. Jim forced himself to smile.

"You were right about this place," Ilyasah said. "Nice and quiet. Ever since they reclaimed that area up north, you can't go there without falling over bodies. Something wrong, Moira?"

"No," Moira muttered.

"Give us half an hour," Ilyasah went on, "and we'll get the food out."

Jim took the hint. "Sure," he said. Ilyasah left and disappeared among the trees. The black girl had still not shaken off the remnants of her rigid Muslim upbringing and wanted to be sure no one observed her with Walt. Moira had returned to her dormitory room with Jim one evening a little too soon. They had calmly excused themselves and gone to one of the lounges instead, but Ilyasah had been embarrassed for days afterward.

"I guess we'd better watch the path," he said to Moira. "I wouldn't want anyone else to embarrass your roommate." Moira shrugged and continued to sit on the wall.

He tried to fight the tightness in his stomach, the feeling of isolation that was once again wrapping itself around him. *Talk to me, Moira,* he thought, *don't make me stand here guessing and worrying.*

The dark eyes looked at him. "I'm leaving next week," she said quickly. "I'll probably come back in August, but my mother's fixing up her new studio and she needs some help." Her eyes challenged him to respond.

"Why?" he cried, suddenly realizing that he had shouted the word. "Why," he said more quietly, "didn't you tell me this before?"

"I didn't know before."

"Oh, you knew it before. She's been after you for a month about it, and you said she had enough help. Now all of a sudden you have to go home."

Moira hopped off the wall and paced in front of him. "I suppose," she said, "I have to go through a whole explanation."

"No," he said. *Of course you do.*

"All right," she went on. "I decided to go home a while ago. I would have told you before, but—"

"Why not? Why didn't you tell me before?"

Moira smiled suddenly. "You really don't understand, do you? If I had told you before, you would have gotten upset and tried to talk me out of it, or acted as though I did something terribly wrong. So I tell you now, so you don't have time to talk me out of it. I thought I was doing you a favor. But of course you're going to act the same way anyway."

"I want to be with you, is that so wrong?" Jim swallowed, worried that he had whined the words. "I don't like to be separated from you, that's all," he said in a lower tone.

"No, you'd rather be underfoot all the time," she said. "I can't even meet your brothers and sister. Every time I mention that I might like to talk to them, you evade the whole thing. Why?"

He was silent. He could feel sweat forming on his face and under his beard.

"I guess," she said, "you're jealous of your own family too."

He shrugged and tried to smile. "It isn't so bad," he said. "You'll be back in August, and we can—"

"No." She stopped pacing and stood in front of him, arms folded across her chest. "No, Jim. I don't know yet. I want to think about things. I don't want to make any promises now. I'll just have to see. Maybe that's hard on you, but . . ."

She sighed, then walked over to the trees. She stood there leaning against a trunk, her back to him.

"Moira."

No answer.

"Moira." She was gone again, having said what she had to say. He could stride over to her, grab her by the shoulders, shake the slender body while shouting at her, and she would look at him with empty eyes.

Do I love you, Moira? Do I even know you? He stared at the girl's back, stiff and unyielding under the soft yellow shirt. *Am I too possessive, too demanding? Or is that just an excuse, a way to avoid telling me that you can't love a freak, that it would be as easy for you to love one of my cloned brothers if you knew them, that we're all interchangeable?*

Moira, look at me, try to understand me, he wanted to shout. He walked over to her, afraid to touch her, afraid to reach out and hold her. She was lost in her own world, and seemed unaware of his presence.

It was over. He was sure of that, in spite of Moira's comments about waiting until August.

She turned around and looked at him, black eyes expressionless. "Surely you realize," she said, "that I'm getting a bit sick of the newsfax guys always asking for exclusive interviews on what it's like to be with a clone, that's one thing. The fact is, you're trying to use me to prove something to yourself, to show everyone that you are an individual, that I only love you, that I'm completely yours. Well, I've got better things to do than build up your ego."

She still refused to speak. *You could at least say what you mean,* Jim thought as he looked at her back.

"Hey!" Jim turned and saw Walt Merton on the path leading into the woods. "Come on," Walt said, "we're getting the food out."

"Yeah," said Jim. "We'll be along in a minute."

Walt looked from Jim to Moira. "Sure," he said. His dark face showed concern. He looked doubtfully at Jim, then turned and went back down the path.

"Let's go," Moira said suddenly. "I'm starving." She smiled and took him by the hand. She was hiding behind a shield of cheerfulness now: *Nothing's wrong, Jim; everything's settled.* "Damn it, Moira," he said harshly, "can't you at least talk it over, or let me try to get through to you?"

She ignored his question. "Let's go," she said, still smiling, still holding his hand.

The rain had started as a summer shower, but was now coming down steadily, forming puddles on the lawn. Jim sat on the front porch of the large house he shared with his brothers and sister. The evening air was cooler and fresher than it had been for several days.

The large house stood at the end of a narrow road amid a grove of trees. Farther down the road, near one of the other houses, Jim could see a group of naked children dancing in the rain. On the lawn in front of him his brothers Al and Mike were throwing a football. Mike was always ready to use any excuse for fooling around and had dragged Al outside almost as soon as the rain began to fall.

Al's thick brown hair was plastered against the back of his neck and shoulders and Mike's mustache drooped on both sides of his mouth. "Whup," yelled Mike as he drew his arm back and made a forward pass. As the ball left Mike's arm, he slipped on the grass and landed on his buttocks, bare muddy feet poking high into the air. Al hooted and caught the ball. He began to run with it, laughing as Mike got up with mud on his shorts.

Jim watched his brothers. They had not insisted that he join them, understanding almost instinctively that he needed some solitude. He had gone to the university early that morning to drive Moira to the monorail that would take her home.

He had tried once again the night before to talk her out of leaving. "I can't believe your mother needs your help with all those others around," he had said. Moira's mother lived with five other women and Moira herself had been raised communally by the group with three other children. She saw her father only rarely. He had retreated to Nepal years before, emerging only occasionally to face a world that frightened him.

Moira shrugged. "She can still use some extra help," she said.

"Come on, Moira," he shouted. "Stop being so evasive and at least be honest about why you're really going."

She was silent as she packed her things. He had finally left her dormitory room, angrily telling her she could take the shuttle from the university to the monorail.

He had relented, of course, driving onto the automated highway, punching a button, leaning back in his seat as the highway took control of his car. He had reached for Moira, pulled her to him. She had watched him, her black eyes seemingly veiled. She unfastened her blue sari and draped it on the back of the seat. Then she unzipped his shorts, crawled onto him, holding his penis firmly with one hand. He was suddenly inside her, clutching her, gazing up at her face. Her eyes were closed.

"Moira," he had whispered to her. "Moira." He came quickly. She withdrew from him and moved back to her side of the seat.

Jim shivered in the air-conditioned car. He zipped up his shorts and looked over at the dark-haired girl. She was fastening her sari while staring out her window at the blurred scenery. *What was it, Moira, a formality because you're leaving? a way of saying you still care? a way of saying, Goodbye, Jim, it's the last time?* She gave him no answer, not even a clue. Once again she had remained unresponsive, giving him no sign that she had taken pleasure in the act.

He grabbed her, pulling her sari from her and pushed her against the seat. Her face was against the back of the seat, hidden from him. Her buttocks pointed up at his face. He crawled on top of her, pushing inside roughly. He pounded against her, waiting to hear her moans, waiting to see her abandon herself to him at last.

He continued to sit behind the wheel, still watching her. She had finished fastening her sari. She turned toward him, a tentative smile formed on her face. *I've never reached you, Moira,* he thought. At last he pulled her to him, and she

lay there, head on his shoulder, her body stiff, her muscles
tight. He was alone once again.

Al stumbled onto the porch, picked up his towel from the
chair next to him, and massaged his head and shoulders
vigorously. "Am I out of shape," Al said. "I'm going over to
the gym tomorrow. I have to go to the library anyway, so I
might as well work out."

"Yeah," Jim said.

"Want to come along? We can play some handball."

"No." Jim looked up at his brother. "I don't think so." He
looked away, sensing what Al was probably thinking: *Is it
that girl, Jim? You've been sitting around for months, no
interest in much else. You haven't even written any poetry
for a while.*

"Well, if you change your mind," Al said. He turned and
went inside the house, towel draped over his shoulders.

"Catch," shouted Mike. He threw the football to Jim as he
followed Al through the front door.

Jim tucked the football under his chair and continued to
watch the rain. Again he felt separated from his brothers,
seeing them as others might: identical people, clones of the
same man, undifferentiated and interchangeable. Some had
thought that they and their sister Kira would be identical in
interests and achievements, as well as exactly like their
father, Paul Swenson. But Paul, who had raised them and
lived with them until his death in a monorail accident two
years before, had different ideas. He had encouraged the
five clones to develop individual interests. Al had become a
student of astrophysics, Mike was studying physics, Ed was
interested in both mathematics and music, and Kira, the
only female clone, was a student of the biological sciences
that had brought them into existence. Jim, however, had
decided to study literature. Although he had been interested
in the sciences and had studied them to some extent, it was
to literature that he responded most deeply. He had often
thought that he was the most emotional of the clones, that he
had inherited somehow, or at least empathized with, a part
of Paul's personality that had not been apparent to most of
them who had known his father.

No, they had not been exactly like Paul. Instead, they were fragments of him. Paul Swenson had made his mark in astrophysics, his achievements culminating in the theoretical groundwork for a star drive that would take humanity beyond the solar system. But he had also studied other sciences, and was an accomplished violinist. In his later life Paul had written several books on the sciences, hoping to communicate what he had learned to others, and had even tried his hand at poetry. He had been honored and respected by the world until, at the very beginning of the century, he had allowed his friend Hidehiko Takamura to make an attempt to produce clones using Paul's genetic material. The scientific community throughout the world had placed a moratorium on cloning during the early 1980s, delaying any application of the procedure to human beings. The moratorium had been part of an automatic twenty-year delay period placed on the application of new scientific innovations. When that time had run out, Takamura had urged Paul Swenson to donate himself for duplication. Then Takamura and other biologists had taken nucleus materials from Paul and introduced them into eggs from which they had removed the nucleus, in order to insure that each potential child should inherit all of its genes from Paul Swenson.

The attempt had succeeded, and the world had been horrified. Legislation had been passed in the United States and Europe outlawing the application of cloning to human beings, and the artificial wombs used to nurture the clones before birth could no longer be used except to aid prematurely born infants. Newsfax sheets had made Paul Swenson out to be an egotist and megalomaniac, although in fact he had been gentle and self-effacing. The clones themselves were the subjects of stories claiming that they had telepathic powers or a communal mind. The stories had been discredited, but some people still believed them.

Jim sighed. His sister Kira, echoing Paul, often said that they all had a responsibility to use their talents as constructively as possible, to show the world that they were, after all, fellow human beings. Al, feeling the pressure of his father's reputation, did little but study. Ed had become shy, retreating from social contact. *And I,* Jim thought, *have done almost nothing except sit around feeling sorry for myself. But don't I have the right to, if I'm like everyone else? Why do I have to do anything noteworthy? Is it up to me to prove something about clones to everyone?*

He had, after all, tried to make Moira understand, and he had failed completely at that. The thought of Moira suddenly saddened him. He had been numb for most of the day and now her absence hit him at last. *I would have been with her now,* he thought, *we would have been running through the rain together.* He felt purposeless, empty, and alone.

A car was coming along the narrow road, a light green Lear model. It stopped in front of the Swenson house, and he saw his sister and a short stocky figure get out. The two raced through the downpour to the porch. Kira was laughing as she shook the water from her hair. The short stocky person turned out to be Hidehiko Takamura.

Jim wanted to disappear, but he sat and nodded to Dr. Takamura.

"What a downpour!" Kira said. "Can I get you something— a beer maybe?"

"Better make it tea," Dr. Takamura replied. "And I think I'll sit out here. I've been inside all day."

Kira looked at Jim. "I'll have some too," he said. She hurried into the house.

Jim looked over at Dr. Takamura as the older man seated himself. The man was still here at the university, still working at the same research center that had produced the clones, and now Kira was studying with him. Jim shuddered. He usually felt uneasy around the original participants in the experiment. He could never be sure whether they regarded him as a subject or were trying to recapture their friendship with Paul.

"How's everything, Jim?" The older man still retained a youthful appearance and was active, in spite of being in his seventies. "I haven't seen you for a while."

"I haven't been around the house much."

"I have seen you from a distance, wandering around the university with a very attractive young woman."

"Oh. Moira," Jim said. He paused, thinking he should say more. "I met her last winter. I was at home here, tuned in to a lit discussion, and we got into a debate. Then after the discussion was over, we stayed on the screen, just talking, so finally I asked her where she lived, and I went over to her dormitory. She's gone home until August," he finished lamely.

Kira returned and sat down next to Dr. Takamura. "Ed'll bring the tea out," she said. Jim looked at her face—his face, only more feminine—high cheekbones, large green eyes. She looked back, eyes questioning him: *Everything all right, Jim?* He tried to smile back at her.

"We were just discussing the young woman I've seen Jim with." Kira appeared startled. She brushed some of her thick brown hair off her face and leaned forward. "You know," Dr. Takamura went on, "she resembles a girl Paul was seeing when he was about your age, when we were both at Chicago. Rhoda something, her name was. She left for Israel a couple of years later. He was very serious about her for a while."

Jim began to feel uneasy. Kira sensed his mood. "It sure is raining," she said. "Must be about three inches by now."

Jim leaned toward Dr. Takamura. "What was she like?" he asked. His hands felt sweaty. Kira was still watching him.

"I didn't really know her that well," the older man said. "She seemed, well, distant somehow. She was always friendly, sometimes very talkative, but she always seemed to be holding something back somehow, never really telling you anything about herself. Paul was always with her. He practically lived at her apartment, and they were thinking of getting one of their own."

The weather seemed to be colder. Kira coughed softly. "Certainly took me back," said Dr. Takamura. "I haven't thought of that whole business in years."

"What happened?" Jim mumbled. "What happened?" he said more clearly.

Dr. Takamura was gazing out at the lawn. "She broke it off. I don't think she ever told him why. Paul was pretty depressed for a while, apathetic about everything, but he pulled together. Jon Aschenbach and I managed to get him through his finals."

Jim shivered. "That was a long time ago," said Dr. Takamura.

Ed came out on the porch carrying a tray with three mugs of tea. Jim took one of the mugs and looked on as his brother exchanged greetings with the older man. Ed was the most austere of the clones; he was clean-shaven and wore his hair cropped close to his skull. He spent most of his time on his mathematical studies or his music, and his only close friends were the clones themselves.

Jim heard their voices but not their words. He saw Paul and Rhoda on the Chicago streets, Paul and Moira. . . . He had thought Moira could not bring herself to accept him because he was a clone. Perhaps it was not that at all, but something else. *That should console me,* he thought.

No.

This was worse.

I'm living Paul's life, he thought. He felt paralyzed. He saw himself as a puppet walking through an ever-repeating cycle. *I'll go through it again,* his mind murmured. *I'll go on feeling the way I do, acting the way I do, and I won't have any choice. It's all happened before and I have no way of changing it.*

Moira was gone. He knew it. Moira was gone from him for good. Rhoda had not come back to Paul. Paul had eventually forgotten Rhoda, and Jim supposed he would forget Moira too. The thought, instead of cheering him, simply sat there in his mind, cold and damp, with no power to move him at all.

The early July weather was hot. The grass was beginning to look scorched, the flowers were wilted. The sun glared down at the earth, only occasionally disappearing behind a cloud and then emerging once again to mock at the stifled world below. Jim sat on his heels removing weeds that threatened the bushes alongside the house. His hair was tied back on his head. He had debated with himself about shaving his beard, and decided against it, knowing he would regret it when winter returned. There was another reason for not shaving it, he knew. The beard was his way of differentiating himself from his brothers.

He put his trowel down, sat back, and looked over at Kira. She was seated under one of the trees reading a book. She held the small microfiche projector to her eyes with one hand, turned a small knob on the projector with the other. Jim still preferred the feel of a book in his hands, enjoyed turning the pages, liked the smell of print and old paper. He had insisted on keeping the books in Paul's library, even though they took up more space than the tiny bits of tape he could have purchased to replace them.

He was like Paul in his attachment to old things. Paul had remained in his old slightly run-down house in the area surrounding the university while other researchers and professors had moved to living units inside one of the new pyramidal structures only a few minutes away from the campus by train. Paul had remained on earth while many of his colleagues in astrophysics had gone to the moon, and he had decided he was too old to go. He had raised the clones in the peaceful, almost timeless atmosphere of the university, feeling that this would best prepare them for the complex, almost chaotic world outside. He had wanted them to have a quieter place where they could discover themselves and gain intellectual tools. The universities, so disorganized during Paul's youth, were once again oases of liberal education. Those who had wished for activism had set up their own colleges in the disorderly cities of the continent; and specialists in many fields had their own research centers on ocean floors, in wilderness areas, and on the surface of the moon and Mars. The university had been, in a sense, a retreat for the clones, and Jim wondered if they might have become too easily adjusted to it and afraid to look beyond.

"Why don't you go inside?" he said to Kira. "It's a lot cooler there."

"It's too cool," she replied. "I don't think the regulator's

working. I shiver all the time and I had to put blankets on
my bed last night."

"I guess I better check it one of these days." He wiped
sweat off his forehead with the back of his arm. He
continued to watch Kira as she resumed reading. She had
pinned her hair up on her head and wore a sleeveless
blue-green tunic that barely reached the tops of her thighs.
To Jim she suggested a woodland sprite who at any moment
might disappear among the trees.

In spite of the heat and some painful blisters on his hands,
Jim felt content, more at peace than he had been in a long
time. He and Kira had been busy since the day Moira had
gone home, making repairs on the house, painting the
kitchen, putting some new shingles on the roof. He had
buried himself in physical work, tiring himself so he could
sleep soundly, hoping to keep the thought of Moira at a
distance. Kira, too, had time on her hands. Dr. Takamura
had gone to Kenya to aid in training scientists there who
wished to clone needed animals for wildlife preserves. He
and Kira had worked together, laughing and joking most of
the time, exhausting themselves. One day Jim had realized
that his sorrow had receded a little, only returning in force
during the night, just before fatigue pushed him into deep
sleep.

Yesterday had been different. They had been sitting with
Ed on the front porch, talking about one of Jim's poems,
listening to Ed play his violin, discussing some of the work
Kira had done with Takamura. They talked for a long time,
their minds drawing together, communicating ideas and
feelings with perfect understanding. Then Al and Mike had
joined them and they sat there until very late, finally giving
in reluctantly to sleepiness, and Jim realized as he lay in his
bed that he had not thought of Moira all day.

"Hey," he said to Kira, "how about driving up to the lake
for a swim? It's too hot to do anything else."

Kira put down her projector. "I'd love to," she said, "but
you know there'll be a mob there. I went up with Jonis last
month, you could hardly find a place to put a towel down,
so we went over to the nude beach and it was worse there.

And there were picnickers all over the woods, and empty containers just thrown all around." Kira sighed and pulled up her legs, wrapping her arms around them. "They think the containers'll just disappear, they don't think it takes months for them to dissolve completely. Jonis said she heard that guys go up and take pot shots at the eagles. They don't care—after all, we can always clone more. It makes me so damned mad. I wish they'd kept it closed after reclamation."

We can always clone more. He looked over at Kira and suddenly felt sorry for the cloned eagles. "We could drive to the park. It's always pretty empty," he said. "It'll be cooler there than here, and we could take some supper for later."

"Great," she said. "At least we'll get away from the house for a while." She stood up, brushed some grass from her tunic, picked up her projector by the handle, and walked toward the house, tanned arms swinging loosely at her sides.

Jim watched her until she disappeared around the corner of the house. She had inherited Paul's gentleness and concern for others. When one of the clones was depressed or worried about something, it was always Kira who was willing to listen or offer moral support. Her creation had been the result of curiosity about how Paul's qualities might manifest themselves in a female. As it happened, she was essentially no different from the brothers, and the concern she expressed for them was probably the product of her studies. She spent as much of her time in seminars discussing ethical problems raised by the biological sciences as in the laboratory. Perhaps she was more mature than he or the others, and there were often times when he thought she was more like Paul than any of them.

He picked up his trowel and followed her inside.

The night air was still warm, but pleasantly so. They had jogged around the perimeter of the park until the heat had subdued them. Then they had climbed up the hill to the stone wall overlooking the automated highway. They sat on the wall, legs dangling over the side, as they drank beer and finished the remnants of supper.

It had been a pleasant afternoon, but Jim had grown more silent as the sun set. He sat quietly, ignored the highway below, and watched the rising moon. Al had often spoken of going to the moon, joining the people there who were carrying on Paul Swenson's work. Jim tried to concentrate on the lunar disk, tried to ignore the tendrils of thought brushing at the edges of his consciousness. A warm breeze stirred the trees behind him.

He sat with Moira on the wall, held her hand lightly. He gestured toward the moon as he told her of his father's hopes and tried to communicate the reasons behind Paul's dreams. He looked at Moira as she sat listening quietly, seemingly interested, then heard her soft sigh of impatience.

He looked at Kira. She, too, was watching the moon. He wondered what Moira was doing now. He had managed to keep from calling her since she had left, afraid that she would misinterpret his motives. He should not have come to the park. It had only deepened his pain, bringing it to the surface once again. Kira turned slightly and her eyes met his.

"I never," he said, "really told you much about Moira, did I? Not even that time . . ." He looked away in embarrassment. *He was standing on the wall, ready to hurl himself toward the brightly lit highway. Kira clung to his arm, silvery tears glistened on her face. "Jump," she shouted. "Jump, but you'll have to take me with you."* "Very melodramatic performance," he mumbled, and felt her hand on his arm.

"Don't degrade your pain, Jim," she said softly.

"She didn't just go home for the summer, you know. I don't think she wants to see me when she returns."

"I know," said Kira. "I could tell. You don't have to talk about it, Jim."

"I don't know what's wrong with me," he went on. "It's funny I should care so much about Moira when, if I were honest about it, I'd have to admit I never really knew her. I know she didn't understand me. She never really tried to, she just withdrew." He looked at Kira. "That sounds so cold," he said.

"Don't dwell on it," said Kira softly. "You can't analyze a thing like that, and you'll just feel worse if you try." She swung her legs over the wall and stood up. "Want to take a walk? My legs feel a little stiff."

"Sure." He picked up the small picnic basket and followed her.

They walked along the narrow path that wound through the woods. The path was lighted by the moon. The trees on either side of them were a dark and impenetrable forest. There was a smell of pine and wildflowers. Above him he could hear the movement of a small creature along the limbs of a tree. An owl hooted and was answered by crickets.

Moira stopped, leaned against one of the trees, and smiled at him. He moved to her side, put his arms around her slender waist, and she rested her head contentedly on his shoulder.

Jim halted to rest against a tree. His stomach was a closed fist inside him, his face was hot and his mouth dry. He struggled to restrain a moan. The picnic basket slipped from his fingers and hit the ground with a muffled thud. The handles clattered loudly against the sides of the basket.

"Jim." Kira stood in front of him, clutching his shoulders. "Jim." She released his shoulders and embraced him, cradling his head with one hand. "I know," she said softly.

He was a child again, curled on Paul's lap. "I know," Paul whispered, stroking his hair. "Let it out, Jimmy. Don't ever be ashamed to cry." He squeezed his eyelids together, but the tears would not come. She brushed his hair from his forehead.

She seemed to understand his pain almost instinctively. He rested against her and felt some of the loneliness subside. "I guess," he said finally, "this place must have brought it all back." The tightness of his stomach began to ease.

He stood up straight, arms still around her, and looked into her green eyes, level with his own. She was a dryad, a part of the forest in her tunic and sandaled feet, and it seemed that she might suddenly release him and vanish. He held her more tightly.

He felt his penis stiffen. Startled, he let go of Kira and stood awkwardly in front of her, arms dangling at his sides. She did not move away but continued to stand with her arms around his shoulders. Her face was pale in the moonlight. She tilted her head to one side. *Don't move away,* her eyes seemed to say. *Don't retreat.* She moved closer to him and kissed his lips gently.

The park had grown silent. He was paralyzed, rooted to the ground as surely as the tree against his back. He strained to hear the sounds of the forest, but there was only a thundering in his ears.

She released him and they faced each other, silent and still. He tried to raise his arms. They trembled slightly as he reached out to her.

She unfastened the sash around her waist and let it flutter to the ground. She grasped her tunic with both hands and pulled it over her head. Then she slipped off her pants, balancing first on one leg, then the other. She moved slowly and as precisely as a dancer. She stood in front of him, and at last she met his eyes again.

He saw apprehension and fear on her face, as well as love and concern. He moved toward her, taking one step, then a second one—and he was in her arms, holding her tightly. He was afraid to speak. Kira, too, was trembling. He began to stroke her hair.

He loosened his shorts with one hand and dropped them on top of Kira's rumpled tunic. He ran his hands along her smooth back to her buttocks, only slightly wider and rounder than his own. She was no longer trembling.

They knelt, then lay on the ground together. He reached out, held her breasts gently as she watched him. Her face looked like Ed's in the moonlight, ascetic and austere. Then she suddenly smiled, reminding him of Mike in one of his playful moods. She touched his penis, running her thumb lightly over its tip, then grasped him firmly.

His fear faded. She thrust her hips up, pulled him to her. He thought of the uncertainty he had always felt with Moira, the lonely climaxes. There was no uncertainty with Kira. She was his female self, reaching for him now with the same urgency and impatience he felt. Her hand held him and guided him inside her.

She drew up her knees and they lay on their sides, facing each other. Still gazing into his own green eyes, he thrust with his hips, ran his hand along her thigh. Her lips parted and he heard a soft sigh. He continued to move and was conscious of her response; she was moaning now, clutching his shoulders tightly. He saw himself as a woman, receiving a man, opening to the hardness that plunged inside her, and knew that she was seeing herself as a man, moving inside the wet and welcoming orifice. They moved together, grinding their hips in perfect rhythm, and he felt the core of his excitement increasing, threatening at any moment to hurl him outside himself for a few timeless seconds.

This has never happened before. He suddenly realized that as he moved inside her, sighing his responses to her moans. *Never before.* He saw generation after generation evolve, become more differentiated, genetic structures changing and mutating. He saw millions of men and women seeking mates, trying to find those who would complete them, make them whole again, yet always separated from them by the differences passed on to them by eons of change. He saw Kira and himself, reflections of each other, able to move along their individual paths and yet meet in perfect communication. She was no longer his sister, but his other self, closer to him than a sister could have been, merging with him so completely and perfectly that they were one being.

He moved with her, breathed with her, sensitive to every movement of her hands on his body. Then he stopped, held his body absolutely still, prepared himself for the final thrust. She was still also, waiting, watching him with wide eyes. Her lips were parted and swollen, the warmth inside her body had grown even more intense.

At last, unable to bear it any longer, he thrust again, and she moved to meet him, gasping quietly at first, then crying out, shattering the night silence. He felt himself spurt inside her, and he trembled, moving with her, suspended in a pocket of timelessness. He was adrift with her in a universe

contained by the skin of their bodies, and he called out as his
pleasure compressed itself in his groin, then erupted throughout his body. He cried out again, could no longer tell which
cries were his and which were Kira's.

Then it was over and he realized with a tinge of sadness
how short a time it had actually been. He withdrew from her
slowly but remained beside her, resting his head in her arms.
He became aware of the sweat that covered their bodies, the
warmth of the night. Now he kept his eyes from meeting
hers.

Kira, as if responding to his fears, held him more closely.
"Don't, Jim," she whispered. "Don't feel ashamed. I love
you. I've known it for a while. How could I help it?" She
was right, of course, the old codes and ancient prohibitions
could not apply to them, had not even allowed for their
existence.

He looked at her face. She lay at his side stroking his hair.
It was Paul's face that watched him, smiling, gently reassuring him with love. He curled up next to her.

The thunderstorm had passed by morning, leaving behind it
cool air and large fluffy clouds. The sun, previously a
malevolent eye peering balefully at the earth, was now a
friendly presence, occasionally hiding behind one of the
white clouds as if ashamed of its former fit of temper. Jim
had carried the light plastic chairs off the porch and placed
them on top of old newsfax sheets and computer print-outs
in the front yard. Aiming his spray can at one, he began to
cover it with a surface of gray paint.

He glanced at Ed and Kira. They had moved two of the
three cars out into the road and were washing them down
with the hose. Their shorts and shirts were plastered against
their bodies. Kira hooted as she aimed the hose at Ed,
drenching him completely. He grabbed the hose from her
and began to spray her with water. Kira danced on her toes,
laughing loudly.

Jim moved to spray the next chair. He had been trying to
accept and understand his new relationship with Kira. He
turned it over in his mind, trying to view it objectively: It

wasn't harming them, it affected no one else, it gave him pleasure. It seemed cold and somehow negative to think of it that way.

"Is it so strange, Jim?" Kira had asked. They were sitting on her bed, legs folded in front of them, elbows on knees, head in hands, perfectly matched. "It would be stranger if we didn't feel this way, weren't drawn to each other."

He continued to spray the chairs. *How do I feel about it?* he asked himself. *I'm able to reach someone else, able to love and communicate without rejection.* He thought of Moira. His love for her had been nervous and feverish, an uneasiness that was always with him occupying his entire mind, refusing to let go. With Kira he was at peace, except for the occasional guilty doubts that nudged him from time to time, then retreated under the onslaught of his rationalizations. With Kira, he could work at his poetry or talk, easily sharing his thoughts and feelings and understanding hers as well.

Kira and Ed were walking toward the house, leaving the hose on the lawn. They seemed to be discussing something. Ed gestured with his right arm as they climbed the steps to the front porch and disappeared into the house. Jim finished spraying the last chair, then glared at the hose. All the clones had inherited an almost obsessive tidiness from Paul, and he was annoyed that Ed and Kira had not rewound the hose. It was not like them.

The chairs would need a little time to dry before he moved them back to the porch. He ambled to the front door, depositing the can on the porch, and went inside.

The house was silent. Al and Mike had gone to the university earlier to do some lab work. Jim wandered through the living room, which was furnished with old overstuffed chairs and sofas. Two learning booths stood in the corner. They resembled large transparent eggs; their screens were blank and their earphones were lying idly on the writing surfaces next to the chairs. Paul had installed two more booths upstairs in the room he had once used as a study. Few people had that many booths in their homes, but Jim knew that few people used the one booth they usually had, preferring to watch the large vidscreens on their walls. Al had left several print-outs on the writing surface of one booth. He was the "pack rat" of the clones and would gather piles of neatly folded printouts until someone, usually Mike, threw them out. He continued through the living room to the kitchen.

The kitchen was empty. Jim was surprised, having assumed Kira and Ed had come in for a sandwich. He left the kitchen, went back through the living room and up the stairs, and decided he would ask them if they wanted help with the hose and if they wanted to have some lunch with him. He walked past Ed's room. The door was open and there was no one inside. He went past Mike's room, then his own, stopped at Kira's door.

It was closed. He knocked, heard the sounds of someone moving in the room. "Kira?" he said. He knocked again, then opened the door.

Kira and Ed were sprawled on the bed. Both were naked. Ed turned and looked at Jim and appeared startled. Kira seemed calm. "Oh, no," said Jim. He clenched his hands into fists. "Oh, no." He felt himself shaking. The twin faces on the bed were watching him.

He wanted to pound his fist into the wall. He turned and fled down the hall to his own room. He stood there, alone, trying to sort out the thoughts that tumbled through his mind. He heard soft footsteps coming down the hall. They stopped at his door. "Jim." He did not move. "Jim." He turned and saw Kira standing in the door, a long red robe draped over her shoulders.

He gestured at the robe. "Your one concession to modesty," he said bitterly. She came into the room and closed the door.

"Why are you so angry, Jim?"

He turned from her and sat on the chair at his desk. "There's no reason to be angry," he muttered. "I found out that we're interchangeable to you too, that's all."

"No, Jim," she said softly, leaning against the door. "That's not what you found out. Do you think for one moment I confuse Ed with you? Forget about yourself for

one minute and think about him. He's just about given up
trying to reach out to anyone, including us. He's so quiet
about his problems, it's easy to pretend he's just shy or not
that interested in people. You know how you felt, how
lonely you were, but at least you kept trying with Moira, and
you could reach me. Ed gave up trying, and about all you've
accomplished today is reinforcing the way he feels. Now
he's sitting in my room feeling guilty."

Jim looked over at Kira. She was looking at the floor,
folding her arms across her chest. "Oh, Jim, I don't know.
Maybe I have my own problems too. Don't I have a right to
solve them, or at least try? Or am I supposed to limit myself
to you, or ignore Ed? Has this business really changed
anything you might have found out through me?" She
sighed. "Maybe it'll be harder for us, Jim. We have to find
our own answers in our own way, and we don't even have
the rough guidelines everybody else has. Some people
would look at us and talk about incest taboos, and others
would probably find it strange if we loved anyone else but
the other clones. The point is, we have to try, and maybe
we'll make mistakes, but . . ."

She turned and opened the door. "I still love you, Jim, just
as much as I did before. Maybe none of us will ever feel the
same way about anyone else. Maybe we really can't, being
the way we are, and that means that Ed needs me too, and
maybe Al and Mike will if they ever look beyond each
other."

She left the room but did not close the door. He sat at the
desk trying to sort out his thoughts. He considered himself
and the other clones, turned over their problems and
relationships in his mind, and wondered what he should do
now.

*He was with Kira, hands on her belly. She looked up at
him as he hovered over her, guided his hand between her
legs. He felt her wetness with his finger, moved forward and
embraced her, embraced himself, and sighed as they merged.*

Jim lifted the suitcase and put it in the back seat of the car.
Al leaned against the open car door. "We'll miss you," he
said.

"I won't be gone long," he replied. He turned to Kira. Her brow was wrinkled with worry. He reached over to her, grasped her shoulders. "Come on, cheer up," he said. "I'll be back in a month or so. I'm not running away. I know what I'm doing, and I know why."

She smiled at him tentatively, and he kissed her lightly on the forehead. Then he climbed into the car, waving his arm at the porch where Ed and Mike sat.

He had explained himself to them as best he could, and he was satisfied that they understood him as well as could be expected. He would drive up to Moira's home first. He would not make demands of her, would not force himself on her. He would not give up if she drew away from him. He would leave and go to a poetry workshop in Minnesota he had heard about, meet people there, be like anyone else.

Kira had come to his room the night before. They lay on his bed, arms and legs entwined, as he told her about his hopes and his plans.

It would be easy to stay with Kira, easy to give up on other people. He would not let himself do it yet, not until he had tried and failed many times.

He started the car and drove away from the house slowly. When he got to the end of the narrow road, he turned his head and saw Kira and Al walking to the front porch. Suddenly he felt doubtful about his actions, wondered if he should leave, asked himself if he really wanted to go.

He continued to drive until the house was out of sight and he was on the road leading to the automated highway. He thought of Kira again, saw her head resting on his shoulder, and wondered if he were making a mistake. *Will I love anyone else as completely?* The image of Kira faded from his mind. She had given him as many questions as answers.

The world out there was just as worthy of his attention as his own personal problems. It was a world very different from the sheltered enclave of the university, a world of neatly organized cities inside pyramids and under domes, and disorganized cities that sprawled across the landscape. It was a world of people who looked beyond the earth to the stars, and people who sought to preserve old customs and ancient ways. It was a world of abundance for many and starvation for some, of green and fertile reclaimed wildernesses and eroded deserts. It was time that he tried to understand his own place in this world.

He drove the car onto the bypass, punched out his destination, and leaned back as the highway control took over, guided his car around the curved bypass, and shot him forward into the stream of cars on the highway.

WHERE LATE THE SWEET BIRDS SANG

Kate Wilhelm

Kate Wilhelm began publishing in 1956, and by now is widely regarded as one of the best of today's writers—outside the genre as well as in it, for her work has never been limited to the strict boundaries of the field, and she has published mysteries, mainstream thrillers, and comic novels as well as science fiction. Wilhelm won a Nebula Award in 1968 for her short story, "The Planners," took a Hugo in 1976 for the novel version of the story that follows, Where Late the Sweet Birds Sang *(perhaps the most famous and acclaimed of all clone novels), added another Nebula to her collection in 1987 with a win for her story "The Girl Who Fell Into the Sky," and won yet another Nebula the following year for her story "Forever Yours, Anna." Her many books include the novels* Margaret and I, Fault Lines, The Clewisten Test, Juniper Time, Welcome, Chaos, Oh, Susannah! , Huysman's Pets, *and* Cambio Bay, *and the collections* The Downstairs Room, Somerset Dreams, The Infinity Box, Listen, Listen, Children of the Wind, *and* And the Angels Sing. *In recent years, she has become well known as a mystery novelist as well with novels such as* The Hamlet Trap, Smart House, Seven Kinds of Death, Sweet, Sweet Poison, Death Qualified, *and* The Best Defense. *Her most recent book is a new mystery novel,* Justice for Some. *Wilhelm and her husband, writer Damon Knight, ran the Milford Writer's Conference for many years, and both are still involved in the operation of the* Clarion *workshop for new young writers. She lives with her family in Eugene, Oregon.*

In the complex and darkly lyrical story that follows, she takes an incisive look at humankind's age-old trait of seeing what they want to see, instead of the unpleasant and uncomfortable truths that are right under their noses.

What David always hated most about the Sumner family dinners was the way everyone talked about him as if he were not there.

"Has he been eating enough meat lately? He looks peaked."

"You spoil him, Carrie. If he won't eat his dinner, don't let him go out and play. You were like that, you know."

"When I was his age, I was husky enough to cut down a tree with a hatchet. He couldn't cut his way out of a fog."

David would imagine himself invisible, floating unseen over their heads as they discussed him. Someone would ask if he had a girl friend yet, and they would *tsk-tsk* whether the answer was yes or no. From his vantage point he would aim a ray gun at Uncle Clarence, whom he especially disliked because he was fat, bald, and very rich. Uncle Clarence dipped his biscuits in his gravy, or in syrup, or more often in a mixture of sorghum and butter that he stirred together on his plate until it looked like baby shit.

"Is he still planning to be a biologist? He should go to med school and join Walt in his practice."

He would point his ray gun at Uncle Clarence and cut a neat plug out of his stomach and carefully ease it out, and Uncle Clarence would ooze from the opening and flow all over them.

"David." He started with alarm, then relaxed again. "David, why don't you go out and see what the other kids are up to?" His father's quiet voice, saying actually, that's enough of that. And they would turn their collective mind to one of the other offspring.

As David grew older, he learned the complex relationships that he had merely accepted as a child. Uncles, aunts, cousins, second cousins, third cousins. The honorary members: brothers and sisters and parents of those who had married into the family. There were the Sumners and Wistons and O'Gradys and Heinemans and the Meyers and Capeks and Rizzos, all part of the same river that flowed through the fertile Virginia valley.

He remembered the holidays especially. The old Sumner house was rambling, with many bedrooms upstairs and an attic that was wall-to-wall mattresses, pallets for the children, with an enormous fan in the west window. Someone was forever checking to make certain that they hadn't all suffocated in the attic. The older children were supposed to keep an eye on the younger ones, but what they did in fact was to frighten them night after night with ghost stories and inhuman sighs and groans. Eventually the noise level would rise until adult intervention was demanded. Uncle Ron would clump up the stairs heavily and there would be a scurrying, with suppressed giggles and muffled screams, until everyone found a bed again, so that by the time he turned on the hall light that illuminated the attic dimly, all the children seemed to be sleeping. He would pause briefly in the doorway, then close the door, turn off the light, and tramp back down the stairs, apparently deaf to the renewed merriment behind him.

Whenever Aunt Claudia came up, it was like an apparition. One minute pillows would be flying, someone would be crying, someone else trying to read with a flashlight, several of the boys playing cards with another flashlight, some of the girls huddled together whispering what had to be delicious secrets, judging by the way they blushed and looked desperate if an adult came upon them suddenly, and then the door would snap open, the light would fall on the disorder, and she would be standing there. Aunt Claudia was very tall and thin, her nose was too big and she was tanned to a permanent old-leather color. She would stand there, immobile and terrible, and the children would creep back into bed without a sound. She would not move until everyone was back where he or she belonged, then she would close the door soundlessly. The silence would drag on and on. The ones nearest the door would hold their breath, trying to hear breathing on the other side. Eventually someone would become brave enough to open the door a crack, and if she was truly gone, the party would resume.

The smells of holidays were fixed in David's memory. All the usual smells: fruitcakes and turkeys, the vinegar that

went in the egg dyes, the greenery, and the thick, creamy
smoke of bayberry candles. But what he remembered most
vividly was the Fourth of July smell of gunpowder that
permeated their hair, their clothes, that lasted on their hands
for days and days. Their hands would be stained purple-
black from berry picking, and the color and smell were one
of the indelible images of his childhood. Mixed in with it
was the smell of sulfur that was dusted on them liberally to
confound the chiggers.

If it hadn't been for Celia, his childhood would have been
perfect. Celia was his cousin, his mother's sister's daughter.
She was one year younger than David and by far the
prettiest of all his cousins. When they were very young they
had promised to marry one day, and when they grew older
and it was made abundantly clear that no cousins might ever
marry in that family, they had become implacable enemies.
He didn't know how they had been told. He was certain that
no one ever put it in words, but they knew. When they could
not avoid each other after that, they fought. She pushed him
out of the hayloft and broke his arm when he was fifteen,
and when he was sixteen they wrestled from the back door
of the Wiston farmhouse to the fence fifty or sixty yards
away. They tore the clothes off each other and he was
bleeding from her fingernails down his back, she from
scraping her shoulder on a rock. Then somehow in their
rolling and squirming frenzy, his cheek came down on her
uncovered chest, and he stopped fighting. He suddenly
became a melting, sobbing, incoherent idiot and she hit him
on the head with a rock and ended the fight.

Up to that point the battle had been in almost total silence,
broken only by gasps for breath and whispered language
that would have shocked their parents. But when she hit him
and he went limp, not unconscious, but dazed, uncaring,
inert, she screamed, abandoning herself to anguish and
terror. The family tumbled from the house as if they had
been shaken out, and their first thought must have been that
he had raped her. His father hustled him to the barn,
presumably for a thrashing. But in the barn, his father, belt
in hand, looked at him with an expression that was furious

and strangely sympathetic. He didn't touch David, and only after he had turned and left did David realize that tears were still running down his face.

In the family there were farmers, a few lawyers, two doctors, insurance brokers and bankers and millers, hardware merchandisers, other shopkeepers. David's father owned a large department store that catered to the upper-middle-class clientele of the valley. The valley was rich. David always supposed that the family, except for a few ne'er-do-wells, was rather wealthy. Of all his relatives his favorite was his father's brother Walt. Dr. Walt, they all called him. He played with the children and taught them grown-up things, like where to hit if you really meant it, where not to hit in a friendly scrap. He seemed to know when to stop treating them as children long before anyone else in the family did. Dr. Walt was the reason David had decided very early to become a scientist.

David was seventeen when he went to Harvard. His birthday was in September and he didn't go home for it. When he did return at Thanksgiving and the clan had gathered, Grandfather Sumner poured the ritual before-dinner martinis and handed one to him. And Uncle Warner said to him, "What do you think we should do about Bobbie?"

He had arrived at that mysterious crossing that is never delineated clearly enough to be seen in advance. He sipped his martini, not liking it particularly, and knew that childhood had ended, and he felt a profound sadness and loneliness.

The Christmas that David was twenty-three seemed out of focus. The scenario was the same, the attic full of children, the food smells, the powdering of snow, none of that had changed, but he was seeing it from a new position and it was not the wonderland it had been, and he knew with regret that the enchantment had vanished and could never be recaptured. When his parents went home he stayed on at the Wiston farm for a day or two, waiting for Celia. She had missed the Christmas Day celebration, getting ready for her

coming trip to Brazil, but she would be there, her mother
had assured Grandmother Wiston, and David was waiting
for her, not happily, not with an expectation of reward, but
with a fury that grew and caused him to stalk the old house
like a boy being punished for another's sin.

When she came home and he saw her standing with her
mother and her grandmother, his anger melted. It was like
seeing Celia in a time distortion, as she was and would be
or had been. Her pale hair would not change much, but her
bones would become more prominent, and the almost-
emptiness of her face would have written on it a message of
concern, of love, of giving, of being decisively herself, of a
strength unsuspected in her frail body. Grandmother Wiston
was a beautiful old lady, he thought in wonder, amazed that
he never had seen her beauty before. Celia's mother was
more beautiful than the girl. And he saw the resemblance to
his own mother in the trio. Wordlessly, defeated, he turned
and went to the rear of the house and put on one of his
grandfather's heavy jackets because he didn't want to see
her at all now, and his own outdoor clothing was in the front
hall closet too near where she was still standing.

He walked a long time in the frosty afternoon, seeing very
little, and shaking himself from time to time when he
realized that the cold was entering his shoes or making his
ears numb. And he found that he was climbing the slope of
the antique forest where his grandfather had taken him once,
a long time ago. He climbed and became warmer, and at
dusk he was under the branches of the tiers of trees that had
been there since the beginning of time. They or others that
were just like them. Forever waiting for the day when they
would reclaim the land and cover the continent once more.
Here were the relicts his grandfather had brought him to see.
Here was a silverbell grown to the stature of a large tree,
while down the slopes, in the lower reaches, it remained
always a shrub. Here the white basswood grew alongside
the hemlock and the bitternut hickory, and the beeches and
sweet buckeyes locked arms.

"David!" He stopped and listened, certain he had imagined it, but the call came again. "David, are you up here?"

He turned then and saw Celia among the massive tree trunks. Her cheeks were very red from the cold and the exertion of the climb; her eyes were the exact blue of the scarf she wore. She stopped six feet from him and started to speak again, but didn't. Instead she drew off a glove and touched the smooth trunk of a beech. "Grandfather Wiston brought me up here, too, when I was twelve. It was very important to him that we understand this place."

David nodded.

"Why did you leave like that? They all think we're going to fight again."

"We might," he said.

She smiled. "I don't think so."

"We should start down. It'll be dark in a few minutes." But he didn't move.

"David, try to make Mother see, will you? You understand that I have to go, that I have to do something, don't you? She thinks you're so clever. She'd listen to you."

He laughed. "They think I'm clever like a puppy dog."

Celia shook her head. "You're the one they'd listen to. They treat me like a child and always will."

David shook his head, smiling. "Why are you going, Celia? What are you trying to prove?"

"Damn it, David! If you don't understand, who will?" She took a deep breath. "People are starving in South America. Not just a few Indians, but millions of people. And practically no one has done any real research in tropical farming methods. It's all lateritic soil, and no one down there understands it. Well, we trained in tropical farming and we're going to start classes down there, in the field. It's what I trained for. This project will get me a doctorate."

The Wistons were farmers, had always been farmers. "Custodians of the soil," Grandfather Wiston had said once, "not its owners, just custodians." Celia reached down and moved aside some matted leaves and muck on the ground, and straightened with her hand full of black dirt. "The famines are spreading. They need so much. And I have so much to give! Can't you understand that?" she cried. She closed her hand hard, compacting the soil into a ball that crumbled again when she opened her fist. She let the soil fall from her hand and carefully pushed the protective covering of leaves back over the bared spot.

"You followed me to tell me good-bye, didn't you?" David said suddenly, and his voice was harsh. "It's really good-bye this time, isn't it?" He watched her and slowly she nodded. "There's someone in your group?"

"I'm not sure, David. Maybe." She bowed her head and started to pull her glove on again. "I thought I was sure. But when I saw you in the hall, saw the look on your face when I came in . . . I realized that I just don't know."

"Celia, you listen to me! There aren't any hereditary defects that would surface! Damn it, you know that! If there were, we simply wouldn't have children, but there's no reason. You know that, don't you?"

She nodded. "I know."

"Come with me, Celia. We don't have to get married right away, let them get used to the idea first. They will. They always do. We have a resilient family, you and me. Celia, I love you."

She turned her head and he saw that she was weeping; she wiped her cheeks with her glove, then with her bare hand, leaving dirt streaks. David pulled her to him, held her and kissed her tears, her cheeks, her lips.

She finally drew away and started back down the slope, with David following. "I can't decide anything right now. It isn't fair. I should have stayed at the house. I shouldn't have followed you up here. David, I'm committed to going in two days. I can't just say I've changed my mind. It's important to me. To the people down there. I can't just decide not to go."

He caught her arm and held her, kept her from moving ahead again. "Just tell me you love me. Say it, just once."

"I love you," she said very slowly.

"How long will you be gone?"

"Three years, I signed a contract."

He stared at her. "Change it! Make it one year. I'll be out of grad school then. You can teach here. Let their bright young students come to you."

"We have to get back, or they'll send a search party for us," she said. "I'll try to change it," she whispered then. "If I can." Two days later she left.

David spent New Year's Eve at the Sumner farm with his parents and a horde of aunts and uncles and cousins. On New Year's Day, Grandfather Sumner made an announcement. "We're building a hospital up at Bear Creek, this side of the mill."

David blinked. That was a mile from the farm, miles from anything else. "A hospital?" He looked at his uncle Walt, who nodded.

Clarence was studying his eggnog with a sour expression, and David's father, the third brother, was watching the smoke curl from his pipe.

"Why up here?" David asked finally.

"It's going to be a research hospital," Walt said. "Genetic diseases, hereditary defects, that sort of thing. Two hundred beds."

David shook his head in disbelief. "You have any idea how much something like that would cost? Who's financing it?"

His grandfather laughed nastily. "Senator Burke has graciously arranged to get federal funds," he said. His voice became more caustic. "And I cajoled a few members of the family to put a little in the kitty." David glanced at Clarence, who looked pained. "I'm giving the land," Grandfather Sumner went on. "So here and there we got support."

"But why would Burke go for it? You've never voted for him in a single campaign in his life."

"Told him we'd dig out a lot of stuff we've been sitting on, support his opposition. If he was a baboon, we'd support him, and there's a lot of family these days, David. A heap of family."

"Well, hats off," David said, still not fully believing it. "You giving up your practice to go into research?" he asked Walt. His uncle nodded. David drained his cup of eggnog.

"David," Walt said, "we want to hire you."

He looked up quickly. "Why? I'm not into medical research."

"I know what your specialty is," Walt said quietly. "We want you for a consultant, and later on to head a department of research."

"But I haven't even finished my thesis yet," David said, and he felt as if he had stumbled into a pot party.

"You'll do another year of donkey work for Selnick and eventually you'll write the thesis, a bit here, a dab there. You could write it in a month, couldn't you, if you had time?" David nodded reluctantly. "I know," Walt said, smiling faintly. "You think you're being asked to give up a lifetime career for a pipe dream."

Grandfather Sumner let out his breath explosively. He was a large man with a massive chest and great bulging biceps. His hands were big enough to grip a basketball in each. But it was his head that you remembered. It was the head of a giant, and although he had farmed for many years, and later overseen the others who did it for him, he had found time to read more extensively than anyone else David knew. And he remembered what he read. His library was better than most public libraries. Now he leaned forward and said, "You listen to me, David. You listen hard. I'm telling you what the goddamn government doesn't dare admit yet. We're on the first downslope of a slide that is going to plummet the world to a depth that they never dreamed of. I know the signs, David. Pollution's catching up to us faster than anyone knows. There's more radiation in the atmosphere than there's been since Hiroshima—French tests, Chinese tests. Leaks. God knows where it's all coming from. We reached zero population growth a couple of years ago, but, David, we were trying, and other nations are getting there too, and they aren't trying. There's famine in a quarter of the world right now. The famines are here, and they're getting worse. There are more diseases than there's ever been since the good Lord sent the plagues to Egypt. And they're plagues that we don't know anything about. There's more drought and more flooding than there's ever been. England's changing into a desert, the bogs and moors are drying up. Entire species of fish are gone, just damn gone, and in only a year or two. The anchovies are gone.

The codfish industry is gone. The cods they are catching are diseased, unfit to use. There's no fishing off the west coast of the Americas, North or South. Every damn protein crop on earth has some sort of blight that gets worse and worse. We're restricting our exports of food now, and next year we'll stop them for good. We're having shortages no one ever dreamed of. Tin, copper, aluminum, paper. Chlorine, by God! And what do you think will happen in the world when we suddenly can't even purify our drinking water?"

His face was darkening as he spoke, and he was getting angrier and angrier, directing his unanswerable questions to David, who stared at him with nothing at all to say.

"And they don't know what to do about any of it," his grandfather went on. "No more than the dinosaurs knew how to stop their own extinction. We've changed the photo-chemical reactions of our own atmosphere, and we can't adapt to the new radiations fast enough to survive! There've been hints here and there that this is a major concern, but who listens? The damn fools will lay each and every catastrophe at the foot of a local condition and turn their backs on the fact that this is global, until it's too late to do anything."

"But, if it's what you think, what could they do?" David asked, looking at Dr. Walt for support and finding none.

"Turn off the factories, ground the airplanes, stop the mining, junk the cars. But they won't, and even if they did, it would still be a catastrophe. It's going to break wide open. Within the next couple of years, David, it's going to break. There's going to be the biggest bust since man began scratching marks on rocks, that's what! And we're getting ready for it! I'm getting ready for it! We've got the land and we've got the men to farm it, and we'll get our hospital and we'll do research on ways to keep our animals and our people alive, and when the world goes into a tailspin we'll be alive and when it starves we'll be eating."

Suddenly he stopped and studied David with his eyes narrowed. "I said you'd leave here convinced that we've all gone mad. But you'll be back, David, my boy. You'll be back before the dogwoods bloom, because you'll see the signs."

David returned to school and his thesis and the donkey work Selnick gave him to do. Celia didn't write, and he had no address for her. In response to his questions his mother admitted that no one had heard from her. In February, in retaliation for the food embargo, Japan imposed trade restrictions that made further United States trade with her impossible. Japan and China signed a mutual aid treaty. In March, Japan seized the Philippines and their fields of rice, and China resumed its long-dormant trusteeship over the Indochina peninsula, with the rice paddies of Cambodia and Vietnam.

Cholera struck in Rome, Los Angeles, Galveston, and Savannah. Saudi Arabia, Kuwait, Jordan, and other Arab-bloc nations issued an ultimatum: the United States must guarantee a yearly ration of wheat to the Arab states and discontinue all aid to Israel, or there would be no oil for the United States or Europe. They refused to believe the United States could not meet their demands. Worldwide travel restrictions were imposed immediately, and the United States government, by presidential decree, formed a new department with Cabinet status: the Bureau of Information.

The redbuds were hazy blurs of pink against the clear, May-softened sky when David returned home. He stopped by his house only long enough to change his clothes and get rid of his boxes of college mementos before he drove out to the Sumner farm, where Walt was staying while he oversaw the construction of his hospital.

Walt had an office downstairs. It was a clutter of books, notebooks, blueprints, correspondence. He greeted David as if he hadn't been away at all. "Look," he said, "this research of Semple and Ferrer, what do you know about it? The first generation of cloned mice showed no deviation, no variation in viability or potency, nor did the second or third, but with the fourth the viability decreased sharply. And there was a steady, and irreversible, slide to extinction. Why?"

David sat down hard and stared at Walt. "How did you get that?"

"Vlasic," Walt said. "We went to med school together. We've corresponded all these years. I asked him."

"You know his work?"

"Yes. His rhesus monkeys show the same decline during the fourth generation, and on to extinction."

"It isn't just like that," David said. "He had to discontinue his work last year—no funds. So we don't know the life expectancies of the later strains. But the decline starts in the third clone generation, a decline of potency. He was breeding each clone generation sexually, testing the offspring for normalcy. The third clone generation had only twenty-four percent potency. The sexually reproduced offspring started with that same percentage, and, in fact, potency dropped until the fifth generation of sexually reproduced offspring, and then it started to climb back up and presumably would have reached normalcy again."

Walt was watching him closely, nodding now and then. David went on. "That was the clone-three strain. With the clone-four strain there was a drastic change. Some abnormalities were present, and life expectancy was down seventeen percent. The abnormals were all sterile. Potency was generally down to forty-eight percent. It was downhill all the way with each sexually reproduced generation. By the fifth generation no offspring survived longer than an hour or two. So much for clone-four strain. Cloning the fours was worse. Clone-five strain had gross abnormalities, and they were all sterile. Life expectancy figures were not completed. There was no clone-six strain. None survived."

"A dead end," Walt said. He indicated a stack of magazines and extracts. "I had hoped that they were out of date, that there were newer methods, or perhaps an error had been found in their figures. It's the third generation that is the turning point, then?"

David shrugged. "My information could be out of date. I know Vlasic stopped last year, but Semple and Ferrer are still at it, or were last month. They may have something I don't know about. You're thinking of livestock?"

"Of course. You know the rumors? They're just not

breeding well, no figures available, but hell, we have our own livestock. They're down by half."

"Can you get materials for the hospital?" David asked.

"For now. We're rushing it like there's no tomorrow, naturally. And we're not worrying about money right now. We'll have things that we won't know what to do with, but I thought it would be better to order everything I can think of than to find out next year that what we really need isn't available."

David went to the window and looked out at the farm. The green was well established by now, spring would give way to summer without a pause and the corn would be shiny, silky green in the fields. Just like always. "Let me have a look at your lab equipment orders, and the stuff that's been delivered already," he said. "Then let's see if we can wrangle me travel clearance, out to the coast. I'll talk to Semple; I've met him a few times. If anyone's doing anything, it's that team."

"What is Selnick working on?"

"Nothing. He lost his grant, his students were sent packing." David grinned at his uncle suddenly. "Look, up on the hill, you can see a dogwood ready to burst open, some of the blooms are already showing."

David was bone-tired, every muscle seemed to ache at once, and his head was throbbing. For nine days he had been on the go, to the coast, to Harvard, to Washington, and now he wanted nothing more than to sleep, even if the world ground to a stop while he was unaware. He had taken a train from Washington to Richmond, and there, unable to rent a car, or buy gasoline if a car had been available, he had stolen a bicycle and pedaled the rest of the way. He had never realized his legs could ache so much.

"You're sure that bunch in Washington won't be able to get a hearing?" Grandfather Sumner asked.

"No one wants to hear the Jeremiahs," David said. Selnick had been one of the group, and he had talked to David briefly. His committee was trying to force the government to admit the seriousness of the coming catastrophe and take strict measures to alleviate it. The government chose instead to paint glowing pictures of the coming upturn that would be apparent by fall. During the next six months, Selnick had warned, those with sense and money would buy everything they could to see them through, because after that period of grace there would be nothing to buy.

"Selnick says we should offer to buy his equipment. The school will jump at the chance to unload it right now. Cheap." David laughed. "Cheap. A quarter of a million, possibly."

"Make the offer," Grandfather Sumner said.

David stood up shakily and went off to bed.

People still went to work. The factories were still producing, not as much, and none of the nonessentials, but they were converting to coal as fast as possible. David thought about the darkened cities, and the fleets of trucks rusting, and the corn and wheat rotting in the fields. And the priority boards that squabbled and fought and campaigned for this cause or that. It was a long time before his twitching muscles relaxed enough for him to lie quietly, and a longer time before he could relax his mind enough to sleep.

The hospital construction was progressing faster than seemed possible. There were two shifts at work; again a case of damn-the-cost. Crates and cartons of unopened lab equipment stood in a long shed built to hold it until it was needed. David went to work in a makeshift laboratory trying to replicate Ferrer's and Semple's tests. And in early July, Harry Vlasic arrived at the farm. He was short, fat, near-sighted, and short-tempered. David regarded him with the same awe and respect that an undergraduate physics student would have felt toward Einstein.

"All right," Vlasic said. "The corn crop has failed, as predicted. Monoculture! Bah! They'll save sixty percent of the wheat, no more. This winter, hah, just wait until winter! Now where is the cave?"

They took him to the cave entrance a hundred yards from the hospital. Inside the cave they used lanterns. The cave was over a mile long in the main section and there were several branches. Deep in one of them flowed a river that was black and silent. Spring water, good water. Vlasic nodded again and again. When they finished the cave tour he was still nodding. "It's good," he said. "It'll work. The laboratories go in there, underground passage from the hospital, safe from contamination. Good."

They worked sixteen hours a day that summer and into the fall. In October the first wave of flu swept the country, worse than the outbreak in 1917 and 1918. In November a new illness swept the country, and here and there it was whispered that it was plague, but the government Bureau of Information said it was flu. Grandfather Sumner died in November. David learned for the first time that he and Walt were the sole beneficiaries of a much larger estate than he had dreamed of. And the estate was in cash. Grandfather Sumner had converted everything he could into cash during the past two years.

In December the family began to arrive, leaving the towns and villages and cities scattered throughout the valley to take up residence in the hospital and staff buildings. Rationing, black markets, inflation, and looting had turned the cities into battlegrounds. And the government had frozen the assets of every business—nothing could be bought or sold without approval. The family brought their stocks with them. Jeremy Streit brought his hardware merchandise in four truckloads. Eddie Beauchamp brought his dental equipment. David's father brought all that he could from his department store. With the failure of radio and television communication, there was no way for the government to cope with the rising panic. Martial law was declared on December 28, six months too late.

There was no child left under eight years of age when the spring rains came, and the original three hundred nineteen people who had come to the upper valley had dwindled to two hundred one. In the cities the toll had been much higher.

David studied the fetal pig he was about to dissect. It was wrinkled and desiccated, its bones too soft, its lymph glands lumpy, hard. Why? Why did the fourth generation decline?

Harry Vlasic came to watch briefly, then walked away, his head bowed in thought. Not even he could come up with any answers, David thought, almost with satisfaction.

That night David, Walt, and Vlasic met and went over it all again. They had enough livestock to feed the two hundred people for a long time, through cloning and breeding of the fertile animals. They could clone up to four hundred animals at a time. Chickens, swine, cattle. If the livestock all became sterile, as seemed likely, then the food supply was limited.

Watching the two older men, David knew they were purposely skirting the other question. If the people also became sterile, how long would they need a continuing supply of food? He said, "We should isolate some of the sterile mice, clone them, and test for the reemergence of fertility with each new generation of clones."

Vlasic frowned and shook his head. "If we had a dozen undergraduate students, perhaps," he said.

"We have to know," David said, feeling hot suddenly. "You're both acting like this is just a five-year emergency plan to tide us over a few bad years. What if it isn't that at all? Whatever is causing the sterility is affecting all the animals. We have to know."

Walt glanced at David and said, "We don't have the time or the facilities to do any research like that."

"That's a lie," David said. "We can generate all the electricity we can use, more than enough power. We have equipment we haven't even unloaded yet . . ."

"Because there's no one who can use it yet," Walt said patiently.

"I can. I'll do it in my free time."

"What free time?"

"I'll find it."

In June, David had his preliminary answers. "The A-four strain," he said, "has twenty-five percent fertility." Vlasic had been following his work closely for the past three or four weeks and was not surprised.

Walt stared at him in disbelief. "Are you sure?" he whispered after a moment.

"The fourth generation of cloned sterile mice showed the same degeneracy that all clones show by then," David said. "But they also had a twenty-five percent fertility factor. The offspring have shorter lives, but more fertile individuals. This trend continues to the sixth generation, where fertility is up to ninety-four percent, and life expectancy starts to climb up again, and then it's on its way to normalcy." He had it all on the charts that Walt now studied. A, A,^{1}, A^2, A^3, A^4, and then the offspring by sexual reproduction, a, a^1, a^2 . . . There were no clone strains after A^4; none had survived to maturity.

David leaned back and closed his eyes. He thought about bed and a blanket up around his neck and black, black sleep. "Higher organisms must reproduce sexually or die out, and the ability to do so is there. Something remembers and heals itself," he said dreamily.

"You'll be a great man when you publish," Vlasic said softly, his hand on David's shoulder. He then moved to sit next to Walt, to point out some of the details that Walt might miss. "A marvelous piece of work," he said, his eyes glowing as he looked over the pages. "Marvelous." Then he glanced back at David. "Of course, you are aware of the other implications of your work."

David opened his eyes and met Vlasic's gaze. He nodded. Walt, puzzled, looked from one to the other of them. David got up and stretched. "I have to sleep," he said.

But it was a long time before he slept. He had a single room at the hospital, more fortunate than most. The hospital had more than two hundred beds, but few single rooms. The implications, he mused. He had been aware of them from the start, although he had not admitted it even to himself then, and was not ready to discuss it now. Three of the women were pregnant finally, after a year and a half. Margaret was near term, the baby well and kicking at the moment. Five more weeks, he thought. Five more weeks, and perhaps he never would have to discuss the implications of his work.

But Margaret didn't wait five weeks. In two weeks she gave birth to a stillborn child. Zelda had a miscarriage the

following week, and in the next week May lost her child.
That spring the rains kept them from planting anything more
than a truck garden.

Walt began testing the men for fertility. He reported to
David and Vlasic that no man in the valley was fertile.

"So," Vlasic said softly, "we now see the significance of
David's work."

Winter came early in sheets of icy rain that went on day
after day after day. The work in the laboratories increased,
and David found himself blessing his grandfather for his
purchase of Selnick's equipment, which had come with
detailed instructions for making artificial placentas as well
as nearly completed work on computer programs for chemical amniotic fluids. When David had gone to talk to Selnick
about the equipment, Selnick had insisted—madly, David
had thought at the time—that he take everything or nothing.
"You'll see," he had said wildly. "You'll see." The following week he hanged himself, and the equipment was on its
way to the Virginia valley.

They worked and slept in the lab, leaving only for meals.
The winter rains gave way to spring rains, and a new
softness was in the air.

David was hardly aware of the spring until one day his
mother found him in the cafeteria. He hadn't seen her for
weeks, and would have brushed past her with a quick hello
if she hadn't stopped him. She looked strange, childlike; he
turned from her to stare out the window, waiting for her to
release his arm.

"Celia's coming home," she told him. "She's well, she
says."

David felt frozen; he continued to stare out the window,
seeing nothing. "Where is she now?" He listened to the
rustle of cheap paper and when it seemed that his mother
was not going to answer him, he wheeled about. "*Where is
she?*"

"Miami," she said finally, after scanning the two pages.
"It's postmarked Miami, I think. It's over two weeks old.
Dated May twenty-eighth. She never got any of our mail."

David didn't read the letter until his mother had left the cafeteria. *I was in Colombia for a while, eight months, I think. And I got a touch of the bug that nobody wants to name.* The writing was spindly and uncertain. He looked for Walt.

"I have to go get her. She can't walk in on that gang at the Wiston place."

"You know you can't leave now."

"It isn't a question of can or can't. I have to."

Walt studied him for a moment, then shrugged. "How will you get there and back? No gas. You know we don't dare use it for anything but the harvest."

"I know," David said impatiently. "I'll take Mike and the cart. I can stay on the back roads with Mike." He knew that Walt was calculating, as he had done, the time involved, and he felt his face tightening, his hand clenching. Walt simply nodded. "I'll leave as soon as it's light in the morning." Again Walt nodded. "Thanks," David said suddenly. He meant: for not arguing with him, for not pointing out what both already knew; that there was no way of knowing how long he would have to wait for Celia, that she might never make it to the farm.

Three miles from the Wiston farm David unhitched the cart and hid it in thick underbrush. He swept the tracks where he had left the dirt road, then led Mike into the woods. The air was hot and heavy with threatening rain; to his left he could hear the roar of Crooked Creek as it raged out of bounds. The ground was spongy and he walked carefully, not wanting to sink to his knees in unsuspected mud here in the lowlands. The Wiston farm always had been flood-prone; it enriched the soil, Grandfather Wiston had claimed, not willing to damn nature for its periodic rampages. "God didn't mean for this piece of ground to have to bear year after year after year," he said. "Comes a time when the earth needs a rest, same as you and me. We'll let it be this year, give it some clover when the ground dries out." David started to climb, still leading Mike, who whinnied softly at him now and again.

"Just to the knob, boy," David said softly. "Then you can

rest and eat meadow grass until she gets here." The horse whinnied.

Grandfather Wiston had taken him to the knob once, when David was twelve. He remembered the day, hot and still, like this day, he thought, and Grandfather Wiston had been straight and strong. At the knob his grandfather had paused and touched the massive bole of a white oak tree. "This tree saw the Indians in that valley, David, and the first settlers, and my great-grandfather when he came along. It's our friend, David. It knows all the family secrets."

"Is it still your property up here, Grandfather?"

"Up to and including this tree, son. Other side's national forest land, but this tree, it's on our land. Yours too, David. One day you'll come up her and put your hand on this tree and you'll know it's your friend, just like it's been my friend all my life. God help us all if anyone ever lays an ax to it."

They had gone on that day, down the other side of the knob, then up again, farther and steeper this time until once more his grandfather had stopped and, his hand on David's shoulder, paused for a few moments. "This is how this land looked a million years ago, David." Time had shifted suddenly for the boy; a million years ago, or a hundred million, was all the same distant past, and he had imagined the tread of giant reptiles. He had imagined that he smelled the fetid breath of a tyrannosaur. It was cool and misty beneath the tall trees, and under them the saplings grew, their branches spread horizontally as if to catch any stray bit of sunlight that penetrated the high canopy, and where the sun did find a path through, it was golden and soft, the sun of another time. In even deeper shadows grew bushes and shrubs, and at the foot of it all were the mosses and lichens, liverworts and ferns. The arching, heaving roots of the tree were clothed in velvet emerald plants.

David stumbled and caught himself against the giant oak tree that was, somehow, his friend. He pressed his cheek against the rough bark, and stayed there for a few minutes. Then he pushed himself away and looked up through the luxuriant branches; he could see no sky beyond them. When it rained, the tree would protect him from the full force of

the storm, but he needed shelter from the fine drops that
eventually would make their way through the leaves to fall
quietly on the absorbent ground.

He examined the farm through his binoculars. Behind the
house there was a garden being tended by five people,
impossible to tell immediately if they were male or female.
Long-haired, jeans, barefoot, thin. It didn't matter. He noted
that the garden was not producing yet, that the plants were
sparse and frail. He studied the east field, aware that it was
changed, not certain how. Then he realized that it was
planted to corn. Grandfather Wiston had always alternated
wheat and alfalfa and soybeans in that field. The lower
fields were flooded, and the north field was grown up in
grasses and weeds. He studied the people he could see and
swung the glasses slowly over the buildings. He spotted
seventeen of them altogether. No child younger than eight or
nine. No sign of Celia, nor of any recent use of the road; it
was also overgrown with weeds. No doubt the people down
there were just as happy to let the road hide under the
weeds.

He built a leanto against the oak where he could lie down
and observe the farm. He used fir branches to roof his
shelter, and when the storm came half an hour later, he
stayed dry. Rivulets ran among the garden rows below, and
the farmyard turned silver and sparkly from this distance,
although he knew that closer at hand it would simply be
muddy water, inches deep. The ground was too saturated in
the valley to absorb any more water. It would have to run off
into Crooked Creek, which was inching higher and higher
toward the north field and the vulnerable corn there.

By the third day the water had started to invade the
cornfield, and he pitied the people who stood and watched
helplessly. The garden was still being tended, but it would
be a meager harvest. By now he had counted twenty-two
people; he thought that was all of them. During the storm
that lashed the valley that afternoon, he heard Mike whinny.
He crawled from the leanto and stood up. Mike, down the
slope of the knob, wouldn't mind the rain much, and he was
protected from the wind. Still he whinnied again, and then

again. Cautiously, holding his shotgun in one hand, shielding his eyes with the other, David edged around the tree. A figure stumbled up the knob haltingly, stopping with bowed head often, not looking up, probably blinded by the rain. Suddenly David threw the shotgun under the leanto and ran to meet her. "Celia!" he cried. "Celia!"

She stopped and raised her head, and the rain ran over her cheeks, plastered her hair to her forehead. She dropped the shoulder bag that had weighed her down and ran toward him, and only when he caught her and held her tight and hard did he realize that he was weeping, as she was.

Under the leanto he pulled her wet clothes off and rubbed her dry, then wrapped her in one of his shirts. Her lips were blue, her skin seemed almost translucent; it was an unearthly white.

"I knew you'd be here," she said. Her eyes were very large, deep blue, bluer than he remembered, or bluer in contrast to her pale skin. Always before she had been sunburned.

"I knew you'd come here," he said. "When did you eat?"

She shook her head. "I didn't believe it was this bad here. I thought it was propaganda. Everyone thinks it's propaganda."

He lighted the Sterno. She sat wrapped in his plaid shirt and watched him as he opened a can of stew.

"Who are those people down there?"

"Squatters. Grandmother and Grandfather Wiston died last year. That gang showed up. They gave Aunt Hilda and Uncle Eddie a choice, join them or get out. They didn't give Wanda any chance at all. They kept her."

She stared down the valley and nodded slowly. "I didn't know it was this bad. I didn't believe it." Without looking back at him she asked then, "And Mother, Father?"

"They're dead, Celia. Flu, both of them. Last winter."

"I didn't get any letters," she said. "Almost two years. They made us leave Brazil, you know. But there wasn't any transportation home. We went to Colombia. They promised to let us go home in three months. And then they came one night and said we had to get out immediately. There were riots, you know."

He nodded, although she was still staring down at the valley and couldn't see. He wanted to tell her to weep for her parents, to cry out, so that he could take her in his arms and try to comfort her. But she continued to sit motionless and speak in a dead voice.

"They were coming for us, for the Americans. They blame us for letting them starve. They really believe that everything is still all right here. I did too. No one believed any of the reports. And the mobs were coming for us. We left on a small boat, a skiff. Nineteen of us. They shot at us when we got too near Cuba."

David touched her arm, and she jerked and trembled. "Celia, turn around and eat now. Don't talk any longer. Later. You can tell us about it later."

She shook her head. "Never again. I'll never mention any of it again, David. I just wanted you to know there was nothing I could do. I wanted to come home and there wasn't any way."

The storm was over, and the night air was cool. They huddled under a blanket and sat without talking, drinking hot black coffee. When the cup began to tilt in Celia's hand, David took it from her and gently lowered her to the bed he had prepared. "I love you, Celia," he said softly. "I've always loved you."

"I love you, too, David. Always." Her eyes were closed and her lashes were very black on her white cheeks. David leaned over and kissed her forehead, pulled the blanket higher about her, and watched her sleep for a long time before he lay down beside her.

The next morning they left the oak tree and started for the Sumner farm. She rode Mike until they got to the cart; by then she was trembling with exhaustion and her lips were blue again, although the day was already hot. There wasn't room for her to lie down in the cart, so he padded the back of the wooden seat with his bedroll and blanket, and let her sit behind him where she could at least put her head back and rest, when the road wasn't too bumpy. She smiled faintly when he covered her legs with another shirt, the one he had been wearing.

"It isn't cold, you know," she said matter-of-factly. "That goddamn bug does something to the heart, I think. No one would tell us anything about it. My symptoms are all in the circulatory system."

"How bad was it? When did you get it?"

"Eighteen months ago. Just before they made us leave Brazil. It swept Rio. That's where they took us when we got sick. Not many survived it. Hardly any of the later cases. It became more virulent as time went on."

He nodded. "Same here. Something like sixty percent fatal, increasing up to eighty percent by now, I guess."

There was a long silence then, and he thought perhaps she had drifted off to sleep. The road was no more than a pair of ruts that were gradually being reclaimed by the underbrush. Already grass covered it almost totally, except where the rains had washed the dirt away and left only rocks. Mike walked deliberately, and David didn't hurry him.

"David, how many are up at the northern end of the valley?"

"About one hundred and ten now," he said. He thought, two out of three dead, but he didn't say it.

"And the hospital? Was it built?"

"It's there. Walt is running it."

"David, while you're driving, now that you can't watch me for reactions or anything, just tell me about it here. What's been happening, who's alive, who's dead. Everything."

When they stopped for lunch hours later, she said, "David, will you make love to me now, before the rains start again?"

They lay under a stand of yellow poplars and the leaves rustled incessantly with a motion that needed no appreciable wind to start. Under the susurrous trees, their own voices became whispers. She was so thin and so pale, and inside her she was so warm and alive; her body rose to meet his and her breasts seemed to lift, to seek his touch. Her fingers were in his hair, on his back, digging into his flanks,

strong now, then relaxed and trembling, then clenched into
fists that opened spasmodically; and he felt her nails
distantly, aware that his back was being clawed, but
distantly, distantly. And finally there were only the susurrant
leaves.

"I've loved you for more than twenty years, did you
realize that?" he said.

She laughed. "Remember when I broke your arm?"

Later, in the cart again, her voice came from behind him,
softly, sadly. "We're finished, aren't we, David? You, I, all
of us?"

And he thought, Walt be damned, promises be damned,
secrecy be damned. And he told her about the clones
developing under the mountain, in the laboratory deep in the
Great Bear Cave.

Celia started to work in the laboratory a week later. "It's the
only way I'll ever get to see you at all," she said when David
protested. "I promised Walt I would work only four hours a
day to start. Okay?"

David took her through the lab the following morning.
The entrance to the cave was concealed in the furnace room
of the hospital basement. The door was steel, set in the
limestone bedrock. As soon as they stepped through the
doorway, the air was cold and David put a coat about Celia's
shoulders. "We keep them here at all times," he said, taking
a second coat from a wall hanger. "Twice government
inspectors have come here, and it might look suspicious if
we put them on to go down the cellar. They won't be back,"
he said. She nodded.

The passageway was dimly lighted, the floor smooth. It
went four hundred feet to another steel door. This one
opened into the first cave chamber, a large, high-domed
room. It had been left almost as they had found it, with
stalactites and stalagmites on all sides, but now there were
many cots, and picnic tables and benches, and a row of
cooking tables and serving tables. "Our emergency room,
for the 'hot' rains," David said, hurrying her through. There

was another passage, narrower and rougher than the first. At the end of this passage was the animal experiment room.

One wall had been cut through and the computer installed, looking grotesquely out of place against a wall of pale pink travertine. In the center of the room were tanks and vats and pipes, all stainless steel and glass. On either side of these were the tanks that held the animal embryos. Celia stared without moving for several moments, then turned to look at David with startled eyes. "How many tanks do you have?"

"Enough to clone six hundred animals of varying sizes," he said. "We took a lot of them out, put them in the other side, and we're not using all that we have here. We're afraid our supplies of chemicals will run out, and so far we haven't come up with alternatives that we can extract from anything at our disposal here."

Eddie Beauchamp came from the side of the tanks, jotting figures in a ledger. He grinned at David and Celia. "Slumming?" he asked. He checked his figures against a dial and adjusted it a fraction, and continued down the row checking the other dials, stopping now and again to make a minor adjustment.

Celia's eyes questioned David and he shook his head. Eddie didn't know what they were doing in the other lab. They walked past the tanks, row after row of them, all sealed, with only the needles of the meters and gauges to indicate that there was anything inside. They returned to the corridor. David led her through another doorway, another shorter passage, then unlocked a door and took her into the second laboratory.

Walt looked up as they entered, nodded, turned again to his desk. Vlasic didn't even look up. Sarah smiled and hurried past them and sat down before a computer console and began to type. Another woman in the room didn't seem to be aware that anyone had come in. Hilda. Celia's aunt. David glanced at Celia, but she was staring wide-eyed at the tanks, and in this room the tanks were glass-fronted. Each was filled with a pale liquid, a yellow so faint that the color seemed almost illusory. Floating in the liquid were sacs, no larger than small fists. Slender transparent tubes connected the sacs to the top of the tanks; each one was attached to a pipe that led back into a large stainless steel apparatus which seemed to be covered with dials.

Celia walked slowly down the aisle between the tanks, stopped midway and didn't move again for a long time. David took her arm. She was trembling slightly.

"Are you all right?"

She nodded. "I . . . it's a shock, seeing them. I . . . maybe I didn't quite believe it." There was a film of perspiration on her face.

"Better take off the coat now," David said. "We have to keep it pretty warm in here. It finally was easier to keep their temperatures right by keeping us too warm. The price we pay," he said, smiling slightly.

"All the lights? The heat? The computer? You can generate that much electricity?"

He nodded. "That'll be our tour tomorrow, or sometime. Like everything else around here, the generating system has bugs in it. We can store enough power for no longer than six hours, and we just don't let it go out for more than that."

She nodded. "Six hours is a lot. If you stop breathing for six minutes, you're dead." With her hands clasped behind her she stepped closer to the shiny control system at the end of the room. "This isn't the computer. What is it?"

"It's a computer terminal. The computer controls the input of nutrients and oxygen, and the output of toxins." He nodded toward the wall. "The animal room is on the other side. Those tanks are linked to it, too. Separate set of systems, but the same machinery."

She nodded again. They went through the nursery for the animals, and then the nursery for the human babies. There was the dissection room, several small offices where the scientists could withdraw to work, the stock rooms. In every room except the one where the human clones were being grown, people were working. "They never saw a bunsen burner or a test tube before, but they have become scientists and technicians practically overnight," David said. "And thank God for that, or it never would have worked. I don't know what they think we're doing now, but they don't ask questions. They just do their jobs."

In August, Avery Handley got through to a shortwave contact in Richmond who warned of a band of marauders working up the valley. "They're bad," he said. "They took over the Phillpotts' place, ransacked it, and then burned it to the ground."

In September they fought off the first attack. In October they learned the band was grouping for a second attack, this time with thirty to forty men. "We can't keep fighting them off," Walt said. "They must know we have food here. They'll come from all directions this time. They know we're watching for them."

"We should blow up the dam," Clarence said. "Wait until they're in the upper valley and flood them out."

The meeting was being held in the cafeteria, with everyone present. Celia's hand tightened in David's, but she didn't protest. No one protested.

"They'll try to take the mill," Clarence went on. "They'll probably think there's wheat there, or something." A dozen men volunteered to stand guard at the mill. Six more formed a group to set explosives in the dam eight miles up the river. Others would be a scouting party.

David and Celia left the meeting early. He had volunteered for everything and had been turned down. He was not one of the expendable ones. The rains had become "hot" again, and the people were all sleeping in the cave. David and Celia, Walt, Vlasic, the others who worked in the various labs, all slept there on cots. In one of the small offices David held Celia's hand and they whispered before they fell asleep. Their talk was of their childhood.

Long after Celia fell asleep David stared into the blackness, still holding her hand. She had grown even thinner, and earlier that week when he had tried to get her to leave the lab to rest, Walt had said, "Leave her be." She stirred fitfully, and he knelt by the side of her cot and held her; he could feel her heart flutter wildly for a moment. Then she was still again and slowly he released her and sat on the stone floor with his eyes closed. Later he heard Walt moving about, the creaking of his cot in the next office. David was getting stiff, and finally he returned to his own bed.

The next day the people worked to get everything up to high ground. Nothing could be spared, and board by board they carried a barn up the hillside and stacked the pieces. Two days later the signal was given and the dam was destroyed. David and Celia stood in one of the upper hospital rooms and watched together as the wall of water roared down the valley. It was like a jet takeoff; a crowd furious with an umpire's decision; an express train out of control; a roar like nothing he had ever heard, or like everything he had ever heard, recombined to make this noise that shook the building, that vibrated in his bones. A wall of water, fifteen feet high, twenty feet high, raced down the valley, accelerating as it came, smashing, destroying everything in its path.

They walked back through the empty hospital, through the long dimly lighted passage, through the large chamber where the people were trying to find comfortable positions on the cots, on the benches, through the smaller passages and finally into the lab office.

"How many people did we kill?" she asked, stepping out of her jeans. She turned her back to lay her clothes on the foot of her cot. Her buttocks were nearly as flat as an adolescent boy's. When she faced him again, her ribs seemed to be straining against her skin. She looked at him for a moment, and then came to him and held his head tight against her chest as he sat on his cot and she stood naked before him. He could feel her tears as they fell onto his cheek.

There was a hard freeze in November, and with the valley flooded and the road and bridges gone, they knew they were safe from attack, at least until spring. The people had moved out of the cave again, and work in the lab went on at the same numbing pace. The fetuses were developing, growing, moving now with sudden motions of feet and elbows. David was working on substitutes for the chemicals that already were substituting for amniotic fluids. He worked each day until his vision blurred, or his hands refused to obey his

directions, or Walt ordered him out of the lab. Celia was
working longer hours now, still resting in the middle of the
day for several hours, but she returned after that and stayed
almost as late as David did.

David was aware of her, as he always was, even when
preoccupied with his own work. He was aware that she
stood up, that she didn't move for a moment, and when she
said, in a tremulous voice that betrayed disbelief, "David . . .
David . . ." he was already starting to his feet. He caught her
as she crumpled.

Her eyes were open, her look almost quizzical, asking
what he could not answer, expecting no answer. A tremor
passed through her and she closed her eyes, and although
her lids fluttered, she did not open them again.

"David, are you going to pull yourself together? You just
giving up?" Walt didn't wait for a reply. He sat down on the
only chair in the tiny room and leaned forward, cupping his
chin, staring at the floor. "We've got to tell them. Sarah
thinks there'll be trouble. So do I."

David stood at the window, looking at the black landscape, done in grays and blacks and mud colors. It was
raining, but the rain had become clean. The river was a gray
swirling monster that he could glimpse from up here, a dull
reflection of the dull sky.

"They might try to storm the lab," Walt went on. "God
knows what they might decide to do."

"I don't care," David said.

"You're going to care! Because those babies are going to
come busting out of those sacs, and those babies are the only
hope we have, and you know it. Our genes, yours, mine,
Celia's, those genes are the only thing that stand between us
and oblivion." He was white, his lips were pale, his eyes
sunken. There was a tic in his cheek that David never had
seen before.

"Why now?" David asked. "Why change the plan and tell
them now, so far ahead of time?"

"Because it isn't that far ahead of time." Walt rubbed his
eyes hard. "Something's going wrong, David. I don't know

what it is. Something's not working. I think we're going to
have our hands full with prematures."

David couldn't stop the rapid calculations he made. "It's
twenty-six weeks," he said. "We can't handle that many
premature babies."

"I know that." Walt put his head back and closed his eyes.
"We don't have much choice," he said. "We lost one
yesterday. Three today. We have to bring them out and treat
them like preemies."

Slowly David nodded. "Which ones?" he asked, but he
knew. Walt told him the names, and again he nodded. He
had known that they were not his, not Walt's, not Celia's.
"What are you planning?" he asked then, and sat down on
the side of his bed.

"I have to sleep," Walt said. "Then a meeting, posted for
seven. After that we prepare the nursery for a hell of a lot of
preemies. As soon as we're ready, we begin getting them
out. That'll be morning. We need nurses, half a dozen, more
if we can get them. Sarah says Margaret would be good. I
don't know."

David didn't know either. Margaret's four-year-old son
had been one of the first to die of the plague, and she had
lost a baby in stillbirth. He trusted Sarah's judgment,
however. "Think between them they can get enough others,
tell them what to do, see that they do it properly?"

Walt mumbled something, and one hand fell off the chair
arm. He jerked upright.

"Okay, Walt, you get in my bed," David said, almost
resentfully. "I'll go down to the lab, get things rolling there.
I'll come up for you at six-thirty." Walt didn't protest, but
fell onto the bed without bothering to take off his shoes.
David pulled them off. Walt's socks were mostly holes, but
probably they kept his ankles warm. David left them on,
pulled the blanket over him, and went to the lab.

At seven the hospital cafeteria was crowded when Walt
stood up to make his announcement. "There's not a person
in this room hungry tonight. We don't have any more plague
here. The rain is washing away the radioactivity. We have
food stores that will carry us for years even if we can't plant

crops in the spring. We have men capable of doing just about anything we might ever want done." He paused and looked at them again, from left to right, back again, taking his time. He had their absolute attention. "What we don't have," he said, his voice hard and flat now, "is a woman who can conceive a child, or a man who could impregnate her if she was able to bear."

There was a ripple of movement, like a collective sigh, but no one spoke. Walt said, "You know how we are getting our meat. You know the cattle are good, the chickens are good. Tomorrow, ladies and gentlemen, we will have our own babies developed the same way."

There was a moment of utter silence, of stillness, then they broke. Clarence leaped to his feet shouting at Walt. Vernon fought to get to the front of the room, but there were too many people between him and Walt. One of the women pulled on Walt's arm, almost dragging him over, screaming in his face. Walt yanked free and climbed onto a table. "Stop this! I'm going to answer any questions, but not this way."

For the next three hours they questioned, argued, prayed, formed alliances, reformed them as arguments broke out in the smaller groups. At ten Walt took his place on the table again and called out, "We will recess this discussion until tomorrow night at seven. Coffee will be served now, and I understand we have cakes and sandwiches." He jumped from the table and moved to the door too fast to let any of them catch up to him. He and David hurried to the cave entrance and went through, locking the massive door behind them.

"Clarence was ugly," Walt muttered. "Bastard."

David's father, Walt, and Clarence were brothers, David reminded himself, but he couldn't help regarding Clarence as an outsider, a stranger with a fat belly and a lot of money who expected instant obedience from the world.

"They might organize," Walt said after a moment. "We'll have to be ready for them."

David nodded. They had counted on delaying this meeting until they had live babies, human babies that laughed and gurgled and took milk from the bottle. Instead they would have a roomful of not-quite-finished preemies, certainly not human-looking, with no more human appeal than a calf born too soon.

They worked all night preparing the nursery. Sarah had enlisted Margaret, Hilda, Lucy, and half a dozen other women. They were all gowned and masked professionally. One of them dropped a basin and three others screamed in unison. David cursed under his breath. They would be all right when they had the babies, he told himself.

The bloodless births started at five forty-five, and at twelve thirty they had twenty-five infants. Four died in the first hour, another died three hours later; the rest of them thrived. The only baby left in the tanks was the fetus that would be Celia, nine weeks younger than the others.

The first visitor Walt permitted in the nursery was Clarence. After that there was no further talk of destroying the inhuman monstrosities.

There was a celebration party, and a drawing was held to select eleven female names and ten male. In the record book the babies were labeled R-1 strain: Repopulation 1. But in David's mind, as in Walt's, the babies were W-1, D-1, and soon, C-1 . . .

For the next month there was no shortage of nurses, male or female, no shortage of help doing any of the chores that so few had done before. Everyone wanted to become a doctor or a biologist, Walt grumbled, but he was sleeping more now, and the fatigue lines on his face were smoothing out. Often he would nudge David and tow him along, away from the nursery, propel him toward his own room in the hospital and see to it that he remained there for a night's sleep. One night as they walked side by side back to their rooms, Walt said, "Now you understand what I meant when I said this was all that mattered, don't you?"

David understood. Every time he looked down at the tiny, pink new Celia he understood more fully.

David watched the boys from the window in Walt's office. There was Clarence, already looking too pudgy—he'd be fat in another three or four years. And a young Walt, frowning in concentration over a problem that he wouldn't put on paper until he had a solution. Mark, too pretty almost, but determinedly manly, always trying harder than the others to endure, to jump higher, run faster, hit harder. And D-4, himself . . . He turned away and pondered the future of the boys, uncles, fathers, grandfathers, all the same age. He was starting a headache again.

"They're inhuman, aren't they?" he said bitterly to Walt. "They come and go, and we know nothing about them. What do they think? Why do they hang so close to each other? Why won't they talk to us?"

"Remember that old cliché, generation gap? It's here, I reckon." Walt was looking very old. He was tired and seldom tried to hide it any longer. He looked up at David and said, "Maybe they're afraid of us."

David nodded. He had thought of that, too. "I know why Hilda did it," he said. "I didn't at the time, but now I know." Hilda had strangled the small girl who looked more like her every day.

"Me too." Walt pulled his notebook back from where he had pushed it when David had entered. "It's a bit spooky to walk into a crowd that's all you, in various stages of growth. They do cling to their own kind." He started to write then, and David left him.

Spooky, he thought, and veered from the laboratory where he had been heading originally. Let the damn embryos do their thing without him. He knew he didn't want to enter because D-1 or D-2 would be there working. The D-4 strain would be the one, though, to prove or disprove the experiment. If Four didn't make it, then chances were that Five wouldn't either, and then what? A mistake. Woops, wrong, sir. Sorry about that.

Behind the hospital, he climbed the ridge over the cave, and sat down on an outcrop of limestone that felt cool and smooth. The boys were clearing another field. They worked well together, with little conversation and much laughter that seemed to arise spontaneously. A line of girls came into view from nearer the river; they were carrying baskets of berries. Blackberries and gunpowder, he thought suddenly, and he remembered the ancient celebration of the Fourth of July, with blackberry stains and fireworks, sulfur for the chiggers. And birds. Thrushes, meadowlarks, warblers, purple martins. Three Celias came into view, swinging easily with the weight of the baskets, a stairway succession of Celias. He shouldn't do that, he reminded himself harshly. They weren't Celias, none of them had that name. They were Mary and Ann and something else. He couldn't remember for a moment the third one's name, and he knew it didn't matter. The one in the middle might have pushed him from the loft just yesterday; the one on the left might have been the one who rolled in savage combat with him in the mud.

Once, three years ago, he had had a fantasy in which Celia-3 had come to him shyly and asked that he take her. And in the fantasy he had taken her; in his dreams for weeks to come, he had taken her, over and over and over again. And he had awakened weeping for his own Celia. Unable to endure it any longer, he had sought out C-3 and asked her haltingly if she would come to his room with him, and she had drawn back quickly, involuntarily, with fear written too clearly on her smooth face for her to pretend it was not there.

"David, forgive me. I was startled . . ."

They were promiscuous, indeed it was practically required of them to be free in their loving. No one could anticipate how many of them eventually would be fertile, what the percentage of boys to girls would be. Walt was able to test the males, but since the tests for female fertility required rabbits, which they did not have, he said the best test for fertility was pregnancy. The children lived together, and promiscuity was the norm. But only with one another. They all shunned the elders. David had felt his eyes burning as the girl spoke, still moving away from him.

He had turned and left abruptly, and had not spoken to her again in the intervening years. Sometimes he thought he saw her watching him warily, and each time he glared at her and hurried away.

C-1 had been like his own child. He had watched her

develop, watched her learn to walk, talk, feed herself. His child, his and Celia's. C-2 had been much the same. A twin, somewhat smaller, identical nevertheless. But C-3 had been different. No, he corrected himself, his perceptions of her had been different. When he looked at her now he saw Celia, and he ached.

He had grown chilled on the ridge, and he realized that the sun had set long ago and that the lanterns had been lighted below. The scene looked pretty, like a sentimental picture titled "Rural Life." The large farmhouse with glowing windows, the blackness of the barn; closer, the hospital and staff building with the cheerful yellow lights in the windows. Stiffly he descended into the valley again. He had missed dinner, but he was not hungry.

"David!" one of the youngest boys, a Five, called to him. David didn't know whom he had been cloned from. There were many people he hadn't known when they were that young. He stopped and the boy ran to him, then past him, calling as he went, "Dr. Walt wants you."

On Walt's desk and spread over a table were the medical charts for the Four strain. "I've finished," Walt said. "You'll have to doublecheck, of course."

David scanned the final lines quickly, H-4 and D-4. He didn't look up, but nodded. "Have you told the two boys yet?"

"I told them all. They understand." Walt rubbed his eyes. "They have no secrets from each other," he said. "They understand about the girls' ovulation periods, about the necessity of keeping records. If any of those girls can conceive, they'll do it." His voice was almost bitter when he looked up at David. "They're taking it over completely from now on."

"What do you mean?"

"W-1 made a copy of my records for his files. He'll follow it through."

David nodded. The elders were being excluded again. The time was coming when they wouldn't be needed for anything—extra mouths to feed, nothing else. He sat down and for a long time he and Walt sat in companionable silence.

In class the following day nothing seemed different. No pair bonding, David thought cynically. They accepted being mated as casually as the cattle did. If there was any jealousy of the two fertile males, it was well hidden. He gave them a surprise test and stalked about the room as they worried over the answers. They would all pass, he knew—not only pass, but do well. They had motivation. They were learning in their teens what he hadn't grasped in his twenties. There were no educational frills, no distractions. Work in the classroom, in the fields, in the kitchens, in the laboratories. They worked interchangeably, incessantly—the first really classless society. He pulled his thoughts back when he realized that they were finishing already. He had allowed an hour, and they were finishing in forty minutes—slightly longer for the Fives, who, after all, were two years younger than the Fours.

The two oldest D's headed for the laboratory after class, and David followed them. They were talking earnestly until he drew near. He remained in the laboratory for fifteen minutes of silent work, then left. Outside the door he paused and once more could hear the murmur of quiet voices. Angrily he tramped down the hallway.

In Walt's office, he raged. "Damn it, they're up to something! I can smell it."

Walt regarded him with a detached thoughtfulness. David felt helpless. There was nothing he could point to, nothing he could attach significance to, but there was a feeling, an instinct that wouldn't be quieted.

"All right," David said, almost in desperation. "Look at how they took the test results. Why aren't the boys jealous? Why aren't the girls making passes at the two available studs?"

Walt shook his head.

"I don't even know what they're doing in the lab anymore," David said. "And Harry has been relegated to caretaker for the livestock." He paced the room in frustration. "They're taking over."

"We knew they would one day," Walt reminded him gently.

"But there are only seventeen Fives, eighteen Fours. Out of the lot there might be six or seven fertile ones. With a decreased life expectancy. With an increased chance of abnormality. Don't they know that?"

"David, relax. They know all that. They're living it. Believe me, they know." Walt stood up and put his arm around David's shoulders. "We've done it, David. Can't you understand that? We made it happen. Even if there are only three fertile girls now, they could have up to thirty babies, David. And the next generation will have more who will be fertile. We have done it, David. Let them carry it now if they want to."

By the end of summer two of the Four girls were pregnant. There was a celebration in the valley that was as frenetic as any Fourth of July holiday any of the older people could remember.

The apples were turning red on the trees when Walt became too ill to leave his room. Two more girls were pregnant; one of them was a Five. Every day David spent hours with Walt, no longer wanting to work at all in the laboratory, feeling an outsider in the classrooms, where the Ones were gradually taking over.

"You might have to deliver those babies come spring," Walt said, grinning. "Might start a class in delivery procedures. Walt-3 is ready, I guess."

"We'll manage," David said. "Don't worry about it. I expect you'll be there."

"Maybe. Maybe." Walt closed his eyes for a moment and said, "You were right about them, David. They're up to something."

David leaned forward, and involuntarily lowered his voice. "What do you know?"

Walt looked at him and shook his head. "About as much as you did when you first came to me early this summer. David, find out what they're doing in the lab. And find out what they think about the pregnant girls. Harry tells me they have devised a new immersion suspension system that doesn't require artificial placentas. They're adding them as fast as they can." He sighed. "Harry has cracked, David. Senile or crazy. W-1 can't do anything for him."

David stood up, but hesitated. "Walt, I think it's time you told me. What's wrong with you?"

"Get out of here, damn it," Walt said, but the timbre of his voice was gone, the force that should have propelled David from the room was not there.

David walked by the river for a long time. Find out. How? He hadn't been in the lab for weeks, months perhaps. No one needed him there any longer. The winters were getting colder, starting earlier, lasting longer, with more snows than he could remember from childhood. As soon as man stopped adding his megatons of filth to the atmosphere, he thought, the atmosphere had reverted to what it must have been long ago, moister weather summer and winter, more stars than he had ever seen before: the sky a clear endless blue by day, velvet blue-black at night with blazing stars that modern man had never seen.

The hospital wing where W-1 and W-2 were working now was ablaze with lights when David turned toward it. As he neared the hospital he began to hurry; there were too many lights, and he could see people moving behind the windows, too many people, elders.

Margaret met him in the lobby. She was weeping silently, oblivious of the tears that ran erratically down her cheeks. She wasn't yet fifty, but she looked older; she looked like an elder, David thought with a pang. When had they started calling themselves that? Was it because they had to differentiate somehow, and none of them had permitted himself to call the others what they were? Clones! he said to himself vehemently. Clones! Not quite human.

"What happened, Margaret?" She clutched his arm but couldn't speak, and he looked over her head at Warren, who was pale and shaking. "What happened?"

"Accident down at the mill. Jeremy and Eddie are dead. A couple of the young people were hurt. Don't know how bad. They're in there." He pointed toward the operating-room wing. "They left Clarence. Just walked away and left him. We brought him up, but I don't know." He shook his head. "They just left him there and brought up their own."

David put Margaret aside and ran down the hall toward the emergency room. Sarah was working over Clarence while several of the elders moved back and forth to keep out of her way without leaving entirely.

David breathed a sigh of relief. Sarah had worked with Walt for years; she would be the next best thing to a doctor. He flung his coat off and hurried to her. "What can I do?"

"It's his back," she said tightly. She was very pale, but her hands were steady as she swabbed a long gash on Clarence's leg and put a heavy pad over it. "This needs stitches. But I'm afraid it's his back."

"Broken?"

"I think so. Internal injuries."

"Where the hell is W-1 or W-2?"

"With their own. They have two injuries, I think." She put his hand over the pad. "Hold it tight a minute." She used her stethoscope deliberately, peered into Clarence's eyes, and finally straightened and said, "I can't do a thing for him."

"Stitch his leg. I'm going to get W-1." David strode down the hall fast, not seeing any of the elders who moved out of his way. At the door to the operating room he was stopped by three of the young men. He saw an H-3 and said to him, "We have a man who's probably dying. Where's W-2?"

"Who?" H-3 asked, almost innocently.

David couldn't think of the name immediately. He stared at the young face, and he felt his fist tighten. "You know damn well who I mean. We need a doctor, and you have one or two in there. I'm going to bring one of them out."

He became aware of movement and turned to see four more of them approaching, two girls, two boys. Interchangeable, he thought. It didn't matter which ones did what. "Tell him I want him," he said harshly. One of the newcomers was a C1-2, he realized, and still more harshly he said, "It's Clarence. Sarah thinks his back is broken."

C1-2 didn't change his expression. They had moved very close. They encircled him, and behind him H-3 said, "As soon as they're through in there, I'll tell them, David." And David knew there was nothing he could do, nothing at all.

He stared at their smooth young faces; so familiar, living memories every one of them, like walking through his own past, seeing his aged and aging cousins rejuvenated, but with something missing. Familiar and alien, known and unknowable. Behind H-3 the swinging door opened and W-1 came out, still in surgical gown and mask, now down about his throat.

"I'll come now," he said, and the small group opened for him. He didn't look at David after dismissing him with one glance.

David followed him to the emergency room and watched his deft hands as he felt Clarence's body, tested for reflexes, probed confidently along the spinal column. "I'll operate," he said, and that same confidence came through with the words. He motioned for S-1 and W-2 to bring Clarence, and left once more.

Sarah had moved back out of the way, and now she slowly turned and stripped off the gloves she had put on in preparing to stitch up the leg wound. Warren watched the two young people cover Clarence, strap him securely, and wheel him out the door. No one spoke. Sarah methodically started to clean up the emergency-room equipment. Sarah finished her tasks and looked uncertainly about for something else to do.

"Will you take Margaret home and put her to bed?" David asked. She looked at him gratefully and nodded. When she was gone, David turned to Warren. "Someone has to see to the bodies, clean them up, prepare for burial."

"Sure, David," Warren said in a heavy voice. "I'll get Avery and Sam. We'll take care of it. I'll just go get them now and we'll take care of it. I'll . . . David, what have we done?" And his voice that had been too heavy, too dead, became almost shrill. "What are they?"

"What do you mean?"

"When the accident happened, I was down to the mill. Having a bite with Avery. He was just finishing up down there. Section of the floor caved in, you know that old part where we should have put in a new floor last year, or the year before. It gave way somehow. And suddenly there they were, the kids, out of nowhere. No one had time to go get them, to yell for them. Nothing, but there they were. They got their own two out of there and up to the hospital like their tails was on fire. David. Out of nowhere."

Several of the elders were still in the waiting room when David went there. Lucy and Vernon were sitting near the window, staring out at the black night. Since Clarence's wife had died, he and Lucy had lived together, not as man and wife, but for companionship, because as children they had been as close as brother and sister, and now each needed someone to cling to. Sometimes sister, sometimes mother, sometimes daughter, Lucy had fussed over him, sewed for him, fetched and carried for him, and now, if he died, what would she do? David went to her and took her cold hand. She was very thin, with dark hair that hadn't started to gray, and deep blue eyes that had twinkled with merriment once, a long, long time ago.

"Go on home, Lucy. I'll wait, and as soon as there is anything to tell you, I promise I'll come."

She continued to stare at him. David turned toward Vernon helplessly. Vernon's brother had been killed in the accident, but there was nothing to say to him.

"Let her be," Vernon said. "She has to wait."

David sat down, still holding Lucy's hand. After a moment or so she pulled it free gently and clutched it herself until both of her hands were white-knuckled. None of the young people came near the waiting room. David wondered where they were waiting to hear about the condition of their own. Or maybe they didn't have to wait anywhere, maybe they would just know. He pushed the thought aside angrily, not believing it, not able to be rid of it. A long time later W-1 entered and said to no one in particular, "He's resting. He'll sleep until tomorrow afternoon. Go on home now."

Lucy stood up. "Let me stay with him. In case he needs something, or there's a change."

"He won't be left alone," W-1 said. He turned toward the

door, paused and glanced back, and said to Vernon, "I'm sorry about your brother." Then he left.

Lucy stood undecided until Vernon took her arm. "I'll see you home," he said, and she nodded. David watched them leave together. He turned off the light in the waiting room and walked slowly down the hall, not planning anything, not thinking about going home, or anywhere else. He found himself outside the office that W-1 used, and he knocked softly. W-1 opened the door. He looked tired, David thought, and wasn't sure that his surprise was warranted. Of course, he should be tired. Three operations. He looked like a young, tired Walt, too keyed up to go to sleep immediately, too fatigued to walk off the tension.

"Can I come in?" David asked hesitantly. W-1 nodded and moved aside, and David entered. He never had been inside this office.

"Clarence will not live," W-1 said suddenly, and his voice, behind David, because he had not yet moved from the door, was so like Walt's that David felt a thrill of something that might have been fear, or more likely, he told himself, just surprise again. "I did what I could," W-1 said. He walked around his desk and sat down.

W-1 sat quietly, with none of the nervous mannerisms that Walt exhibited, none of the finger tapping that was as much a part of Walt's conversation as his words. No pulling his ears or rubbing his nose. A Walt with something missing, David thought. They all had something missing, a dead area. Now, with fatigue drawing his face, W-1 sat unmoving, waiting patiently for David to begin, much the same way an adult might wait for a hesitant child to initiate a conversation.

"How did your people know about the accident?" David asked. "No one else knew."

W-1 shrugged. A time-consumer question, he seemed to imply. "We just knew."

"What are you doing in the lab now?" David asked, and heard a strained note in his voice. Somehow he had been made to feel like an interloper; his question sounded like idle chatter.

"Perfecting the methods," W-1 said. "The usual thing."

And something else, David thought, but he didn't press it. "The equipment should be in excellent shape for another ten years or more," he said. "And the methods, while probably not the best conceivable, are efficient enough. Why tamper now when the experiment seems to be proving itself?" For a moment he thought he saw a flicker of surprise cross W-1's face, but it was gone too swiftly and once more the smooth mask revealed nothing.

"Remember when one of your women killed one of us a long time ago, David? Hilda murdered the child of her own likeness. We all shared that death, and we realized that each of you is alone. We're not like you, David. I think you know it, but now you must accept it." He stood up. "And we won't go back to what you have."

David stood up also, and his legs felt curiously weak. He gripped the edge of the desk. "What exactly do you mean?"

"Sexual reproduction isn't the only answer. Just because the higher organisms evolved to it doesn't mean it's the best. Each time a species has died out, there has been another higher one to replace it."

"Cloning is one of the worst ways for a higher species," David said. "It stifles diversity." The weakness in his legs seemed to be climbing, and he felt his hands start to tremble. He clenched the desk harder.

"That's assuming diversity is beneficial. Perhaps it isn't," W-1 said. "You pay a high price for individuality."

"There is still the decline and the inevitable slide to extinction. Have you got around that?" David wanted suddenly to end this conversation, to hurry from the sterile office and the smooth unreadable face with the sharp eyes that seemed to know what he was feeling.

"Not yet," W-1 said slowly. "But we have the fertile members to fall back on until we do." He moved around his desk and walked toward the door. "I have to check my patients," he said, and held the door open for David.

"Before I leave," David said, "will you tell me what is the matter with Walt?"

"Don't you know?" W-1 shook his head. "I keep forget-

ting, you don't tell each other things, do you? He has cancer.
Inoperable. It metastasized. He's dying, David. I thought
you knew that."

David walked blankly for an hour or more, and finally
found himself in his room, exhausted, unwilling yet to go to
bed. He sat at his window until dawn, and then he went to
Walt's room. When Walt woke up he reported what W-1 had
told him.

"They'll use the fertile ones only to replenish their supply
of clones," he said. "The humans among them will be
pariahs. They'll destroy what we worked so hard to create."

"Don't let them do it, David. For God's sake, don't let
them do it!" Walt's color was bad, and he was too weak to
sit up. "Vlasic's mad, so he'll be of no help. You have to
stop them somehow." Bitterly he said, "They want to take
the easy way out, give up now when we know everything
will work."

David didn't know if he was sorry or glad that he had told
Walt. No more secrets, he thought. Never again. "I'll stop
them somehow," he said. "I don't know how, or when. But
soon."

A Four brought Walt's breakfast, and David returned to
his room. He rested and slept fitfully for a few hours, then
showered and went to the cave entrance, where he was
stopped by a Two.

"I'm sorry, David," he said. "Jonathan says that you need
a rest, that you are not to work now."

Wordlessly David turned and left. Jonathan. W-1. If they
had decided to bar him from the lab, they could do it. He
and Walt had planned it that way: the cave was impregnable.
He thought of the elders, forty-four of them left, and two of
that number terminally ill. One of the remaining elders
insane. Forty-one then, twenty-nine women. Eleven able-
bodied men. Ninety-four clones.

He waited for days for Harry Vlasic to appear, but no one
had seen him in weeks, and Vernon thought he was living in
the lab. He had all his meals there. David gave that up; he
found D-1 in the dining room and offered his help in the lab.

"I'm too bored doing nothing," he said. "I'm used to working twelve hours a day or more."

"You should rest now that there are others who can take the load off you," D-1 said pleasantly. "Don't worry about the work, David. It is going quite well." He moved away, and David caught his arm.

"Why won't you let me in? Haven't you learned the value of an objective opinion?"

D-1 pulled away, and still smiling easily, said, "You want to destroy everything, David. In the name of mankind, of course. But still, we can't let you do that."

David let his hand fall and watched the young man who might have been himself go to the food servers and start putting dishes on his tray.

"I'm working on a plan," he lied to Walt again and again in the weeks that followed. Daily Walt grew feebler, and now he was in great pain.

David's father was with Walt most of the time now. He was gray and aged but in good health. He talked of their boyhood, of the coming hunting season, of the recession he feared might reduce his profits, of his wife, who had been dead for fifteen years. He was cheerful and happy, and Walt seemed to want him there.

In March, W-1 sent for David. He was in his office. "It's about Walt," he said. "We should not let him continue to suffer. He has done nothing to deserve this."

"He is trying to last until the girls have their babies," David said. "He wants to know."

"But it doesn't matter any longer," W-1 said patiently. "And meanwhile he suffers."

David stared at him with hatred.

W-1 continued to watch him for several more moments, then said, "We will decide." The next morning it was found that Walt had died in his sleep.

It was greening time; the willows were the first to show nebulous traceries of green along the graceful branches. Forsythias and flaming bushes were in bloom, brilliant yellows and scarlets against the gray background. The river

was high with spring runoffs up north and heavy March
rains, but it was an expected high, not dangerous, not
threatening this year. The air had a balminess that had been
missing since September; the air was soft and smelled of
wet woods and fertile earth. David sat on the slope
overlooking the farm. There were calves in the field, and
they looked the way spring calves always looked: thin legs,
awkward, slightly stupid. No fields had been worked yet,
but the garden was green: pale lettuce, blue-green kale,
green spears of onions, dark green cabbage. The newest
wing of the hospital, not yet painted, crude compared to the
finished brick buildings, was being used already, and he
could even see some of the young people at the windows
studying. They had the best teachers, themselves, and the
best students. They learned amazingly well from one
another, better than they had in the early days.

They came out of the school in matched sets: four of this,
three of that, two of another. He sought and found three
Celias. He could no longer tell them apart; they were all
grown-up Celias now, and indistinguishable. He watched
them with no feeling of desire; no hatred moved him, no
love. They vanished into the barn, and he looked up over the
farm, into the hills on the other side of the valley. The ridges
were hazy and had no sharp edges anywhere. They looked
soft and welcoming. Soon, he thought. Soon. Before the
dogwoods bloomed.

The night the first baby was born, there was another
celebration. The elders talked among themselves, laughed at
their own jokes, drank wine, the clones left them alone and
partied at the other end of the room. When Vernon began to
play his guitar and dancing started, David slipped away. He
wandered on the hospital grounds for a few minutes, as
though aimlessly, and then, when he was certain no one had
followed him out, he began to trot toward the mill and the
generator. Six hours, he thought. Six hours without electricity would destroy everything in the lab.

David approached the mill cautiously, hoping the rushing
creek would mask any sound he might make. The building
was three stories high, very large, with windows ten feet

above ground, on the level where the offices were. The ground floor was filled with machinery. In the back the hill rose sharply; David could reach the windows by bracing himself on the steep incline and steadying himself with one hand on the building. He found a window that went up easily when he pushed it, and in a moment he was inside a dark office. He closed the window, and then, moving slowly with his hands outstretched to avoid any obstacles, crossed the room to the door and opened it a crack. The mill was never left unattended, but he hoped that those on duty tonight would be down with the machinery. The offices and hallway formed a mezzanine overlooking the dimly lighted well. Grotesque shadows made the hallway strange, with deep pools of darkness and places where he would be clearly visible should anyone happen to look up at the right moment. Suddenly David stiffened. Voices.

He slipped his shoes off and opened the door wider. The voices were below him. Soundlessly he ran toward the control room, keeping close to the wall. He was almost to the door when the lights came on all over the building. There was a shout, and he could hear them running up the stairs. He made a dash for the door and yanked it open, slammed it behind him. There was no way to lock it. He pushed a file cabinet an inch or so, gave up, and picked up a metal stool by its legs. He raised it and swung it hard against the main control panel. At the same moment he felt a crushing pain in his shoulders, and he stumbled and fell forward as the lights went out.

He opened his eyes painfully. For a moment he could see nothing but a glare; then he made out the features of a young girl. She was reading a book, concentrating on it. Dorothy? She was his cousin Dorothy. He tried to rise, and she looked up and smiled at him.

"Dorothy? What are you doing here?" He couldn't get off the bed. On the other side of the room a door opened and Walt came in, also very young, unlined, with his nice brown hair ruffled.

David's head began to hurt, and he reached up to find

bandages that came down almost to his eyes. Slowly memory came back and he closed his eyes, willing the memory to fade away again, to let them be Dorothy and Walt.

"How do you feel?" W-1 asked. David felt the cool fingers on his wrist. "You'll be all right. A slight concussion, badly bruised, I'm afraid. You're going to be pretty sore for a while."

Without opening his eyes, David asked, "Did I do much damage?"

"Very little," W-1 said.

Two days later David was asked to attend a meeting in the cafeteria. His head was still bandaged, but with little more than a strip of adhesive now. His shoulder ached. He went to the cafeteria slowly, with two of the clones as escorts.

Most of them were in the cafeteria. D-1 stood up and offered David a chair at the front of the room. David accepted it silently and sat down to wait. D-1 remained standing.

"Do you remember our class discussions about instinct, David?" D-1 asked. "We ended up agreeing that probably there are no instincts, only conditioned responses to certain stimuli. We have changed our minds about that. We agree now that there is still the instinct to preserve one's species. Preservation of the species is a very strong instinct, a drive, if you will." He looked at David and asked, "What are we to do with you?"

"Don't be an ass," David said sharply. "You are not a separate species."

D-1 didn't reply. None of them moved. They were watching him quietly, intelligently, dispassionately. David stood up and pushed his chair back. "Then let me work. I'll give you my word of honor that I won't try to disrupt anything again."

D-1 shook his head. "We discussed that. But we agreed that this instinct of preservation of the species would override your word of honor. As it would our own."

David felt his hands clench, and he straightened his fingers, forced them to relax. "Then you have to kill me."

"We talked about that, too," D-1 said gravely. "We don't want to do it. We owe you too much. In time we will erect statues to you, Walt, Harry. We have very carefully recorded all of your efforts in our behalf. Our gratitude and affection for you won't permit us to kill you."

David looked about the room again, picking out familiar faces. Dorothy. Walt. Vernon. Margaret. Herbie. Celia. They all met his gaze without flinching. Here and there one of them smiled at him faintly.

"You tell me, then," he said finally.

"You have to go away," D-1 said. "You will be escorted for three days, downriver. There is a cart loaded with food, seeds, a few tools. The valley is fertile, the seeds will do well. It is a good time of year for starting a garden."

W-2 was one of the three who accompanied him for the first three days. They didn't speak. The boys took turns pulling the cart of supplies. David didn't offer to pull it. At the end of the third day, on the other side of the river from the Sumner farm, they left him. W-2 lingered a moment and said, "They wanted me to tell you, David. One of the girls you call Celia has conceived. One of the boys you call David impregnated her. They wanted you to know." Then he turned and joined the others. They vanished among the trees very quickly.

David slept where they had left him, and in the morning he continued south, leaving the cart behind, taking only enough food for the next few days. He stopped once to look at a maple seedling sheltered among the pines. He touched the soft green leaves very gently. On the sixth day he reached the Wiston farm; alive in his memory was the day he had waited there for Celia. The white oak tree that was his friend was the same, perhaps larger, he couldn't tell. He could not see the sky through its branches covered with new, vivid green leaves. He made a leanto and slept under the tree that night, and the next morning he told it good-bye solemnly and began to climb the slopes overlooking the farm. The house was still there, but the barn was gone, and the other outbuildings. Swept away by the flood they had made so long ago.

He reached the antique forest late in the afternoon. He watched a flying insect beat its wings almost lazily and remembered his grandfather telling him that even the insects here were primitive—slower than their more advanced cousins, less adaptable to hot weather, dry spells.

It was misty and very cool under the trees. The insect had settled on a leaf spread out horizontally to catch what sun it could. In the golden sunlight the insect was also golden. For a brief moment David thought he heard a bird's trill—a thrush. It was gone too fast to be certain, and he shook his head. Wishful thinking, no more than wishful thinking.

In the antique forest, a cove forest, the trees waited, keeping their genes intact, ready to move down the slopes when the conditions were right for them again. David stretched out on the ground under the great trees and slept, and in the cool, misty milieu of his dream saurians walked and a bird sang.

FURTHER READING

NOVELS

The Multiple Men, Ben Bova
Cyteen, C.J. Cherryh
Imperial Earth, Arthur C. Clarke
Clone, Richard Cowper
Joshua, Son of None, Nancy Freedman
The Boys from Brazil, Ira Levin
Solution Three, Naomi Mitchison
Cloned Lives, Pamela Sargent
The Iron Dream, Norman Spinrad
The Ophiuchi Hotline, John Varley
Steel Beach, John Varley
Where Late the Sweet Birds Sang, Kate Wilhelm
The Fifth Head of Cerberus, Gene Wolfe

NON-FICTION

The Biological Time-Bomb, Gordon Rattray Taylor

SHORT STORIES

"Let's Be Frank," Brian W. Aldiss
"Trading Post," Neal Barret, Jr.
"A Special Kind of Morning," Gardner Dozois
"The Death Artist," Alexander Jablokov
"The Relic," Gary Jennings
"Think Like a Dinosaur," James Patrick Kelly
"By the Mirror of My Youth," Kathe Koja
"Sex Education," Nancy Kress
"Across the Darkness," Geoffrey A. Landis
"The Dakna," Jamil Nasir
"Guest of Honor," Robert Reed
"The Clone Zone," Robert Silverberg

"When You Care, When You Love," Theodore Sturgeon
"He-We-Await," Howard Waldrop
"Lethe," Walter Jon Williams
"Solip: System," Walter Jon Williams
"The Fifth Head of Cerberus," Gene Wolfe